David Perry–the national bestselling author of *The Cyclops Conspiracy*–once again demonstrates his consummate skill as a thrill master with another exhilarating, poignant tale. . .

Second Chance

Hospital pharmacist Alex Benedict is engulfed in a perpetual battle against death in his professional life and haunted by its grim specter on a personal level. Benedict happens upon a shocking piece of evidence, leading him to conclude that one of Tidewater Regional Medical Center's own pharmacists, Michael Watson, may be involved in the demise of several patients.

Watson leaves Benedict a recording implicating himself while purporting an incredible claim and urging Benedict to become the steward of a powerful compound. Watson has separated the compound's formula into three pieces and disguised their locations in the form of quatrains. If Benedict can bring the sections together, he is promised the opportunity to lift the black cloud of death from his own life.

After witnessing the compound's power, Benedict embarks on the quest to solve the riddles. A frantic, life-and-death pursuit ensues, stretching up and down the east coast. Benedict must elude the lethal grip of the secret cabal that wants the formula back as Tidewater Regional Medical undergoes a crucial inspection. In the story's stunning climax, Benedict races to alter his fate and is asked to make an incredible, life-altering choice.

Second Chance is another brilliantly woven tale of suspense and intrigue in the world of pharmacy. Perry challenges his readers with a clever, fast-paced plot offering bombshell twists at every turn.

Praise for David Perry's Books

The Cyclops Conspiracy

"Taut and gripping, The Cyclops Conspiracy is a top-notch thriller that you won't want to put down!"

—David Compton, bestselling author of Executive Sanction

The Cyclops Conspiracy features a well-crafted plot, skillfully written action scenes, and credible characters. Perry unravels the storyline with increasing speed as he introduces characters and effectively reveals what motivates them to reach their goals. Perry's descriptions are detailed and evocative. . .his plot, characters, and descriptions, as well as his choreography of action scenes are intricate, strong, and clear. Perry quickly builds—and deftly sustains—a momentum that will have readers engrossed in this page-turner.

—Maya Fleischmann, Clarion Foreword Reviews

In *The Cyclops Conspiracy,* we read a story about ordinary people, who find themselves in extraordinary situations and who somehow discover within them the necessary wealth of psychological stamina to endure all the ill fortune that life throws at them. The second half of the book is so fast-paced that it leaves the reader almost breathless, something that adds some points to the overall affect of the narration. . .this is the author's first book, and as such it comes very close to genre perfection. 9/10.

—Lakis Fourouklas, Reviewer

Second Chance

There [are] not many books that keep me up reading all night but this one I could not put down it had my interest from the very first page. . .Shame I could not give more stars than five.

—Julie Banton, NetGalley Reviewer

What a thriller! I could not put this book down once I started reading. Very believable characters that the reader can relate to [in] their own lives. The villains are numerous and sinister. The good guys are loveable and smart. Hopefully this is not the last we have heard of Alex Benedict.

—Cindy Musslewhite, Reviewer

Set at a fast pace. . .you will speed through, hanging on every last word. [Second Chance] is a great book to read during the holidays or on your next trip. National Best Sellers also make great gifts! If you have any book worms on your list this is a great way to make sure to get them something that they'll love!

—Maggie Franz, Reviewer

Second Chance is a beautifully spun tale of corruption, greed and intrigue. . .This book is well written. . .I strongly suggest reading this book.

—Kerry Marsh, Reviewer

SECOND CHANCE

Also by David Perry

The Cyclops Conspiracy

SECOND CHANCE

Roger,
Enjoy this Prescription
for Excitement

DAVID PERRY

David Perry

9·19·2015

Pettigrew
ENTERPRISES

Copyright © 2013 by Pettigrew Enterprises, LLC

Published in the United States by Pettigrew Enterprises, LLC. Cataloging-in-Publication data is on file with the Library of Congress

Library of Congress Control Number: 2013912520

ISBN 978-0-9836375-4-7 (hardcover)
ISBN 978-0-9836375-3-0 (softcover)

PRINTED IN THE UNITED STATES OF AMERICA
10 9 8 7 6 5 4 3 2 1
First Edition

For Anne,

Shared with you, life is a joyous adventure.

"And this maiden she lived with no other thought
than to love and be loved by me."
Edgar Allen Poe

"The path of duty lies in what is near, and man
seeks for it in what is remote."
Mencius

ACKNOWLEDGMENTS

The following individuals have provided me with invaluable assistance in researching this work:

Clinical pharmacists Pete LeBel, PharmD and Sunao Slayton, PharmD for their insight into hospital pharmacy and clinical drug issues;

Dr. Lisa Casanova, Dr. Cheryl Lawson and Dr. Joe Wilson for all matters medical;

Sherrie Capotosto and Carmelou Aloupas for their legal input and counsel;

Anne Alberti, a wonderful aunt, and Alberta Pedroja for their assistance on Joint Commission procedures;

Orin "Chip" Booth, Carlyle Gravely, Mary Sellen and David Cecil, my fellow Rotarians, for their assistance and support;

Shelly Sapyta, Tim Snider, Victoria Maximovich, my friends at BookMasters;

Chris Serra, my long lost and newly rediscovered friend; thanks for your artistic input into the cover design, we've come a long way since dodging cars during the street hockey days;

Brian and Debbie Tate at the Cigar Vault and the long list of friends who are too numerous to list here. Thanks for all the support. I can't wait for the re-opening;

Sara Brooks, thanks for your marketing and promotional tenacity;

Alex: remember, no matter what happens, I'll always be your dad and never stop giving you unsolicited and unwanted advice;

Katlyn and Sarah, two wonderful young women: Though I never had a daughter of my own, the Lord saw fit to bless me twice by bringing both of you into my life. Thanks for sharing Momma Anne with me;

Mom and Dad, my two biggest fans;

To my growing number of readers, thank you for the support and encouragement. On those stressful and busy days in pharmacy, the words, "I really enjoyed your book" make the early mornings and late nights worthwhile.

PART ONE

CHAPTER 1

Pharmacist Alex Benedict lived with death as a constant companion. It lurked everywhere, whispering foreboding and permanence. But Benedict never relented. His life had become a vigil dedicated to keeping that unwanted guest at bay.

The physical signs of his battle had become gradually more evident each morning when he looked in the mirror. The color of his intelligent caramel eyes had fogged with fatigue. The whites were mapped with broken capillaries. The eyes themselves seemed to have sunk deeper into his skull. He'd lost fifteen pounds in the last few months and the pasty skin beneath those eyes hung from his cheeks.

Today's victim, though, was Augustus Palladine.

Benedict and the rest of the Tidewater Regional Medical Center's Code Blue team had been working on Palladine for almost ten minutes. Benedict manned the crash cart, delivering medications in the correct sequence and at exacting intervals.

He watched the raven-haired nurse Katherine Diehl, perched on a step-stool, pumping her balled hands on the man's chest. Benedict noticed in that moment that Diehl herself looked haggard. Strain pulled at the corners of her eyes.

A respiratory therapist, stationed at the patient's head, squeezed a green, vinyl ambu bag every eight seconds. Air forced its way into the man's lungs through the endotrachial tube in Palladine's throat with a shrill, caustic hiss.

"Stop compressions, Katherine," John Edward Kyle commanded in his thick Scottish accent. Kyle was Tidewater Regional Medical Center's chief hospitalist. The salt-and-pepper haired man, rail-thin and whose white, pasty skin was blotched with eczema, was the most influential physician in the hospital.

Palladine was a large man and retired shipyard worker who'd been diagnosed with mesothelioma a few months back. The fact that his stage I cancer had been diagnosed early offered a glimmer of hope for the number of years the man had left. That is up until this morning. Palladine's cardiac arrest had been witnessed by one of the nurses. He'd shot upright in bed, clutched at his chest as blood dripped from his nose, then immediately collapsed. The nurse had activated the Code team and begun compressions. As the team arrived, the large, black-purple bruising covering the man's torso had begun to materialize. It portended another defeat. The rivulet of blood oozing from his nose had begun creeping down his cheek.

Katherine Diehl stood erect. The team gazed at the green, un-coordinated squiggle traversing the cardiac monitor.

"He's still in V-fib," Kyle announced. "Let's shock him with 120 joules."

The young resident physician assigned to Kyle hit a button on the defibrillator. It whined to a climax. "Clear," the resident announced.

He pressed another button and the charge was transferred to the pads on the patient's blackened chest. His muscles contracted and his torso jerked slightly.

Benedict noticed Kyle's mouth opening to bark out another command. Benedict beat him to it.

"I've got the amiodarone ready, Dr. Kyle," Benedict said, the syringe poised. "Three hundred milligrams."

But the doctor did not respond. His blue eyes darted back and forth absorbing every action and nuance of the team under his leadership.

"Shall I give the amiodarone?" Benedict urged.

"Give it," Kyle replied.

Benedict stepped to the bed and screwed the syringe into the port of the IV line. When the dose was given, Benedict stepped back to the crash cart.

Katherine Diehl, her turn over, was replaced by another nurse. As the new nurse began compressions, Katherine Diehl stepped around the bed and passed by the crash cart.

Benedict nodded to her, raising an eyebrow in a silent question. *"Are you okay?"*

She raised a hand half-heartedly in response. *Not now!*

The Code continued. Benedict administered doses of epinephrine, calcium chloride and atropine. The patient was shocked with a higher dose of current. The electrocardiogram still showed no heart rhythm.

Kyle shot a challenge at his first year resident. "What would you do now?"

The blond-haired youngster's eyes widened. "How about some magnesium for the V-fib?"

"Excuse me?" Kyle shot back insulted. "Did you just say magnesium, really?"

Kyle addressed the whole group as they worked on the dead man. "Anybody want to remind our young resident here what we use magnesium for?"

"That would be Torsades!" Benedict responded.

Kyle smiled begrudgingly and turned back to the young doctor. "That's right."

The team ignored the man's embarrassment and continued their work. Benedict disposed of a spent syringe, placing it in the unit mounted on the wall over a trash can.

Benedict glanced into the trash can. The item resting atop the pile of discarded plastic and paper debris caught Benedict's eye. He bent closer, turned the object over with his gloved hand and inspected it.

A cold dagger sliced through his belly.

ΩΩΩ

"I can't do this anymore," Michael Watson declared softly later that morning. "I'm getting out."

Katherine Diehl shook her head at the aging pharmacist. "How are you going to get out of it? We're both in too deep. You can't leave. It will put everything in jeopardy. What about me? I'll be implicated. You can't do this! I have two small children."

"I can exit all this without implicating you. But we have to stop, Kathy. The consequences of continuing are too devastating."

"What are you talking about?"

"Patients are dying, remember? We've had a hand in their deaths."

"You don't need to remind me. We killed another one this morning."

"I know," Watson shot back. "Do you know how many it's been so far?"

They were sitting in Watson's rusting Ford Taurus. Their anxiety-filled conversation had fogged the windows. Diehl wiped a curved arc along the window, clearing a view. She concentrated on the gray skies of the approaching storm for a moment then lowered her head into her hands.

"Yeah, I do. It's six. Six damned patients. And I'll never be able to forgive myself no matter how much money I'm being paid." Her words were muffled through the sweaty hands cover-ing her face.

"We won't be killing anymore patients," Watson declared. Diehl could sense his forced smile even though she wasn't looking at him.

She raised her head to look at Watson. The skin on his face coated with a two-day beard hung from his cheek bones. "That doesn't change the past. We're still murderers."

"Let's not think about that right now. Listen to me for a second. There's another reason all this needs to stop...."

Diehl peered at him, waiting for that reason.

"I've found the answer. It works."

Diehl blinked hard.

"Did you hear me?"

"If it works, why did my patient die this morning?"

"I prepared that mixture three days ago. I prepared a newer formulation just forty hours ago. I've discovered the right ratio of ingredients along with an overlooked procedure, one that's not in any of the literature. It's more of a ... non-scientific step. This newer formula is the right one."

"Non-scientific?"

Watson shook his head, embarrassed by what he was about to reveal. "Do you believe in incantations?"

"No."

"Well believe it."

Diehl pushed out a sigh. "How do you know this one works?"

"I tested it on the one of the monkeys. Her name is Cupid. She was covered in tumors. If the formula isn't exactly right, death en-sues within hours and the recipient exhibits massive bruising. I gave her the dose two days ago. The cancer is gone and Cupid is still alive."

"I don't know. It sounds all too incredible."

"Trust me, Katherine. It works. Unfortunately, there are other, more dire consequences that have to be taken into account."

CHAPTER 2

The answers to the questions created by what Benedict had found in Augustus Palladine's hospital room trash can resided in the anteroom to the pharmacy I.V. room.

Four chest-high ivory-colored filing cabinets in the anteroom housed the documents Benedict needed to find. Benedict leafed through the files, walking his fingers over the hanging folders trying to decipher Michael Watson's filing system.

Michael Watson, the pharmacist assigned to the IV room today at Tidewater, was not at his station. Watson had departed the pharmacy two minutes earlier. His absences had been increasing. This had become expected behavior for the man and it irritated Benedict. Watson's performance had steadily declined over the last months and Benedict meant to discuss it with him, again, very soon. For the moment, Benedict was glad he had some privacy.

It was in the anteroom that technicians and pharmacists collected vials, diluents and intravenous solutions which would be prepared under the three sterile laminar flow hoods housed in the

6

clean room proper. The anteroom housed the voluminous paper trail for all intravenous products prepared by the pharmacy and distributed throughout the institution.

Benedict pushed back his fatigue. He was fighting his own personal struggle that denied him sleep. But he willed himself on, refusing to succumb. He was not going to let his issues affect his work.

The object he'd found in the trash can was a spent IV minibag. When full, it held one hundred milliliters of normal saline. To this particular minibag, a dose of the drug Nonarc had been added. At least, that's what the computer-generated label on the bag read. Benedict had his doubts.

Nonarc, whose generic name was cycloabinazepam acetate, was a potent derivative of the benzodiazepine family. The benzodiazepine class of drugs included Valium and Xanax. Nonarc's molecular structure had been modified and tweaked by its manufacturer, Cardwell-Wolfe Pharmaceuticals, in such a way that the drug could relax muscles and relieve pain. It had become a mainstay of pain therapy management for oncologists in the last three years and named Nonarc because of its non-addictive, non-narcotic properties.

The Code Blue had ended shortly after Benedict had found the bag. The patient, Augustus Palladine, never stood a chance. Nonetheless, the team had worked faithfully attempting to reverse the irreversible. When it was over, Palladine lay dead and exposed, his chest covered in the deep, ugly bruise and the curved endotrachial tube protruding from his mouth like a giant fish hook.

During the commotion of the chest compressions and barked orders, Benedict had lifted the bag out of the can and pressed it against his clipboard, hiding it. The label and the dregs of the contents immediately clued him into the fact there was a problem.

After nearly fifteen minutes of searching, Benedict found the file he was looking for.

The files were organized by date. For every intravenous solution, hyperalimentation or pre-filled syringe that had to be prepared under a laminar flow hood, a hard copy record was kept and signed by the preparing technician and the pharmacist who checked it. He removed a manila folder and opened it on the counter beside the computer terminal, reading the information quickly.

He cursed and found the other files for which he was searching. They all held the same message.

Tidewater had a big problem on its hands.

ΩΩΩ

"What other considerations?" Katherine Diehl asked.

"This formula," Watson continued, "cannot ever see the light of day without a careful analysis of its effects. A strategy must be developed to prevent its abuse and misuse. I don't know what that strategy should be. I am an old and tired man. If I turn this over and it is put out there, there will be chaos."

"Michael, you're not making any sense. This whole project has been a fantasy. It's a sham. I'd blow the whistle on the whole thing except I'd end up as dead as the people we've killed and the nurse that disappeared before me. You know that as well as I do."

"We all made our choices."

"I needed the money. I had no idea it would involve patients dying. I was lied to. I was told it was a simple post-marketing drug study. But I'm as guilty as you are."

"Katherine, we were both deceived and manipulated."

"Now you tell me that all this risk we've taken has been for nothing! You say you've found the answer and we can't use it?"

"That's exactly what I'm saying."

"But the benefits of the formula are so profound, so dramatic. How could society not see its benefit?"

"The benefits are far greater than imagined. Society will do just that. It will be sought after by all mankind. Our professions will no longer be needed. Don't you see? Man will turn upon man to possess its power. Countries will go to war over it. Societies and economies will collapse. There will be anarchy. This formula is the best and the worst thing to ever happen to mankind. Trust me; you'll see when the next dose is delivered."

"You have no right to do this to me! For the past year, I've lived my life looking over my shoulder. I want this to end. I want my life back!"

"Katherine, this is much larger than both of our lives. We're pawns. No matter what happens both of our lives are over. I have found a way out that works for me. And I will take it."

"What is it? Maybe it will work for me?"

"That, my dear, is a truly personal choice, one you will have to make for yourself. You'll know soon enough what my choice is."

"Just destroy the formula! It can't be misused if they don't have it."

"Unfortunately, they already know it has worked on Cupid. The monkey's turnaround was discovered just yesterday. If I don't produce the first dose and its formulation today, I will not live to see tomorrow. I have some things to attend to before that happens. You will be asked to give the dose tonight. Don't worry, it will work."

"What if I never give the next dose? No one will ever know."

Watson smirked at the naive question. "Then they'll find someone else to do it. And you'll end up like Penny Lewis."

"What should I do?"

"Give the next dose just like all the others. You will not be mourning another death. By that time, I will have finished taking the necessary precautions."

"What precautions?"

"The formula has twelve distinct steps. I have separated it into three parts of four steps each. Two of which are already hidden.

I'll place the third one tomorrow. The person who brings all three sections of the recipe together will possess its benefits and curses. I have identified the person who will find and guard the formula. His name is written on the case."

Watson removed a CD case from the console between the front seats. A name was scribbled across the front. He handed it to her. "I have to get back before I'm missed. Katherine, for your own benefit, do *not* listen to this recording."

"Why don't you give it to him yourself?"

"I'm sure we are being watched right now. I cannot be seen giving him anything. They have eyes everywhere. Right now, they probably just assume that we are talking about the next dose to be delivered. Put that disc in your purse before you leave the car."

"When should I give it to him?"

"When you see the formula's power, it will be time. You will know when."

"He won't believe any of this."

"That man has a very big stake in the formula's power. You must make him believe."

CHAPTER 3

"We have a major problem," Benedict said in a dry-throated whisper.

"Alex," Melissa Harrison replied. "I've never known you to be overly dramatic. How bad can it be?"

Harrison, the Director of Pharmacy Services, was Benedict's boss. Benedict had charged into her office, demanding an audience. Harrison had been on the phone. Benedict stared at her, shaking the papers in his hand at her. She'd furrowed a brow, ended the call, motioning for him to sit.

Now, she sat behind her oak desk with her hands tented in front of her. Benedict tried to summon some saliva but failed.

"I've discovered a drug error. Perhaps more than one."

"What kind of error?" Harrison leaned forward.

"I noticed it during the Code this morning." Benedict dropped the IV bag on Harrison's desk. "I found that in the trash can. What do you notice about it?"

Harrison put on her glasses and studied the bag. The expensive tennis bracelet slid down her arm as she lifted the bag. The individual diamonds on it were larger than the single stone Benedict had given his wife when he asked her to marry him.

Harrison's visage turned sour. The soft wrinkles at the corner of her eyes became sharper. Benedict assumed she understood the problem.

"It's a bag of saline labeled as having Nonarc in it. It has the patient's name on it. I don't see any problem."

"Look at the remnants of the solution in it." Benedict took the bag from her. "You see this. The liquid left in the bag isn't right! When a vial of Nonarc is mixed with five milliliters of diluent, the resulting solution holds a milky white consistency. After the resultant mixture is added to a one hundred milliliter IV bag of saline or dextrose for administration to a patient, the milky solution dissolves completely leaving a clear solution. That bag, administered to Augustus Palladine, has a green solution in it. Yet, the label on the IV bag clearly states the contents to be Nonarc."

"Are you sure?"

"Yes, Mel. I even tested it. I mixed up a vial just a few minutes ago then inserted it into a minibag. Here it is. The solution is clear." Benedict held up the unlabeled test bag.

Benedict watched Harrison's face cloud over. "We don't need this now."

"Do we ever need something like this?"

"You know we're overdue for our Joint Commission survey?"

"Yes, I do."

"It's going to happen soon."

"How do you know that? Those visits are always unannounced."

"Ben Roberts has a friend who has a friend at The Joint Commission. Roberts has it on good authority that our visit will happen any day." Ben Roberts was Tidewater Regional Medical Center's president. Harrison tapped a pen on the desk as she spoke. "The

Joint Commission could hit us with an Immediate Jeopardy citation if this is discovered. You're sure about this?"

The Joint Commission was the nation's oldest and largest accrediting body in healthcare. Hospitals were only a part of the many healthcare organizations certified by them on a regular basis. Their findings could range from a Gold Seal of Approval to the more ominous Immediate Jeopardy citation.

Failure to be granted certification could spell financial ruin, in the form of diminished or eliminated reimbursements from government entities including Medicaid and Medicare. Private insurers would soon follow suit. Tidewater Regional Medical Center, as all hospitals were, was in a perpetual state of preparation for a Joint Commission survey. Preparation for the next visit began the moment the previous inspection ended.

And as the days for an expected visit neared, the tension and stress on hospital employees grew exponentially. Thousands of man-hours and hundreds of thousands of dollars were hurled at the preparation for a visit from painting walls to crossing every "t" and dotting every "i" in the mountains of paperwork kept by each department.

"It gets worse, Mel."

"What?"

"You remember those two other deaths that the Morbidity and Mortality Committee asked every department to investigate? The ones with the bruises on their chests?"

Harrison nodded.

"Augustus Palladine—today's Code Blue patient—had a large bruise all over his chest. The same as the other two. Palladine is the third patient to demonstrate this kind of hemorrhaging and ecchymosis...."

"Let me guess," Harrison interrupted as the color drained from her face. "Those other two patients both received Nonarc before they died."

"Yes."

"Who else knows about this?"

"You're the first."

Harrison stood up, shuffling some papers on her desk. It was a nervous action, appearing to allow her time to collect her thoughts rather than actually tidying up. Benedict noticed small beads of sweat forming on her forehead.

Her entire outfit was visible to him now. They were always top-of-the-line. Benedict was far from a fashion expert, but today's ensemble was a white silk double-breasted jacket over a blue sapphire top with matching white slacks. He'd seen her wearing a pink tan Gucci Wool coat on her way into the office. He guessed the suit was Gucci as well. Benedict's wife Rose had met Harrison on several occasions and educated her husband on Harrison's fashion. Rose had commented on how expensive her wardrobe was, guessing each outfit must cost between four and five thousand dollars, well beyond what a Director's salary should be able to afford. When the subject came up, Harrison chalked it up to "good investments."

"Keep it that way for now," Harrison said about the IV bag. "I need to get with administration and the lawyers to find out how we're going to handle this. I'm late for a meeting upstairs. I'll take it up with the brass as soon as we're done." She picked up the IV bag and motioned for Benedict to give her his reports. Harrison stood and came around the desk and took them.

Benedict could also see the bulge under her jacket. Benedict was privy to the fact that the woman carried. Harrison had received death threats a number of years ago when the hospital underwent some downsizing and cuts had to be made. She had a concealed carry permit and always holstered a pistol.

"Mel, there's something else."

CHAPTER 4

"Re-raise," Ari Spanos said as he waved away a cloud of smoke from his face. He dropped a stack of chips into the pot. "Are all you guys ready for this storm?" Spanos asked the eclectic group seated under a low-hanging cloud of pipe and cigar smoke at the poker table set up in Benedict's garage.

The television reports about approaching Hurricane Lorraine were increasing in length and number as the Category Three storm bore down on southeastern Virginia. The television meteorologists were predicting it would make land fall within forty-eight hours. Lorraine was a late-season October cyclone raising anxiety in the area.

"Those storms always turn to the north before they reach us. I'm not worried." Devin McGuire, the lawyer whose over-the-top television commercials had made him a local icon, frowned at his hand and tossed his cards into the muck pile.

"I've got my water, flashlights and canned food all set," Gregor Jablonski stated. "The plywood is ready. I'll put it over the windows of the shop at the last possible moment." Jablonski owned a local cigar and tobacco shop named the Cigar Vault on Route 17 in York County.

"You're such a Boy Scout, Smokes. I fold." Joseph Bellini said as he puffed on one of Jablonski's Rocky Patels.

McGuire said, "I'll fly out of here as soon as those technicians have my plane serviced. They should have been done yesterday. Those guys don't work like an Indy 500 pit crew. With the prices they charge, they ought to."

Bellini turned to Benedict seated beside him.

"I hope Rose doesn't mind us crashing in your garage."

Benedict folded as well. "She's okay with it. It's better that I'm here in case she needs anything. Thanks for asking, Joe." Bellini owned a towing service, Bellini's Towing.

"How's she doing?"

"Yeah, how goes the good fight?" McGuire chimed in.

"She has good days and bad days. Today's been a pretty good day."

"We're waiting on you there, Manny," Spanos barked at the large black man across from him. "You in or out?"

Tyrone Manville sipped his Miller Lite, took a drag on his large cigar and blew a stream of blue smoke at Spanos. "You want a stogie, Ari?"

"You know I don't smoke, Squid."

Manville was a Navy SEAL stationed at the Little Creek Naval Amphibious Base in Virginia Beach. "Doesn't it bother your sensibilities to be sitting here with all us smokers? Aren't you afraid you'll catch some kind of cancer?"

"I always worry about catching something from you guys. I only hang out with you guys 'cause I'm recruiting new patients," Spanos shot back. A leading physician in the area, Aristotle Spanos, had been friends with Benedict and Benedict's wife Rose for nearly a decade. "Are you in or out?"

"I call," Manville said, tossing in his chips.

Jablonski, the cigar shop owner and this hand's dealer, called.

"Pot's good. Roll it," Manville, the SEAL, ordered.

The cigar shop owner burned the top card and turned the next one over. Spanos immediately bet large, chasing out Manville. Jablonski called.

Spanos showed his hole cards. He had a ten high straight to the cigar man's three of a kind.

"Thank you, Greg. My wife thanks you and so does the United States Navy."

"Bite me."

"Let's take a break," Benedict said as Spanos raked in his winnings.

The group walked out the open garage door to talk, sip beer and puff on their cigars and pipes, leaving Spanos and Benedict at the table.

"Are you going to be at the appointment tomorrow?" Spanos asked in low voice, as he stacked and re-stacked his chips.

"Of course. Did you get her results yet?"

"No. The radiologist promised I'd have them first thing in the morning. I asked them to rush it."

"Joint Commission could walk in any day now," Benedict said, changing the subject.

"I heard. What are you going to do about the drug error?"

Benedict had filled Spanos in on the Nonarc IV bag and the patient's death earlier today. "I don't know. I discussed it with my boss. It's in her court at the moment. When I told her about the two other deaths she nearly soiled her expensive pants."

Benedict had outlined the three deaths at the end of their meeting today. Benedict watched the color empty from her face so much so that even her expensive makeup couldn't hide it. He showed her copies of the paperwork he'd collected from the filing cabinets in the anteroom. But the only smoking gun was the empty IV found in the trash can.

"That pharmacist, Watson, really mixed all the doses that killed each patient?"

"According to the paperwork, he did. His is the only name on the paperwork. Normally, IV products are mixed by the technicians and then checked by the pharmacist. In these cases, Michael Watson mixed and checked everything. But I can only verify that one bag was mixed incorrectly. Today's. I can't be sure the others were wrong."

"And you're sure, all three patients died after they were given a dose of intravenous Nonarc? I order that drug all the time. I've never seen any problems with it."

"I guess you wouldn't. But remember the contents left in the bag today were not consistent with Nonarc. So maybe Michael Watson made a mistake."

"Yeah, but three times. And all three times it resulted in death?"

"That's a good point. I did a little more digging. They were all cancer patients in varying stages of their diseases. Palladine, today's death, had early stage mesothelioma. His prognosis was pretty good. The other two patients were closer to death. Not that that matters." Benedict recited the names of the other two patients. "Were either of them yours?"

"The names don't ring any bells."

Benedict nodded. "The hospital's in a bad spot. If Joint Commission finds out the deaths are associated with a pharmacist's negligence, we will be in a world of hurt."

ΩΩΩ

Michael Watson had spent two years working full-time in the subterranean laboratory.

The dank, underground air seeped into his bones, chilling him. With the approaching storm, the humidity was higher and penetrated the earth, making his work space thick and musty. This place was a chemist's dream, an amalgamation of advanced technology and ancient compounding. He swiveled on his stool and surveyed the area.

He was fifteen feet below the surface, directly under the science building on the John Ratcliffe University campus. The architecture of the lab contained no corners. The massive circular room stretched over a fifty foot diameter beneath a ten foot ceiling. The curved, unvarnished oak work benches sat flush to the arced wall and were topped by highly-polished, black granite.

A continuous string of fluorescent lights, curved to match the contour of the room, hung from the ceiling and glowed softly. A second bank of fluorescent lights formed a cross in the center of the circle shedding light on more work benches, several desks and large refrigerator-sized pieces of equipment.

The outer workbench was interrupted by five large, water-tight doors. They were the kind of doors found on a battleship or a submarine. You had to step over a foot high bulkhead. Each one had a large metal spinning handle that rotated watertight pins into place. The sound of dripping water and slick passageways in the tunnels were a constant down here. And unless you were entering or leaving, the doors were always closed.

Four entryways were positioned at the twelve, three, six and nine o'clock positions of the room. The twelve o'clock portal was the tunnel access back to the science building; the three o'clock door allowed entry into the small apartment, the six o'clock opening was a dead-end hallway with one door which Watson had never been allowed to open. Behind the nine o'clock exit resided a small animal lab housing monkeys, mice and rats and a utility room consisting of generators, a high capacity water pump and heater and the air handling units. Watson was seated at the five o'clock position beside the last doorway. One which he had also never seen opened.

He read the signs suspended from the ceiling above. Hanging from chains in the tiles, the professionally crafted signs were stationed at each of the twelve clock positions. Each one represented a step in the manufacturing process Watson had perfected for his employers, and now was hiding from them.

Watson craned his neck to see the word on the sign right above him.

Rubedo

It was Latin, meaning "reddening." Whereas the other stations sported high tech equipment, this work station looked like it belonged in an eighteenth century pharmacy. Black-capped amber bottles filled with various powders were scattered about. The gummed labels, peeling and yellowed, were stained with powdery finger prints. An eight inch thick tome of faded, cracked leather entitled *United States Dispensatory* rested open amidst the jars. The ceramic mortar and pestle was the size of a family-sized salad bowl and was coated with the remnants of a red powder Watson had been triturating into fine granules. He lifted the amber bottle and read its label:

Reddo Sulum

Red sulfur.

Deciphering the correct formulation had been more than just finding the exact ratios of ingredients. The formula consisted of twelve steps, twelve different ingredients. He had toiled to perfect it for two years with no success until a few days ago.

The Rubedo step involving the red sulphur had been the most elusive. Watson had discovered its secret only by chance, in the writings of H.P. Lovecraft. He was an author, the Edgar Allen Poe of science fiction. Watson had been reading him for years. It was buried in a novella entitled *The Case of Charles Dexter Ward.*

The money he was being paid was incredible, more than he could earn in five years as a pharmacist. But, he'd finally learned what this concoction was being used for and that knowledge was clawing at his soul like a desperate prisoner. If Watson was right—and he prayed he was—Augustus Palladine would be the last human subject to give his life for the cause.

Initially, the formula had been tested on the rats and monkeys, resulting in quick, ugly deaths. Red sulphur, he'd learned, was the problem. He tweaked its proportions making adjustments in milligrams, keeping everything else constant. With each batch, he achieved marginally better results. The animals lived longer before they died from massive internal hemorrhaging. Until last night, the longest any animal had survived after administration had been sixty-three minutes.

Despite his lack of complete success, Watson was ordered to compound doses large enough for larger primates, apes and orangutans. What confused him was the lack of larger animals in their possession. They were housed at another facility, he was told. The vials were taken from him and the results communicated back to him later. All were failures. *Keep working* was the standing order.

It was through Katherine, the nurse, that he learned about the human subjects. It wasn't hard to make the connection. They were testing the recipe on live patients. Watson should have seen it coming. And now he was haunted by the deaths and his involvement.

Watson had approached Ashan Habib, the same man who had delivered the red sulphur, demanding the testing be stopped. The stout Iranian had threatened his family in a combination of English and Farsi. His children and grandchildren were being watched, Watson was warned. Harm would befall each and every one of them if he did not keep quiet and, furthermore, did not produce results.

Watson had calculated and prepared two doses of the correct recipe. One dose of the new formula had been confiscated and would be delivered in the next twenty-four hours by Katherine Diehl to an unsuspecting patient. Watson had managed to hide the last remaining dose from his employer.

At sixty-five years old and working two jobs, he was exhausted. His full-time duties at Tidewater and his covert sessions in the lab were sapping his strength and mental alertness. He was so focused on his work in the lab that his work at Tidewater was suffering. Between the two jobs, he was working almost fifteen hours a day, leaving little time for the basic functions of life. He was eating like a starved bird and with the mounting stress, his sleep was all but non-existent.

The stress had mushroomed now. Not only was he burdened with the knowledge that he'd had a hand in the several deaths. In the last twelve hours, he'd learned that the results of his work were no longer a secret. The deaths had been noticed—by his supervisor Alex Benedict. Watson had caught a glimpse of Benedict's computer screen, confirming the deaths and the connection to Nonarc.

Benedict had been in Melissa Harrison's office when Watson had returned from his clandestine meeting with Katherine Diehl. Benedict's office door was open and the report was loaded on his computer screen. The key words jumped off the screen: *massive internal hemorrhaging*. The name Augustus Palladine cemented it. Watson almost threw up then and there. It would only be a matter of time before it all fell apart.

When word of the unethical and illegal testing leaked, he would be finished as a pharmacist. A conviction and prison time was a certainty. His name would be reviled. To add massive insult to all of his transgressions, once his formula and its power were made known, it would lead to world-wide chaos.

The first inkling of a way out had begun to take shape in his mind, one that would keep the promise of the recipe alive so it could be brought to the world in the proper way and, at the same time, end Watson's involvement. His employers could not ever be allowed to possess it. Watson had to pass on the Materia Prima—as it was called—to someone with the wisdom, courage and fortitude, someone who would not shrink from the formidable challenges this dilemma would present.

All that remained would be for that righteous man to follow Watson's clues. Watson had worked at Tidewater long enough to know such a man. He'd seen him in action many times, taking on the minority of difficult doctors and stuffy administrators with integrity and fairness. He was a man who'd been kind to Watson, keeping him on over younger, more energetic but less experienced pharmacists. A man for whom Michael Watson held a great deal of respect.

That man didn't know it yet, but he would soon hold in his hands the ability to bring mankind the greatest gift it would ever see. Or destroy it completely.

ΩΩΩ

In the last eighteen months, Rose had been through the entire arsenal in medicine's armory against late stage ovarian cancer. Surgery had removed her ovaries and the tumor. Following the surgery, Rose had endured cycles of various chemo treatments at Ari Spanos's office and treatment center. Beginning with a six cycle course of carboplatin and Taxol, it hadn't taken long for her gorgeous locks to begin shedding. The trips to the bathroom to puke her guts out were endless bouts of agony for her and heart-rending episodes for Benedict.

Benedict sat on the sofa, aiming the remote at the flat screen television. He stopped on a National Geographic show about the African plains. A sleek cheetah was chasing down a doomed gazelle. A moment before the cheetah made its final leap, Benedict began surfing again. The channels raced by. Rose was curled up beside him, reading Robert Louis Stevenson's *Treasure Island*. Her floral head scarf covered the scraggily threads of what was once a gorgeous head of caramel hair.

"Did you see Jason when you picked up the medication?" She asked him absent-mindedly

Benedict had stopped by The Colonial Pharmacy this afternoon to pick up three of Rose's prescriptions. The new pharmacy manager, Jason Rodgers, had been an upperclassman of Benedict's at MCV, graduating two years before Benedict more than a decade ago.

"Yeah, he was there."

"How's he doing?"

Rose, an adjunct professor of literature at John Ratcliffe University in Newport News near the hospital, was on medical leave. She stayed in touch with her colleagues and students through Facebook, Twitter and e-mail.

"He's got the place under control now. I think he's involved with Christine Pettigrew, Thomas's daughter. They were looking at each other like love-struck teenagers behind the counter."

The Colonial's long-time owner Thomas Pettigrew had died in a car wreck about a year ago. Benedict had heard rumors about Jason who had spent some time in the hospital. Benedict had asked about it, but Rodgers had rebuffed him saying it was nothing.

"Well, good for him," Rose said.

When the Carbo and Taxol hadn't worked, Ari Spanos had started Rose on a round of liposomal doxorubicin with its penchant for cardiotoxicity and more nausea and vomiting. That was followed by topotecan for five days every three weeks.

On several occasions, Rose's treatments had to be withheld because her platelet and neutrophil counts had dropped to dangerous levels. Each time that happened, Benedict would become frustrated with his good friend, Spanos. Every day he delayed her treatments was another twenty-fours that allowed the tumors to grow and spread.

As a clinical pharmacist who'd completed a residency in oncology, Benedict knew full well the dangers of continuing chemo on patients with low blood counts. But as a caregiver and husband, he also knew the angst and hours of worry it created.

And throughout it all, Rose had been prescribed generous amounts of OxyContin, Percocet and Vicodin for her varying degrees of pain. Not to mention the anti-nausea medications and laxatives. Benedict couldn't remember the last time Rose had taken a decent shit. She had also had to have fluid removed from her abdomen twice in the last six months.

Despite all of it, Rose never complained. Her faith was the bedrock of a simple, honest life. "It's God's will," she often said.

"I have my appointment with Ari tomorrow," she reminded him.

"I know," Benedict replied softly.

"Did he say anything to you during poker in the garage?"

"He'll have the results of the latest PET/CT scan in the morning."

"What do you think it will show?"

Benedict wrapped his arm around her. Her head rested against his chest. He squeezed her close. "It's going to be good news."

"I hope so."

"It will."

Benedict filled his chest with air and let it out slowly. He didn't want Rose to feel any tremor in his body. If he pushed it out too fast, he was afraid he'd lose it, something he never did in front of her.

Rose snuggled up closer to him. "I love you, baby."

"I love you more."

"If I ask you a question," she whispered, "will you answer it honestly?"

"I always have. You know that."

"Have I lived a good life?"

ΩΩΩ

Katherine Diehl strode hesitantly into the darkened room, carrying the small IV bag. It was close to midnight. She stopped just inside the door and waited, watching and listening. The patient was surrounded by four crying family members, standing alongside the bed.

She asked the family to step outside while she finished up. When they were gone, the nurse closed the door, and observed the dying woman. Satisfied the patient was sleeping; Katherine made her way to the bedside, still traumatized by what happened yesterday with patient Augustus Palladine.

Guilt, brought on by the violation of the complete trust they were placing in her filled her. Before coming to work, she'd taken several doses of generic Ativan, slugged down a healthy dose of vodka and slept off the drama.

Katherine checked the patients arm band. Margaret Queen was in her eighties.

Queen's skin was pasty and shriveled. Her muscle mass had melted away revealing the slight bones beneath. The thinning hair had been combed and set. A green nasal canulla affixed under her nose hissed oxygen from green tubing running from the wall behind her bed. The woman's chest rose and fell every few seconds.

Advanced colon cancer with metastases to the lung and liver.

As with the others before this one, administration of this particular intravenous medication would show up in the patient's medical record as the drug Nonarc.

With the generous money she was being paid, she'd managed to pay off her car and the substantial credit card bills left by that double-dealing, unfaithful, gambling addict of an ex-husband. She prayed for forgiveness every time she deposited the cash.

The steadily increasingly amounts of vodka could not numb the guilt. The remnants of her imbibitions lingered now in the form of a throbbing headache in her temples.

She was neck-high in an evil taking place at Tidewater Regional Medical Center, violating the Nightingale Pledge. Katherine was knowingly administering an altered medication to the patient, one with deadly consequences. *Or would Michael Watson's promise to her come true? Had he found the true formula?*

The thought of exposing the plan had crossed her mind thousands of times. It would take a mountain of courage to reveal her complicity. And her current reserve was nothing more than an ant-hill. A paraphrased quote jumped into her head: *Evil triumphs when good men—or women—do nothing.*

Once hung at the bedside, it would take about thirty minutes for the tainted liquid to infuse. And when it had infused, Katherine would return, remove the IV bag and place it in her handbag. She would secretly turn it back over to *them.*

Katherine was determined not to repeat the mistake she'd made the other night. After administering the Nonarc, she was called to assist with another patient. A series of patient episodes diverted her attention away from Augustus Palladine and the IV bag. One patient seized. Katherine was called in to assist. When the crisis was over, the night shift hospitalist wanted her to help him with the placement of a central line. As she left that patient's room thirty minutes later, an urgent phone call from the doctor of another patient required she take a stat verbal order for a diuretic.

When she had finally returned to retrieve the IV bag, Katherine entered the room and found the nursing assistant removing it. The nurse looked at her watch. An hour and fifteen minutes had passed.

Panicked that her transgression would be discovered, Katherine retreated to the nurse's station in the center of the circular. She looked around every few minutes for the phalanx of authorities she knew would appear. But nothing happened.

Afraid to go back into the patient's room, she busied herself with other duties in a completely distracted manner. Later, she learned the LPN had removed the bag and thrown it in the trash. Then Augustus Palladine's heart stopped and the Code Blue was initiated. Her employer was not pleased.

Two IV lines snaked their way into Margaret Queen's bloodstream, one in either arm. One was a patient-controlled analgesic, morphine. When pain relief was needed, the patient pushed a button to self-administer a dose according doctor-prescribed parameters.

The button lay untouched at Queen's side. Katherine walked around the bed, lifted the small device and depressed the button. The controlling pump whirred and buzzed. The plunger pushed the prescribed volume of fluid through the tubing and into the patient's veins. Satisfied the dose of narcotic had been administered and that this patient would not wake, she walked back around the bed and began the procedure of hanging the illicit solution.

She lifted the 100 milliliter bag holding the green liquid with golden specks to the hook on the IV stand. The specks suspended in the liquid seemed to glow. It had never done that before. Inserting the pointed end of the tubing, her lips moved silently as she mouthed the words to a childhood prayer. The patient stirred, startling her. She jumped as the patient stared up at her.

"Are you my angel?" the old woman said. "What is that light?"

Katherine regained her poise and said, "No, ma'am. I'm just fixing your IV."

The old woman closed her eyes and fell back into a deep sleep.

Katherine inserted the tubing into the port in the main IV tubing running into Margar's—the patient's—arm. Katherine opened the clamp again allowing the teal solution to begin infusing. Each droplet slammed into the small pool of fluid in the collection chamber like tiny bomblets.

Katherine silently completed her prayer and began to sob as she turned to leave.

CHAPTER 5

The next morning, a break in the clouds allowed a weak ray of orange sunlight to slice through the gray morning air. Michael Watson navigated his aging Ford Taurus through the thickening traffic slowing at the exit leading to the Norfolk Naval Base. He was running behind. His flight to New York was leaving in ninety minutes. He'd forgone his shift at the hospital, not even bothering to call out.

The package sat on the seat beside him. It was a single sheet of white paper inside a manila envelope wrapped in a plastic bag.

Watson parked in the short-term lot at Norfolk International Airport and strode towards the terminal.

ΩΩΩ

He parked the Dodge sedan across from the entrance to the terminal. The driver followed Watson in. The aging pharmacist passed through the security checkpoint and headed towards the

American Airlines check-in. The driver removed his cell phone and dialed a number.

"It's Timothy. He's about to board a flight.... Okay, I will."

Timothy walked to the monitors and read the American Airlines listing. He found three cities and flight numbers listed scheduled for departure: Cincinnati, Charlotte and Philadelphia.

He removed his cell again and dialed another number.

"Hey, Chuck, It's Tim.... I'm fine, thanks for asking.... I need the flight manifests for three American Airlines flights leaving Norfolk in the next thirty minutes. I'm looking for a guy named Michael Watson."

ΩΩΩ

"Are we ready, John?" Ben Roberts asked. "Three years ago, your medical staff was cited in several different areas."

"I assure you, Ben," J. Edward Kyle replied. "All those issues have been addressed and corrected."

"Let's hope so. You know that as the only remaining stand alone hospital in Hampton Roads combined with the fact that our bottom line is so fat, we are ripe for a takeover. Several health systems have been inquiring. We need a good showing with Joint Commission."

Three knocks on the oak door interrupted Roberts.

"They just showed their badges at the front desk," Gladys, the administrative secretary, said as she stuck her head in the door. "We went on to the website and verified their identities."

"Who?"

"Two Joint Commission surveyors just walked in."

ΩΩΩ

She knew she would never give him children.

He had talked about starting a family all the time. They had tried but failed. Since she'd been diagnosed, her husband had not brought up the subject once. Rose wiped away a tear. If he was ever to be blessed with a son or daughter, it would be by another woman after she was gone.

Alex was in the shower and had lifted himself from the bed a few minutes earlier. Rose had not slept well and was awake when Alex rose. She had kept her eyes closed pretending to be asleep. It was an act designed not to be deceptive, but for his benefit.

When he was around her, he was tuned to every sound she made, ready to jump to her aid. A drained look filled his eyes these days. Her deteriorating condition was taking a massive toll on her husband. As much as he tried to hide it from her, Rose saw it sapping his strength.

He was a devoted and loving man, who had spent the last eighteen months taking care of her every need: waking in the middle of the night to place a cool towel against her forehead, picking up her growing inventory of prescriptions or kneeling beside as her innards were turned inside out by the vomiting and then cleaning up the mess. As much as her disease devastated her, she knew her catastrophic situation was sucking the soul out of her husband almost as much as it was her. She hated to be the cause of his ordeal.

That same devotion and love would one day make him a wonderful father. Their house had been built and designed around growing a family that would flourish. Alex talked about how their personalities meshed perfectly for parenthood. Rose, as mothers should be, would be the disciplinarian, the motivator and the one who would pay strict attention to their studies. She would mold these little persons into fine, caring adults with a drive to excel and a compassion for those less fortunate. Mothers were the builders of character, the definers of expectations and the shaper of souls. Fathers were the teachers, the philosophers and the fixers. Alex would teach his sons to throw and hit the ball. Rose would make them get back up to the plate after they struck out, refusing to let them feel sorry for themselves. He would encourage his daughters to try harder and never give up. She would chastise them for lack of discipline and self-pity. Alex would fix the flat tires on their bikes and Rose would teach them how to dress and care for themselves.

Rose had struggled for weeks with the enormous stress her illness had created for him. As hard a decision as it was to make, she'd found a quicker way to ease his torment.

CHAPTER 6

R ose's delicate frame was swallowed by the office chair.

She was leaned forward towards Spanos's desk. The piles of papers and patient charts on his desk put Benedict's to shame in both number and thickness. Spanos had Rose's thick file spread before him, nestled in the small canyon created by two paper skyscrapers.

Benedict smiled at Rose who returned the smile weakly then averted her eyes. His gut was knotted tight as he took in the sight of his strong-willed wife battling to remain un-phased. Despite her attempt to do so, it made her look more vulnerable.

Benedict then locked eyes with his college friend and wife's oncologist.

Ari Spanos's six-three Greek frame was draped in a white lab coat. His murky brown eyes peered from under large brows. Spanos preferred a completely clean-shaven head. Three tightly coiled rolls of muscle-fat wrapped the base of his thick neck.

"We have a lot to discuss," Spanos said quickly. "The PET/CT Scan results arrived early this morning." Positron emission tomography (PET) scans were often read in conjunction with CT scans, giving physicians and radiologists a metabolic and an anatomic picture.

Benedict reached over and placed his hand on Rose's resting in her lap. He turned towards her and absorbed the sight of her profile against the far wall. With her head bowed and wrapped in a floral scarf, she refused to look at him as she gently stroked the top of his hand. Benedict couldn't shake a sense of foreboding. It was more than just the anticipation of the news Spanos was about to deliver. Even in her diminished physical state and under the enormous emotional strain, she seemed distracted. Her caresses were nervous distractions rather than loving strokes.

Spanos spoke in a business-like fashion, delivering facts devoid of emotion. "We see metastases. The last round of chemo had very little effect. Your liver is now involved as well as your intestines."

Spanos continued, answering Benedict's unasked question.

"I know this was the last round of conventional treatment. This is most definitely a setback. But, there are other options. I have a colleague up at Samford who's been doing some great work with an experimental therapy. He's having some success. I think Rose would be a good candid...."

"Stop, Ari," Rose interrupted. After a brief moment of silence, she continued. "I want to say something."

"Sure, Rose. By all means," Spanos replied.

"How long have we known each other? Thirteen years?"

"Sounds about right."

Benedict nodded in agreement.

Rose stroked Benedict's face. "Alex, baby, you know I love you more than anything."

Benedict took her hand in both of his, pressing it against his cheek.

"It's all too much," she said. "It's time to stop."

"Stop what?" Benedict asked.

"I'm going to stop my treatments."

"We can't give up. There's still much that can be done," the doctor said.

Benedict felt like he'd been hit with a tsunami. He sat stunned, listening to Rose and Spanos going back and forth. The words seemed to crawl over his skin.

"There may be much that can be done. But, sometimes, you have to leave it in His hands," Rose replied.

"I believe in God, Rose. I believe He works through me. I am an instrument of His power. I see it every day."

"You're a good man, Ari. I love you for everything you've done. You have done a wonderful job. I couldn't have received better care...."

"I'm not finished," Spanos interjected.

"No!" Rose said, slicing through his words. "But I am."

"Rose, how can you do this?" Benedict started.

Rose moved her hand and placed it over Benedict's. "Baby, I'm tired of all the pain and vomiting. I'm tired of all of it."

"No!" Benedict groaned. "You can't give up!"

"I can and I will," she admonished him. "This is my life and my body."

He swallowed hard several times. Benedict let his head fall, stopping as his chin hit his chest. The sum total of Benedict's fear, frustration and fatigue which had gestated over the last year crowned, spilling forth.

"I'm sorry, honey."

"You can't give up!" He leaned over, closer to Rose. She did the same. "I'm sorry, Rose. It's selfish of me. But, I love you more than anything. I wish it were me."

Rose smiled. "So do I."

Benedict smiled back and pressed his lips against Rose's for several long seconds. "I love you, Rose. I love you very much, baby."

Spanos watched this exchange with no hint of embarrassment or desire to be anywhere else. He waited until they were both looking up at him.

"Are you sure about this, Rose?"

Rose nodded. "No, I'm not. But my decision is final."

ΩΩΩ

Timothy managed one of the last seats, near the cockpit and the forward lavatory. Watson was seated in the middle of the aircraft. Fearing Watson might be trying to flee, Timothy was instructed to follow him. Like Timothy, Watson had no suitcase or carry-on bags. He carried only the manila envelope wrapped in plastic.

The plane landed in Newburgh, New York in the lower part of the state near the Connecticut border. Timothy's contact had informed him that Watson had booked a connecting flight on U.S. Airways from Philadephia to Newburgh, New York. Timothy had done the same. They each rented a car and Timothy trailed his mark to the cemetery of the West Point Military Academy. There Watson entered the grounds. Timothy, not wanting to be made, waited near the entrance to await Watson's return. His orders were to stay with Watson. If he was fleeing, Timothy needed to know where he was going. Watson's actions had been inconsistent of late. Timothy's employer was worried that he was coming unraveled.

Thirty minutes later, Watson drove out of West Point and headed north back to Stewart International Airport in Newburgh. Once Timothy confirmed Watson was returning to Norfolk, he purchased his return tickets for his connecting flights home on U.S. Airways and American Airlines. He noticed that Watson no longer carried the manila envelope.

Back home, he tailed Watson on Interstate 64 across the Hampton Roads Bridge Tunnel, heading west. He phoned Ashan, informing him that the subject was back in town. The Iranian asked where he'd gone and what he'd done. Timothy told him.

"Okay, just keep an eye on him and let me know if anything important happens."

Ten minutes later, Watson took the off ramp for Exit 247. When he connected with Yorktown Road, Watson continued north along Yorktown Road crossing over Jefferson Avenue. Timothy stayed a hundred yards behind. Watson's driving indicated he was unconcerned he might be followed.

Half a mile up Yorktown Road, the Taurus turned right onto the long path leading to Endview Plantation. Timothy slowed as he neared the entrance road and continued past.

He rounded a bend, performed a three-point turn and headed back. He parked a quarter of a mile from the mansion with a view of the Taurus on the access road. Peering through the dusty windshield, he saw that Watson was out of his car, standing at the open trunk. Timothy leaned over the steering wheel for a closer look.

Watson's vehicle was the only one on the property. Without a hint of concern, he stripped to his underpants, tossing his shirt and pants to the ground near the car.

"What the hell?" Timothy whispered.

Then Watson pulled more clothes from the trunk and donned them. In three minutes, he was outfitted in what appeared to be a dark blue Civil War Union officer's uniform, complete with brass buttons and a sword hanging from his belt.

"This guy's deck is a couple aces light," he said out loud.

Watson, fully dressed now, reached into the trunk and removed something. Timothy could not make out what it was. Watson strode to the middle of the field fronting the white mansion and stood at attention for a few moments. Without warning, the pharmacist raised the item in his hand to his temple.

The report took a fraction of a second to travel to Timothy's ears. Even at this distance, the plume of exploding crimson was visible.

CHAPTER 7

"**I** hope you're rested up, big guy. 'Cause you're not getting much sleep tonight," Rose had said with a come-hither smile.

Those words, ones she'd spoken many months ago, had replayed themselves in Benedict's head for the last week. Rose had said them in that low, sexy growl that always made him want her. He remembered them now as he lay in bed beside his sleeping wife, his arm wrapped around her thin body, waiting for another day to begin. He'd lain in bed most of the night unable to sleep.

Benedict wondered if they would ever share another night like that one.

They had eaten at Ruth's Chris's Steakhouse in Virginia Beach, laughing and talking about the future then strolling along the boardwalk. Their world lay before them like yawning canyons, waiting to be explored. During dessert, Rose presented him with the gold jet lighter, engraved with the words she'd whispered in his ear at their wedding. The words that represented the sum total of their feelings for each other.

I burn for your love!!

"I want you to use it when you play golf with Ari and your buddies. I want you to remember me when you do," she'd said. Benedict's passion outside of pharmacy was golf. He was a scratch golfer. But he'd only played once since the day Rose announced she had cancer. It was his worst score ever. He hadn't picked up his clubs since.

After dinner, they'd raced back home to Newport News. The summer light was just beginning its descent behind the trees as they raced into the bedroom. Rose pushed him back out the door, telling him to wait downstairs while she prepared herself.

When she called down to him, Benedict launched himself up the stairs taking them three at a time. He pushed open the door and saw his Rose standing splendidly naked in the early evening glow. The light slanted into the room through the blinds, a sunburst filling the space. It seemed to find only her. Her body was perfect, curved and firm. Her hair framed her face as those green eyes beckoned him forward.

Benedict was looking at a living, breathing Renaissance painting. One side of her was bathed in the glow of diminishing sunlight, the other cast in shadow. Her curves and the texture of her perfect skin were enhanced by the side light. Her nipples were erect as her breasts rippled with each sensuous step she made towards him.

He always thought Rose was the most beautiful woman he'd ever laid eyes on. Tonight, she was a fertile goddess.

She cradled his head in her hands as she gently placed her lips on his. A volcanic shiver erupted down his spine. Rose reached for his belt and began unbuckling it. Benedict became instantly hard, hard enough to hammer nails. Rose led him to the bed.

They made love until the sunlight faded into a deep, rich blackness. They lay spent, sweating, caressing each other. Benedict had always cherished making love with his wife. But that night he had been to the mountaintop and viewed the light and passion inside her like never before. It was the last and best time they'd made love. A few weeks later, Rose began experiencing symptoms.

Now, Benedict opened his eyes, shocked back to his tormented present with a blast of cold reality. He lay behind Rose, spooning her, inhaling her medicated scent as her chest danced a slow rise and fall, thinking about life without her. Of course, they never talked about death. The subject was skirted, avoided as if even uttering it could unleash its demonic power.

As the gray light of morning cut through the bedroom, Benedict's mind shifted, as it always did after remembering their lovemaking, flashing to the seemingly minor snippets he'd taken for granted. At this moment, they took on the magnitude of a condemned man's last meal.

They told each other how much they loved each other every day. But, Rose always showed Benedict that she cherished him. Unexpected cards dripping with romantic writings left on the windshield of his car. Ironing his shirts before every shift he worked. Lovingly prepared dinners by candlelight after ten hour shifts followed by spine-tingling lovemaking. Her fingers caressing his cheek as she leaned in to kiss him goodbye; the soft, crinkle at the edge of her eyes every time she laughed. Sitting on the couch in the dark watching a movie her head nestled in the crook of his neck; the way her hands pulled his ass into her urging him deeper when they made love.

Those acts had died off with the progression of her disease. And it became Benedict's turn to take care of her.

Tender, simple acts!

Benedict had just been promoted to Assistant Director of Clinical Pharmacy Services. Rose had been complaining about abdominal problems, cramps and bloating. At first, her primary care doctor thought it was intestinal, irritable bowel syndrome, perhaps. He prescribed antispasmodics and muscle relaxants. Then she began to have problems with her period and the focus shifted to her uterus. Finally, after a referral to her gynecologist, a more extensive battery of tests had been performed. When the cancer had been confirmed, Ari Spanos was brought in.

He'd watched his lovely Rose shrivel from a healthy, vibrant woman with blushing cheeks and sparkling green eyes into a shadow of herself. Her hair was a memory. Wisps of sickly tendrils sprouted from her scalp like weeds on a driveway. She always kept it covered by a fashionable patterned scarf. Even Benedict wasn't allowed to see her uncovered. But on a few occasions, he'd walked in on her unexpectedly and caught a glimpse. The sight turned his stomach.

Of course, all of his self-pity could not hold a candle to what Rose must be going through. It was only in the lonely darkness as he lay in bed trying to sleep would his demons swell. During the day, he was too busy trying to concentrate on his duties at the hospital and caring for Rose to worry about the future.

As the Assistant Director of Clinical Pharmacy Services at Tidewater Regional Medical Center in Newport News, Virginia, Benedict was responsible for the proper usage of medications and their outcomes. He oversaw education of the pharmacists, nurses and physicians, ensuring they were in-serviced on the vast array of pharmaceutical weapons in the hospital's arsenal. It was a job he loved. And his sparkling performance reviews spoke to his mastery of it.

Until Rose became ill.

Now, it was merely the duty he fulfilled until he could get back to his wife. At the moment, the worry, the lack of sleep and the impending visit from the Joint Commission which had become a reality simply overwhelmed him.

As with the countless days before this one, he summoned the strength to rise. Another in a seemingly endless string of sunrises and sunsets, counting down to the day when he would awake and Rose would not be beside him in bed.

Benedict slipped his hand out from under her arms and carefully swung his legs over the side of the bed. He filled his chest with air several times and tried unsuccessfully to rub the fatigue from his burning eyes. A headache had blossomed at the base of his neck and was threatening to explode.

Reluctantly, he started to enter the closet. A magazine on the night stand on Rose's side of the bed caught his eye. He wasn't sure why he stopped to look at it. The assortment of colors and lines on the cover were not consistent with the types of magazines Rose read. She was a *People, Southern Living, Martha Stewart* kind of woman who had more fashion sense in her thumbnail than Benedict would ever accumulate in a lifetime. The lower right hand corner of the magazine lay exposed from under a stack of Rose's normal collection. The mood of the cover art was dark and burnished with a muted emotion.

He glanced at Rose. She lay on her side with her back to him, sleeping. Benedict slipped the magazine from under the pile. He realized it was not a magazine, but a catalog. He read the title and wanted to vomit: *Parilla Burial Caskets.*

CHAPTER 8

"Oh, my God," she said softly to herself, lifting the tie and letting it flop in her hand. "You are the love of my life. But, you have got to learn how to dress."

Rose took the tie and headed into the closet. She selected a red silk that would stand out magnificently against his navy blazer and khaki trousers. She laid the tie on the shirt and gently smoothed it with her hand.

Alex selected his tie every day. And Rose would go behind him and pick out a better one, the right one. He'd begun to learn which tie went with which outfit. Her husband was a brilliant man. He could pick out a tie. Yet, he always selected the wrong tie. It had become a ritual they performed every workday. Benedict would choose his tie and Rose would go behind him and find the one that best fit his mood and outfit.

Rose bowed her head, grasped the bedpost and cried.

"Are you okay?" Benedict was standing in the bathroom door, a towel wrapped around his waist, drying his hair with a second towel.

Rose quickly stood up and wiped her tears. "I'm fine."

Benedict went to her and wrapped his arms around her. They stood there for along moment until he finally said, "I love you."

"I love you, too."

"What is this?" Benedict walked to the night stand and showed her the casket catalog.

Rose frowned then shrugged.

"Exactly how long have you been thinking about stopping your treatments?"

"About three or four weeks."

"And you never thought to ask me for my advice?"

"Honey, I wasn't sure until just a few days ago. And besides, it's my decision."

Benedict sank on to the bed. Rose sat beside him. "Tell me why?"

ΩΩΩ

A shudder passed through Melissa Harrison.

All department heads, administrators and other hospital management were gathered in the large first floor conference room to meet the two Joint Commission surveyors.

She watched the physician surveyor for the Joint Commission pull president Ben Roberts aside as the Opening Conference and Orientation was about to begin. As the physician spoke in his ear, wagging a piece of paper in front of him, Roberts cast a concerned glance in Harrison's direction.

His next movement caused her concern to swell into panic. Roberts moved behind Harrison's chair, leaned over and whispered in her ear.

"I need a moment," he said.

Harrison excused herself and followed Roberts and the surveyor out into the hallway.

"This is Dr. Preston Mason with the Joint Commission," Roberts said.

He handed the letter to her. "We have received a complaint from a pharmacy employee. We are withholding that person's name for the time being. It's a rather disturbing complaint. It is being alleged that some patient's have died in your institution because of some quote, 'irregular pharmacy activities,' end quote. The complainant has given us days, times and patient names."

Harrison looked at the letter but did not really see or read it. The page wavered in her hand. She swallowed hard.

"We need to get to the bottom of this," she said firmly, hoping her anxiety was not evident.

"Yes, we do," the surveyor said. "We will conduct our regular survey according to the agenda we've outlined. However, in addition, we would like you to make available to us your intravenous compounding records for the last three months for our team to review. The complainant also mentioned another employee by name. This person has intimate knowledge of what's happening. We would at some point like to speak to Alex Benedict."

ΩΩΩ

"I've been having a dream. It's a message from God. He's telling me it's time to leave things in His hands."

Rose had been raised in a devoutly Catholic household and still attended mass when her strength allowed.

"The Lord speaks in many ways," she continued. "Often times, we do not recognize them for what they are. A subtle sign shrugged off. The Lord is behind all of it. Even my cancer is the Lord's work. I don't understand it—and don't like it. But He has a plan. My dream is the Lord speaking to me. I refused to accept it at first. But He is a patient God who just keeps sending me His message."

"You're basing your decision on a dream?"

"One of the reasons I made the choice was the dream," she replied.

"So there are other reasons?"

"They're not important."

"Tell me about the dream," Benedict said.

"Okay, but you can't interrupt."

Rose talked slowly at first, hesitating because it was difficult putting everything into words. But as the words flowed, she organized her thoughts and they flowed as if she'd rehearsed them for weeks.

"I'm seven or eight, playing with the focused intensity young children have when they are left to their own devices. The large tire swing hanging from the huge oak tree in my friend Myrl's spacious backyard was home base. We talked constantly, climbing up and down the tree. The limbs branched out parallel to the ground, thick and sturdy. Myrl's father had even nailed several wooden slats into the trunk to allow us to reach the lowest branch. This tree was huge. Me, and my two friends, Myrl and Dora, were totally absorbed in summer. It was perfect, sweet innocence.

"We called it the Tree of Dreams.

"When the sun went down, Myrl's mother called to us from the back porch. The words are burned into my brain. Alex, this happened many years ago. This scene is true. It happened when I was a young girl. Now, God is using it to tell me it's time," she said.

"*Rose, darling, your mother called. It's time for you to come home!*"

Rose's own mother had passed several years ago succumbing to her own bout with cancer, the same version that was killing Rose.

Rose continued. "The dream always starts with us climbing the massive oak. It ends the same way, with Myrl's mother echoing those words.

"In past nights," she went on. "I was always a young girl. Two nights ago was different. I was sitting in the tree all those years ago. But this time as a fully-grown woman, a married woman who knew she was really sick.

"Rose, darling, your mother called. It's time for you to come home!" Rose took Benedict's hand. "Those are the words. They can't mean anything else."

"Are you sure about this?"

"With each hour that passes, yes, I'm more certain. Do you know why?"

Benedict shook his head. Moisture collected in his eyes.

"Because I'm calm. I have no more anxiety."

Rose could see the pain in his face. She had been enveloped by the calm that came with finally making a tough decision that had been agonized over; solace blossomed in committing to doing something you knew you had to do but feared admitting it or saying it out loud. She'd grabbed her rosary from the night stand, fingered the beads and prayed with her husband, reciting a Hail Mary.

"I'm sure we'll have plenty of time together," she lied, wiping his eyes then hers. "Now get dressed. I feel good today. I'll make you breakfast."

Benedict went into the closet. Rose watched him sorting through socks and underwear then headed for the bathroom and the toilet. When her hand touched the doorknob, the dreadful spinning began. Vomit welled in the back of her throat. Rose forced it back down. She took several heavy breaths. The feeling passed and she stood more erect.

Without warning, like a thunder bolt coursing through her body, the pain rocketed from the base of her spine into her brain. The room took on unfathomable Dali-like dimensions. Plummeting towards the floor was the last sensation she felt before everything turned black.

ΩΩΩ

The shower had reenergized Benedict in a miniscule way. But his just-concluded conversation with Rose had just sucked that energy out of him. He looked back to the bedroom. Rose had gone into the bathroom.

Benedict bent at the waist, pressing his hands against his knees and drawing in quick, short breaths to calm himself. Sweat dripped from his brow onto the carpet. His legs muscles quivered.

Parilla Burial Caskets!

Rose was shopping for caskets as if she were flipping through the L.L. Bean catalog. She had been contemplating her decision for some time. Of course, that was the case. No one made such a decision lightly. It hurt him that she'd kept it from him. He felt betrayed.

A part of him hoped this was not real, that it was a just a circuitous route she would take on the path to making the right choice.

The catalog and her dream shattered those hopes.

A dream?

Benedict slipped on his underwear and socks. He walked back into the bedroom and saw Rose lying in a heap on the carpet.

A gash and a smear of blood lined her forehead. His heart clogged his throat. He dropped to his knees and scampered to his wife.

"Oh, my God!" he cried out. "Rose! Rose! No! Please! Not now! Please not now!"

CHAPTER 9

Rose turned her head to fully gaze at her husband. "Come close," she whispered.

Benedict placed his ear beside her pale lips.

Benedict could feel her soft breaths against his ear. "I won't be coming home, Alex. This will be it."

They were in the emergency room at Tidewater Regional. Benedict had slipped his hand into hers. He squeezed involuntarily at her words. He lowered his head and placed his cheek against hers so his lips were an inch from her ear.

"Don't talk like that."

"No, it's true. I want you to be strong for me. I'm ready. Help me die, Alex. Please, help me die."

Rose's words were whispered. Benedict looked up and flicked his head. Connie Stevens, their neighbor who had followed the ambulance to the hospital and was holding Rose's hand, nodded and departed.

He turned back to Rose. "Rose, I will do no such thing. Don't ask me to do that again!"

"I didn't mean it that way. I want you to be with me. I want your face to be the last thing I see. Will you promise me that?"

Tears filled his vision, dropping onto the blanket covering Rose's chest. He nodded ever so slightly. A gauze bandage had been placed above Rose's right eye.

He peered into Rose's eyes. "How are you feeling?" he asked as he stroked the fabric of her head scarf.

"My head is killing me."

"You took a nasty fall, baby."

"The pain's not from the fall. It's deeper. The back of my head feels like it will explode."

A tall, thin man with close cropped blonde hair dressed in green scrubs with a stethoscope draped sideways behind his neck entered the alcove. Benedict wiped his tear-stained face.

"I'm Dr. Gustaffson. You're one of the pharmacists here, aren't you?"

Benedict nodded still unable to speak, wiping his eyes with his fingers.

"I recognized you from the emergency medicine committee meeting you attended a few months ago. You discussed the results of the stroke treatment protocol study. It was well done."

"Thank you," Benedict croaked. "I remember." Benedict paused then spoke once more.

"She's in a lot of pain, Doc. Can we get her something for the pain?"

"Rose is experiencing unilateral weakness on her left side. I've ordered a CT scan of her head. I want to make sure she hasn't had a stroke of some kind. They should be coming to get her soon. She's under seizure precautions. I've asked for a neuro consult as well. Who is her oncologist?"

"Ari Spanos."

"We'll let him know she's going to be admitted. We'll get her something for the pain as soon as we can."

"Rose! Rose!" Connie, who was peeking through the curtain, began to shriek. "What's happening?"

Benedict turned and saw Rose shaking uncontrollably as the seizure began. Before her eyelids closed completely, he glimpsed her eyes rolling into her head.

Gustaffson pushed Benedict aside, stepped over to Rose. "Angela, get me 1 mg of IV Ativan stat!"

ΩΩΩ

"Are you okay? You look like you're going to be sick."

He looked at everyone at the table. Benedict had barely managed to calm down before entering the room. Melissa Harrison had paged him shortly after Rose's second seizure had been brought under control. Connie walked with the nurses as they wheeled her into Radiology for the CT scan.

"I'll be fine," he croaked.

"Alex," Ben Roberts began. "Melissa informed me about your wife's condition. I'm sorry both for that and the fact that you've had to take her to the ER today. I know this is not easy for you especially since we're now dealing with the Joint Commission. I want to tell you how much I appreciate you being here. Tidewater needs you. I'm not sure...."

His words trailed off in a sincere gush of emotion.

He recomposed and said, "I just want you to know how much I—and Tidewater—appreciate your dedication and commitment. We also have some very bad news."

"Oh?"

Harrison jumped in quickly. "Michael Watson killed himself this morning."

"What?"

The thought hung over the table between the four of them awkwardly.

"Melissa," Roberts said, "tells me he was a valuable member of the pharmacy."

Benedict nodded.

"Unfortunately, we do not have time to dwell on his death at the moment. We must forge ahead," Roberts began again. "We have one objective. That's to get through this Joint Commission survey and maintain our accreditation. Our long term goal is to keep TRMC strong and healthy so we can serve our community. Pharmacy is a vital part of that success. And you are a key factor in that equation. That said, we are under the gun right now. The Pharmacy conference is scheduled to begin in a few hours. And we," he motioned to everyone in the room, "have to get a few things cleared up."

Benedict locked eyes with each of them in turn, blinking away the burn.

Roberts continued. "Melissa tells me that you have discovered some very disturbing news. News that suggests that patients have died as a result of some medication errors. Is that correct?"

"That's right."

"Have you discussed this issue with anyone outside this room?"

"No," Benedict lied. He had discussed it with Spanos last night at the poker game.

"Good, let's keep it that way for now."

"We will have to discuss it sooner or later," Benedict added.

"And we will, Alex. Steps will be taken, have already been taken. You must remember if these deaths occurred as a result of negligence of the pharmacist Watson, Tidewater is at serious legal risk. The Joint Commission received a complaint against the hospital mentioning the deaths. We need to develop our strategy in response to this crisis. The Joint Commission is out and about in the hospital right now conducting tracers. The surveyors will meet with the pharmacy staff this afternoon. They asked for you by name. We just wanted to make sure we are all on the same page about this matter.

"What I'm about to tell you is strictly confidential," Roberts continued. "You know what's going on. Centurion Health is chomping at the bit to swallow us whole. You know what they do. They're going to come in here and strip this place to the bone. They'll cut staff. If we have any negative publicity, our research funds will dry up and Centurion will have more leverage. We need to keep Centurion at arm's length until we can cut a better deal with someone else. A great Joint Commission certification is key. If we get the certification, then we continue to operate as usual. If Joint Commission finds issues, especially your results and they give us an Immediate Jeopardy citation, the Board will be more inclined to sell to Centurion. You know what's going to happen then?"

Benedict remained silent and met the administrator's gaze.

"Think about your future, Alex. What happened to those patients is history. We can only deal with the future."

Benedict eyed Dr. Kyle and Melissa Harrison who to this point had remained silent but addressed Roberts.

"Mr. Roberts...."

"Please call me, Ben."

"Are you asking me to lie about these deaths, Ben?"

"Tell me what you know."

Benedict outlined the facts. Then he said, "I'm sure the Joint Commission expects good faith and honesty in the information they receive from us. If I am asked direct questions, I will tell the truth."

"I'm not asking you to lie, Alex," Roberts implored. "I'm asking you to choose your words very carefully. Okay?"

Benedict hesitated. "We'll see."

ΩΩΩ

"What did the CT Scan say?" Benedict asked.

Spanos walked him over to the monitor on the wall. He punched the keyboard and Rose's CT image and results appeared on the screen. Rose was awake but very groggy and not hearing their conversation.

"These are preliminary," Spanos replied. "The radiologist has not finished his report but he forwarded these as a favor to me. I can discuss them with you because Rose has given her permission."

"And?"

"She has two tumors in her brain. The small one is two centimeters located in the parietal lobe. That one is not much of an issue. The second and larger tumor is five centimeters in diameter and in the cerebellum. That's the one causing the problem."

Benedict's world was on unsteady ground. Michael Watson was dead. And Rose's cancer had spread from her ovaries to her lungs and intestines and now, her brain. "That caused the seizure?"

"The tumor's located in this area causing obstruction with flow of the cerebrospinal fluid causing hydrocephalus."

"Water on the brain?"

"That's the non-clinical term. She's experiencing swelling in her brain caused by a blocked fourth ventricle."

"So what can we do?"

"We could operate. I'd have one of the neurosurgeons install a shunt which is the traditional treatment. The newer procedure called an ETV or endoscopic third ventriculostomy is less invasive but very complicated. We'd have to transfer her to Norfolk. I'm not sure Rose would want that based on her recent declaration about her treatment."

"What do I do, Ari?"

"Let me make a few calls and get more info. In the meantime talk to Rose when she comes around. The neurosurgeon has ordered her some Decadron for the swelling and some IV Ativan to keep her comfortable. Does she have a written medical directive?"

A medical directive was a legal document indicating a patient's wishes about medical care in the event that they could not make decisions for themselves.

"Yeah, but I don't like what it says."

ΩΩΩ

"Will he cooperate?" Roberts asked.

"You heard him," Harrison replied. "He said he wouldn't lie."

"Then perhaps we can just ask Dr. Benedict to skip the pharmacy conference. And we can keep him away from the survey process. That shouldn't be so hard, considering he's looking after his wife."

"The surveyor mentioned Alex by name, remember? They will want to talk to him personally," Kyle responded.

Roberts cupped his chin in his hand, thinking.

"Melissa, John," Roberts swiveled his head between the two of them. "When the subject of these deaths comes up in the pharmacy conference this afternoon, the two of you had better have a plan to neutralize Alex Benedict."

ΩΩΩ

"Just take it one order at a time," he pleaded with Julia Spillane and Shanique Jones, the two technicians seated before the two large laminar flow hoods.

Success today was a rapidly disintegrating target.

Benedict was having a hard time keeping the IV room technicians focused. Keeping his mind on his work was a Herculean task for Benedict as well. He'd begun to discuss the surgery option with Rose. She'd starting shaking her head before he could finish. "It's in God's hands now," she'd said. Benedict kissed her, told her he'd be back soon and left Rose with Connie Stevens.

He had returned back to the pharmacy to cover Michael Watson's vacant shift. The two technicians were swiping back tears as they gamely tried to accomplish their tasks. They were an hour behind in their production of the one hundred or so intravenous products that needed to be delivered by noon.

This was the first time he'd had a chance to process the news of Michael Watson's death. It stunned him. Watson had been a great pharmacist whose performance had suffered over the last year. He was constantly late, missing delivery of medications and he looked drawn and haggard. Benedict had spoken to Watson about it on several occasions, including having to write him up the last time. Benedict felt their once good relationship had become strained. He wondered what had been going on in his life that would cause such a decline. Perhaps Watson had known about the deaths and the mistakes and had been covering them up. It might also explain why he took his own life. Benedict managed to ask a few questions about Watson's suicide. The man had stood in full Civil War dress on the front acreage of Endview Plantation and placed a Civil War-era pistol to his temple and pulled the trigger.

He shook his head. Nothing that had been happening in Benedict's world made much sense to him at the moment.

The list of orders for intravenous products from overnight and previous days was growing as new orders written by doctors this morning grew. The printer spewed forth labels and order documents every few minutes. Benedict felt himself pushing back a growing stress.

Quan Li, the small Chinese pharmacist, stuck her head in the door.

"What is it, Quan?"

"You need to write a TPN order on the third floor." TPN stood for total parenteral nutrition. It was a way of feeding a patient intravenously.

"Doctor wants it started ASAP."

ΩΩΩ

"I don't believe what I seen," one nurse said.

"It's the work of the Lord," said another.

The third nurse with large breasts and equally wide hips on which her hands were planted saw Benedict approach. "What's going on?" he asked.

Benedict had arrived on the oncology unit to find the nurses huddled around someone sitting at the nurse's station in distress.

The oncology unit occupied the entire third floor of the Archer Tower. The building was a tall cylinder, ten stories high. Twenty patient rooms ringed the outer perimeter of the floor plan, except for the area filled by the elevator shafts and stairwells. The center of the floor plan was filled by the nurse's stations, the head nurse's office, a nurse's lounge, patient waiting areas and storage facilities. In fact, Rose was now a patient on this very floor.

The nurse had a cold compress pressed against the woman's neck; another was squatted down face to face with the nurse who appeared to be stunned or in shock for some reason, talking quietly into the nurse's ear. The three remaining nurses stood in a semi circle watching and commenting.

It was then that Benedict saw the nurse who was the focus of all the attention. Katherine Diehl.

"Katy, here, took a tumble," the large-breasted nurse replied. "She's seen a miracle."

Benedict knelt beside Katherine. "Are you okay?"

"Yeah, I just need a minute," she answered as she placed her head in her hands.

"So what happened?"

The third nurse wagged a finger at Benedict and said, "Come on, I'll show you."

The nurse's name tag read "Sheila." Benedict followed her to a patient room where more nurses and aides were gathered.

"This here is Margaret Queen." Queen's room was diametrically opposite Rose's on this floor.

Benedict peered into the room. The patient wearing the traditional backless hospital gown was surrounded by onlookers watching her do a slow-motion jig in the middle of the room to the whoops and hollers of the employees and three people in street clothes. They appeared to be family members.

Benedict looked between the patient and Sheila twice.

"Last night, Maggie here," Sheila held her thumb and forefinger close together, "this close to meeting the Almighty. She was drugged up, cancer riddling her body. She wasn't expected to make it through the night. Her family's here. They were saying their good-byes." Sheila pointed to the dancing woman. "Now, look at her."

Benedict watched the woman for a moment as she two-stepped over to a man who looked to be her son. They waltzed spinning in circles.

"Are you sure it's the same patient?"

"She was my patient yesterday. I assure you it's the same woman."

"How did this happen?"

Sheila looked at Benedict's name badge. "Honey, your guess is as good as mine."

"So what's wrong with Katherine?"

"I guess she walked in and saw Maggie, sitting up, jabbering like there was no tomorrow. She musta been caught by surprise and fainted. It's a friggin' miracle. You just never know," Sheila said. "You just never know. I guess it wasn't her time to go."

Benedict walked to the nurse's station and looked over Margaret Queen's chart. She'd been admitted for a pleural effusion secondary to lung cancer and pain management. He carefully reviewed her medication chart. When he pulled up her Medication Administration Record, he noticed that Queen had been prescribed Nonarc. Benedict inspected the doses that had been given. Katherine Diehl had given Queen a dose late last night.

He went to the nurses around Diehl. "I need to speak with Katherine. Privately," he said.

The nurses dispersed. Benedict knelt beside her. Her hand was over her mouth, trembling.

"Katherine, what happened?"

She looked at him, but did not see him. Her eyes were unfocused and distant.

"Katherine," he repeated. "Tell me what happened."

Benedict grabbed her gently by the shoulder and shook her.

"Katherine, did this have anything to do with the Nonarc?"

Her trance seemed to lift. She became instantly alert to his question.

"How did you know?"

Benedict wanted to ask, "Know what?" But he caught himself. Instead, he said, "It's my job to know. Katherine, it's okay. You can tell me."

"This changes everything."

"What does it change?"

"He figured it out," she said. "The son of a bitch figured it out."

Benedict steered Katherine Diehl down the hall to an empty patient room. He studied the woman as she removed a cigarette from the pocket of her nursing uniform. She brought it to her lips and was about to light it.

"Katherine, there's oxygen in this room. Don't light that."

She looked at him as if seeing him for the first time, then shifted her gaze to the unlit cigarette. After a brief pause, she put the cigarette between her lips. Katherine sucked on it as if it were lit, closing her eyes and savoring it.

"Katherine," Benedict said. "What's going on?"

"You know they killed him," she said.

"Who?"

"Michael, the pharmacist."

"Katherine, he shot himself in the head. It was suicide."

"Michael may have pulled the trigger. But *they* killed him. *They* forced him into a position where he had no other options. He told me he had found a way out. I never thought it would be suicide."

Benedict grabbed her by the shoulder and shook her. "What are you talking about?"

"It started about seven months ago," Diehl began slowly. "I was asked if I wanted to make some extra cash. The first nurse left and was never seen again. They needed a nurse to administer medication in a drug study. It would not be very often. But when I did, I would be paid ten thousand dollars each time."

Benedict wanted an answer to his question about Watson's involvement. But he sensed Diehl was about to reveal a lot more than he bargained for.

"You gave intravenous Nonarc each time?"

Diehl nodded.

"How was the medication delivered to you?"

"The patients were always on Nonarc. And each time when I was giving meds, the IV bag mixed with Nonarc would be delivered to my locker at the beginning of my shift. It had the patient's name and room number on it. When the time came, I gave the dose. It was that simple."

"Didn't you realize that's not the proper way for us to send medications to the floor?"

Diehl wiped her red, swollen eyes. "I needed the money, Alex. My ex left me high and dry with a lot of debt. I guess it was easier to just pretend it was okay."

"When did you realize these patients were dying?"

The tears began to flow harder. Her lower lip quivered. "You know?"

It was Benedict's turn to nod. "When, Katherine?"

"I realized it three patient deaths ago. That's about six weeks. Michael Watson's name was on all of the IV bags. When I made the connection, I found him and asked what he knew."

"How many have died?"

Katherine began to cry again. Her head was tucked to her chest and moved with each sob.

"I ... know of ... six. There have been more."

"What was in the IV bags?"

"I don't know," Katherine whimpered. Saliva and nasal discharge coated her lips. "I truly don't. I asked Michael that. But he refused to tell me. He said they were testing a compound. When I told him it was killing people, he seemed surprised. He didn't know. He was shocked then angry."

Katherine leaned against the empty patient bed.

"Was Michael being paid, as well?"

Diehl confirmed.

"So why did you continue?"

"There was a nurse who was giving doses before me. Her name was Penny Lewis. She disappeared about three weeks before I was recruited. Michael told me about her the day I confronted him. I knew her, but not well. She disappeared suddenly one day on her day off. He told me she was killed because she wanted out of the program."

"What made him think she was murdered?"

"He showed me a picture of her naked body ... Her chest was covered in bruising. He said his bosses had given her the formulation. She died like her patients did."

"Why didn't you go to administration? Call the police?"

"Michael and I are just as guilty. He said we'd end up dead as well. But he said he was close to finding the answer."

"What answer?"

"The formula?"

"What formula?"

Katherine removed the CD case from her pocket and handed to Benedict. "Michael told me to give you this when the time was right. He said I would know when that was. I guess this is it."

Benedict turned the case over in his hands.

"Michael said you are the one who should take up his cause. Now that he's dead he wants you to have the formula. Michael said the formula has great power. But it is so powerful that if the world gets a hold of it without proper guidance, it will be very bad."

"Why me?"

"It's all on the disc," she said. "Michael believed in you. He wants you to be the guardian of the formula."

"What power does it possess?"

"Whoever Michael was working for was trying to find the correct combination of ingredients. Michael called it several things. I don't remember the names. Once he found it, its power would be greater than anything ever created."

"What kind of power?"

"Ask Margaret Queen."

PART TWO

CHAPTER 10

"*B*y now Alex, you know that I am dead...."
As low hanging clouds swirled above, Benedict had slipped the disc into the CD player in his aging, second hand Jaguar parked in the hospital's employee parking lot. He desired privacy. Whatever Michael Watson had recorded; he did not want it being overheard.

The disc drive had whirred and a few seconds later Michael Watson's voice, gruff and low, spoke to Benedict.

"*... For the last two years, I have been involved in an experiment. An unethical and illegal experiment. I was hired to perfect a formula.*"

The rustle of papers on the recording and the monotone pitch of Watson's voice indicated he was reading the words.

"*This formula is one that has eluded scientists and alchemists for centuries. My employer has paid me well to find the exact combination of ingredients that would unleash its power. It has taken nearly two years. I finally succeeded. It is both a miracle and a curse.*"

"*The formula has been tested on patients at Tidewater without their knowledge or consent. The formula was given in IV bags of the drug Nonarc. All of those patients died. They experienced cardiac arrest and massive bruising over their chests. These patients were chosen because they were sick and dying, mostly from end stage cancer.*

"*You must believe me, Alex. In the beginning, I had no knowledge of this horrible fact. I was kept in the dark until I happened upon the fact only three days ago. Even before I came to know about the testing—and the deaths—I came to the conclusion that the formula's power must never see the light of day. Unfortunately, those who employ me know of my discovery. I, with your help, must prevent the formula from being made public or used more widely. I promised myself to find a way to prevent its use and misuse.*

"*My name and work will be linked with this atrocity forever. I continued searching for the correct formulation during the last three days, hoping to put an end to the deaths. In the small hope that if I found the correct combination at least no more patients would die. I was monitored around the clock, guarded to make sure the work would continue. I was forced to relinquish the results at the end of each and every lab session. My house was watched. I was followed everywhere.*

"*A more courageous man would have simply refused to continue. But when you know your life is over because of the mistakes you've made, it is still very hard to say no to the barrel of a gun.*"

Watson cleared his throat several times followed by several sniffles. Emotion had seeped into the monologue.

"*In those two weeks, under extreme pressure and depression, Alex, I found the answer. I found the answer to the riddle with the help of H.P. Lovecraft. The formula goes by many names: Materia Prima, the Elixir of Eternal life, the Philosopher's Stone, and the Fountain of Youth are the most common. I refer to it as the Materia Prima.*

"*The legends are many and scattered across all continents. It has been purported to change lead into gold and to heal the sick or provide eternal youthfulness. But I can tell you, the formula I have discovered does heal, Alex. Did you hear what I just said?*

"The Materia Prima works. It cured a capuchin monkey riddled with cancer. My employer knows that it works. I was ordered to prepare a dose for testing on a human patient. I actually prepared two doses. The first dose was confiscated from me and it will be tested on another patient at Tidewater Regional within twenty-four hours of my making this recording. If you are listening to this, that means the dose was delivered and it worked. I don't know who the patient is—was—but check their medical record and see what the prognosis was. Compare it to their current health status.

"I managed to give those responsible an incorrect formula. I jotted two sets of notes during my final experiment. I gave them the wrong one and saved the real one. They will find out soon enough that the formula they have is not the real one. However, as an added precaution, the correct formula can only be unlocked with the help of the writer, Lovecraft.

"It is the greatest discovery in the history of mankind. And, at the same time, it could be the most devastating. We cannot let it fall into the hands of those that hired me.

"The healing power of the Materia is so powerful it will destroy societies and economies. Men will kill for it. Countries will go to war for it. Only those with the resources to afford it will receive it. Anarchy will rule.

"Alex, I have chosen you to guard this secret. You must find the recipe and decide how it is to be used, if at all. I cannot do it. I am an old man. I do not have the strength to see it through. And I do not have the will power to destroy something that might be so beneficial if used judiciously.

"My paranoia required that I make finding it as difficult as possible. I apologize, but they are necessary precautions. If I were to leave you the formula on this recording or in one place, it would be too risky. My employer is quite resourceful. Therefore, I have separated *the formula into three pieces. Each piece has been hidden in plain sight. The first two pieces of the formula have with them clues which will lead you to the next piece of the recipe. The final piece of the recipe has with it a gift for you—and your beautiful wife, Rose.*

"As you recall, I am a re-enactor. I play the parts of two Generals. Sometimes I play the part of Confederate Brigadier General Joseph R. Anderson; I also play Ethan Allen Hitchcock. Hitchcock was a Union General and an aide to Lincoln. He was an interesting man. To find the first clue, check Hitchcock's boots!

"If you remember, earlier, I said I prepared two doses of the real formula. The first dose was confiscated; the second I saved. That second dose is for you. Find the hidden pieces of the formula and you will find a chance to save your wife."

ΩΩΩ

"I thought I'd find you here."

Benedict spun and saw Ari Spanos grinning at him. Benedict had retreated for a moment's peace to the hospital museum. In the last hour, he'd been bombarded with several seemingly impossible, if not, implausible claims. Claims left him by a dead man.

Watson's suicide shocked him. But combined with the information Benedict had just heard, it hit him like a pile driver to the gut. Rose's looming prognosis and gargantuan treatment decision stacked atop the thinly veiled threat he'd just received from the hospital's president regarding the Joint Commission complaint, he needed time to regroup and gather himself.

When he had the time, which was rare these days, he liked to wander around the old building and scan the artifacts. The Archer House Mansion, lovingly restored and preserved to its pre-antebellum glory, sat nestled as the focal point of the hospital campus among the modern, glittering glass and brick structures of

Tidewater Regional Medical Center. The former plantation house now served as the Archer House Historical Society, funded and run by TRMC. Looking at remnants of history reminded him that despite all the fulminating issues in his life and Rose's, we were all a small tick on the timeline of the universe.

"You can't be here for the tour?" Benedict asked.

A docent, a plump, middle-aged woman, was giving a tour to a gaggle of middle school students, lecturing them on the history of the Archer House and how it blossomed into a medical center with a service population of hundreds of thousands. She was standing in the recreated dining room near the front of the house.

"No," Spanos replied. "I just finished rounds. I went by the pharmacy to find you. They said you stepped out for a minute. So I figured you were here."

"I'm flattered one of the area's top oncologists took time out of his busy schedule to come and find me."

In the next hour and in a soothing, Southern drawl, Benedict knew, for he had taken the tour twice, the docent would explain that the hospital had been founded more than one hundred and fifty years ago before the War between the States—or as true Southerners called it—the War of Northern Aggression. At that time, it was your typical, run-of-the-mill Southern mansion spreading over fifty plus acres, staffed by as many as thirty slaves, and owned by a prominent cotton farmer named Rufus Archer. When the war broke out, Archer, with a little coaxing from the Confederate government, donated the Archer House Mansion to the Confederacy for use as a hospital.

"I need your help," Spanos said, ignoring the jibe. "I'm admitting a patient later. I'd like you to consult on her treatment. She's going to be considered a VIP."

Benedict looked upon a series of black and white photographs of the Archer property during the war, showing its change over the years. It was thick with copses of trees scattered among the fields of cotton and tobacco. The trees had long since been removed, cut down for use in the war effort. With the threat of the Union Army always present, the perimeter of the old grounds had been ringed with earthworks and cannons and manned with war-hardened veterans. An elaborate network of tunnels was constructed allowing a means of escape for generals, prominent citizens and other high-ranking officers should the Yankees get too close. The shafts, burrowed in every direction along the compass, had been barricaded decades ago, the docent explained.

"A VIP? Anyone famous?"

"The patient's not famous. But she's connected to Waldo Paige."

"The *senator?*"

Spanos nodded.

Benedict continued reading the plaques under the photographs. After the war, Archer Mansion continued to treat wounded soldiers and civilians. Federal troops were transported here when the Union took possession of the property. Eventually, it was returned to Rufus Archer who re-donated it and dedicated it as a hospital. Today, the mansion served as a museum and visitor's center, replaced in its clinical duties by two cylindrical medical towers reaching ten stories skyward and connected by skywalks at the third, sixth and eighth floors. The east tower was named for Rufus Archer; the west tower for Matthias Huntington, a hospital benefactor. The spires were bisected by the tree-lined drive named Archer Boulevard carved in a serene, expertly-landscaped acreage.

Benedict said, "Can I ask you a question?"

"Sure."

Benedict didn't exactly know how to phrase it. How did you ask one of your best friends if you'd been told about a cure for cancer without sounding like he'd needed psychotropics?

"Maybe later," he said, thinking better of it. "Tell me about this patient. If they're one of yours, they must not be in good shape."

ΩΩΩ

"Is that the most recent IV bag?"

"Yes, Dr. Kyle."

Katherine Diehl squirmed in her chair. Dr. Kyle and the nurse were seated in his spacious den, one of thirty rooms in his palatial home, nestled in the Menchville area of Newport News. The used minibag rested in the nervous nurse's lap.

"The one that worked?"

"Yes, sir."

Kyle held out his smallish hand, covered with flaking psoriasis and blotches of eczema. She handed it to him. The doctor nodded and Timothy, one of the men in his employ, came forward and took the bag from him.

"Make sure this is analyzed. I want to know the exact make-up of what's in it."

Timothy departed. Kyle lifted the cup from its saucer and sipped his Earl Gray tea. "You really should try some, Katherine. It's quite good," Kyle added, lifting the cup.

"No, thank you. I really need to be going." Katherine Diehl began to lift herself from the cushioned wing chair.

"Not so fast."

She stopped. Kyle studied her and after a moment, she sank back into the fabric.

"You and Michael Watson met in his vehicle the other day. What was the nature of your conversation?"

Katherine looked away and rubbed her hands along her thighs. "He was telling me that he was close to finding the formula ... that we were almost finished."

"Did he tell you anything else?"

"No."

Kyle took another sip of tea. "You're not being very truthful, Katherine. He told you other things. What were they?"

"That was all. I swear." Katherine licked her dry lips.

"I don't believe you, Katherine."

"Dr. Kyle, I'm telling the truth."

"Did he tell you the formula?"

"No, sir, he said it was hidden."

"We know that. Michael left me a note saying as much. You see, young lady. You have already lied to me. You just told me you didn't know anything else. Then you tell me, it is hidden."

Katherine looked at her lap and began to cry.

"What else?"

Her sobs intensified. She had a white knuckle grip on the arms of the chair.

"No worries, we'll find out everything," Kyle said in a soothing tone.

Kyle nodded to Ashan who was standing in the shadows. The Iranian moved behind the nurse. He lifted her up by the hair and put her in a choke hold.

"Take her downstairs," Kyle commanded in a whisper as he took another sip of tea.

CHAPTER 11

"We understand that there may have been some sentinel events associated with the administration of the drug Nonarc," Preston Mason, the physician surveyor stated. "This anonymous letter was e-mailed to our home office in Chicago. It indicates that there have been some deaths associated with the use of this drug in your institution."

Melissa Harrison buried her head in a trembling hand. Kyle's eyes paralleled Roberts's as the two men glared at Benedict, each communicating evil, unsettling intentions. Harrison pushed back her chair and walked out of the room.

Benedict's heart thumped in his chest with a depth and rapidity he'd never experienced before. This was what Ben Roberts, the President of Tidewater had been warning him about. *Had they known this question would come up?*

"The dosing parameters for this drug are rather specific and can be confusing. Some adverse reactions are to be expected," Benedict said, stalling.

He was still trying to gather his wits about him. The effects of Michael Watson's recording felt like they were sewn into a lead-lined blanket draped around him. At the moment, it was the only thing he could think about.

"I see," the nurse surveyor said evenly with a furrowed brow.

As Benedict indicated to Ben Roberts, J. Edward Kyle and Melissa Harrison, if the surveyors asked about Nonarc, he would not lie. He would use his evasiveness to the question as evidence with Ben Roberts that he'd placed the hospital before other interests. If he could extricate himself from this predicament, he would demand that Roberts have prescribing of Nonarc halted until they could find out what was going on. As Rose was doing with her own future, Benedict had left it the hands of Fate. And Fate had decided. Unfortunately, Benedict knew now it wasn't a drug error. And it wasn't any fault of the drug itself. It was an intentional, man-made catastrophe.

"Do you have firsthand knowledge of patient deaths, Dr. Benedict? We would like a complete and forthright answer," Preston Mason, the physician surveyor and the team leader persisted.

Kyle glared at him. Benedict met Kyle's menacing gaze in equal measure with one of his own of steadfast defiance. Out of the corner of his eye, he could see Ben Roberts bristling. The veins in his neck and face popping under the perfect, tanned skin. His eyes repeatedly flashed to the door through which Harrison had just exited.

Benedict broke his eye-lock with Kyle when the nurse surveyor asked a question.

"Dr. Benedict, Dr. Mason just asked you a question," the surveyor persisted.

Benedict shuffled the papers before him. "There is a temporal relationship between the administration of...."

With a quick, desperate whoosh the door opened. Melissa Harrison darted back in.

"I'm sorry to interrupt," she said with a quaking voice. "Alex, you're needed at home."

"What is it?"

"It's Rose."

"Rose isn't at home. She was admitted to the hospital this morning. I told you that earlier. That's why I was late getting here today."

"Oh ... right." Harrison seemed befuddled. "That's what I meant. She's upstairs."

Preston Mason wagged his head between the two of them. "What seems to be the problem?"

Harrison responded before anyone else could. "Alex's wife is very ill. It seems she's taken a turn for the worse."

Benedict darted for the door. He stopped and turned back to the surveyors. "Dr. Mason, I'm sorry."

"Nonsense," Mason replies. "Take care of your family. We will adjourn until tomorrow perhaps. We will continue our survey in other areas. We are *very* interested in what Dr. Benedict has to say."

ΩΩΩ

Katherine Diehl lay naked on the stretcher under a brilliantly white light. She was close to breaking. Michael Watson had been right; she should not have listened to that CD.

Her hands and feet were fastened to the gurney with plastic ties, the kind used by the police. She had given up struggling thirty minutes earlier.

The pain was constant, a permanent part of her existence now. Her body was drenched in sweat, mixing with the blood oozing from her wounds. The skin around her nipples had been expertly sliced with the scalpel. Her jet-black hair had been shaved off and pieces of her scalp had been pulled back, flayed in strips from front to back. The same had been done to her arms and legs.

She spoke to the unseen man and his accomplice standing in the shadows. "I can't believe you're doing this. I've been loyal to you. I've cared for Edgar like he was my own. I gave the doses of Nonarc as I was supposed to. I thought you were a good man."

A sinister cackle was her only response. The sickly aroma of pipe tobacco managed to penetrate her senses through the agony as a thin veil of smoke drifted into the light.

"Katherine," Kyle's voice called out from the darkness, "you will tell us what I want to know. This situation is much bloody bigger than just one man or woman. This project has consequences for all mankind. The price of your life is only a fraction of a farthing in the scheme of things. Now what did Michael Watson tell you before he killed himself?"

"I've already told you everything!"

Katherine only knew Alex Benedict in a professional way. She'd heard rumors that his wife was ill. She really had no allegiance to the man other than the fact that he was involved in this sordid matter by no choice of his own. Katherine felt she needed to protect anyone else from being consumed. But as the pain increased, her will shrank.

Katherine heard the crinkle of paper. "Michael left me this note before he shot himself like a coward. It says, 'the formula will be left for the only man who is worthy enough to possess it. This man will guard it and see that it is released properly.' I'm only going to ask one more time. Who is he?"

"You're going to kill me anyway. Just like Penny Lewis," Katherine spat. "Why should I tell you?"

The man with the accent clicked the pipe between his teeth. A large, capped syringe filled with a pink fluid landed on her exposed belly.

"That syringe contains Euthasol. It's what they use to put dogs down. It contains a combination of pentobarbital, a sedative, and phenytoin, an anti-seizure medication. To it, I've added a large dose of potassium to stop your heart and succinyl choline which as I'm sure you are aware relaxes the muscles including those used to breathe. When I inject you with this, Katherine, the last thing you will feel will be the prick of the needle. Then you'll just go to sleep. It will be painless, but I will be able to say you died like a dog."

"I told you I don't know anything else. You will be caught, you understand that, don't you? All murderers are."

Katherine heard an electrical whine. The man's hand moved something long and silver under the light. It looked like a large food thermometer. But attached to the end of it was a four-pronged claw. It was being held by a hand wrapped around a black rubber handle from which a thin black electrical wire ran into the darkness.

"What is that?"

"This, my dear, is a rectal probe. It was designed for torture. It works quite well. These claw-like fingers on the end ensure that we get maximum contact with the tissues." The man turned to his accomplice. "Turn it up."

The whine increased and a spark arced between two of the prongs. The device was turned off and the man slathered on some lubricant. "This will also increase the conductivity." He looked at her once again. His eyes scanned the entire length of her body.

J. Edward Kyle looked down at Katherine Diehl. He had made love to this woman once many months ago in a moment of professional weakness. "Such a waste, Katherine. Edgar will miss you greatly. I think you were his favorite nurse."

He leaned over her and held up the syringe and brought the probe beside it. "Which will it be the syringe or old Sparky here?" Kyle moved a button back and forth. Katherine watched the prongs of the probe open and close.

Katherine began to sob and shook her head.

"You will tell us. We will do this until you tell us."

A pair of gloved hands spread her cheeks apart as the cold implement was inserted. A click followed and the prongs of the probe pressed themselves against her tissues. Kyle nodded. The whine began again.

Katherine's body arched in spasm. Her tongue had been caught between her teeth and blood began to flow down her throat. She let out a cry.

Before she passed out, she heard herself screaming Alex Benedict's name.

CHAPTER 12

Benedict hesitated with his thumb over the numbers, willing himself to make the phone call he'd been dreading. His hand shook with nervousness. The anxiety he felt was a combination of two forces. The growing sense of unease about how he would tell his father-in-law about Rose's latest development mixed with the residual panic from the abruptly ended conference with the Joint Commission.

Melissa Harrison had caught up with Benedict as he raced to the elevator following her storming through the door. Harrison had informed him that her interruption had been a ruse. Rose, as far as she knew, was no better or worse than the last time Benedict had seen her. She was simply saving Benedict the trouble of lying to the surveyors, she'd said.

Benedict's first impulse had been to slam his fist into his boss's face. His second was to simply say, "You make me sick." He'd turned and taken the stairs to check on Rose. She was in fact as fine as she could be under the circumstances. He'd kissed her and told her he'd be back later. Benedict decided it was time to go home and pack a suitcase. He would be spending many consecutive hours at the hospital. He needed time to recover from the shock of the phony scare Harrison had delivered. Connie Stevens had stayed with Rose while he did. When he'd arrived home, the tension in his body was a palpable entity but slowly subsiding.

As he calmed, he thought about the other man whose life would be devastated by the news he was about to deliver. Finally, he dialed.

"Hey, Grumps, it's Alex."

The gravity in Benedict's voice registered and his tone became tense. "What's happened?"

Ronald Blackmon was a robust man but his daughter, Rose, had the ability to turn the former banker to mush.

"Rose is in the hospital."

Rose had bestowed the nickname, "Grumps," on her father when she was ten years old. It was a well-deserved moniker. He would bark and grumble when Rose or her sister would interrupt his reading, football games or nap. Everyone knew Grumps was to be left alone when he was partaking of these simple pleasures. Even Benedict had once forgotten and changed the channel while he was "resting his eyes" during a lopsided Notre Dame victory over Georgia Tech. The old man woke spewing a string of expletives so garbled and incoherent it sounded like a foreign language.

"Give it to me straight."

The Blackmon women were a loving, devoted trio who would throw themselves in front of a runaway train to save their husbands or children. Grumps would regale Benedict with stories from Rose's childhood demonstrating her intransigence to perceived wrongs despite her father's pleading, threats of corporal punishment or withdrawal of privileges. Invariably, Rose would end the standoff by saying, "You can punish me all you want, Daddy. But I'm right!"

"She had a doctor's appointment yesterday. Her tumors have spread."

His wife, Rose's mother, had died of ovarian cancer a decade ago. He'd spent thirty years as a bank executive and retired to Florida to play golf and spend time working in his garage woodshop. Rose had told him she was sick four months ago, underplaying it and convincing him that she was fine. Nonetheless he came for a visit every couple of weeks to check on his eldest daughter.

Blackmon swore. "Where?"

"To her liver and intestines. And her brain. That's what caused the seizure."

"Oh, my God! I'll fly up right away."

"Thanks."

"Alex?"

"I'm a banker not a doctor. How long does she have?"

ΩΩΩ

The small human form looked like a neglected child's doll. The room was dark. The bony, blanket-covered bumps undulated smoothly across the bed to a small head poking from beneath the covers. A tube of a clear intravenous solution snaked its way through the stainless steel railing and under the blanket. The intermittent blip of the intravenous pump kept a regular tempo as the liquid dripped into Angel Blair's emaciated arm. Benedict noticed a small, brown teddy bear nestled on the pillow beside the sleeping child's head.

He had spent the rest of the day between going on rounds and checking on Rose. He managed to write a few reports on his laptop at her bedside as she slept off her seizure. He'd been instructed to stay away from the Joint Commission surveyors.

Darkness had descended agonizingly over Hampton Roads. The night seemed to push itself into the room through the closed window, helped along by strong gusts preceding the hurricane. Benedict's dark mood had deepened in concert with the evaporating sunlight.

The attractive, dark-haired woman occupying the chair rested her head on the stainless steel rail. Her face lugged the same weariness visible even through sleep that Benedict himself felt. It was the relentless, bone-weary vigil only a mother could endure and survive.

He rested the chart on the railing of the bed and flipped through the history and physical:

Angel Blair, 8yo white female diagnosed with chronic myeloid leukemia one year ago, admitted for an elevated temperature and weakness. Patient was started on Gleevec, a tyrosine kinase inhibitor, approximately one year ago and has progressed to the blast crisis phase of her condition.

Benedict winced. The diagnosis was extremely poor. Chronic Myelogenous Leukemia, CML, occurred mostly in middle-aged and elderly patients, but had been documented in all age groups. Angel Blair had been dealt a bad hand. Her blood work showed twenty-four percent myeloblasts, large clusters of both myelo- and lymphoblasts in the bone marrow on biopsy and the development of a chloroma in the left thigh.

Benedict had completed an oncology specialty residency after a one year general pharmacy residency after pharmacy school. He hadn't seen a pediatric case of CML for at least two years.

The woman sensed his presence and looked up.

"Are you Angel's mother?" he inquired.

The woman nodded. It was a slow, fatigued movement.

"Dr. Spanos asked me to review Angel's chart and make sure we're doing everything we can for your daughter," Benedict said through the mask he was wearing because Angel was under neutropenic precautions to prevent infection.

"Thank you," she said weakly. "Yes, I'm Angel's mother. And you are a *doctor*?"

"I'm Dr. Benedict. I'm a pharmacist." He reached out his hand across the sleeping child.

The woman smiled weakly, slowly raised her arm and squeezed Benedict's hand.

"Lauren Blair."

"That's a beautiful arrangement," Benedict said. A large bouquet of flowers sat on the bedside table along with a giant stuffed panda bear.

"Yes, it is. It's from my boss."

"I understand you work for Senator Paige?"

"I'm his chief of staff."

Waldo Paige was the senior senator for the Commonwealth of Virginia. He'd been a mainstay inside the beltway for more than twenty-five years and chaired the powerful Armed Services and Justice Committees. His influence had siphoned many millions of dollars off to the Virginia economy, most notably to the defense contractors in the Hampton Roads. It was widely rumored that he was going to forego another run for the Senate.

"Do you understand what's going on with Angel?"

"Unfortunately, yes," she replied. "I'm the local CML president."

"I didn't realize there were that many cases in the area."

"The chapter encompasses most of the Mid-Atlantic region, not just this area."

Lauren Blair spoke with the confidence of a fourth year oncology resident. "CML's progression is divided into three phases. Most patients are diagnosed in the chronic phase which demonstrates mild symptoms of fatigue, left-side pain due to enlarged spleen, joint pain and abdominal fullness. Early treatment can delay advancement to the accelerated phase. The accelerated phase signifies that the disease is progressing and that the next phase, blast crisis, is imminent. Drug treatment is often less effective. The final stage, blast crisis, represents the final phase. Its rapid progression leads to a very short survival rate."

"You know your stuff."

"I've read everything I can get my hands on about it."

"I see from her chart that stem cell transplantation was not an option."

"That's right. Angel is an only child so she doesn't have any siblings. Her father passed away and I'm not a match. It looks like she's relapsing despite the Gleevec."

A single tear snaked down her cheek.

Angel Blair, for reasons known only to God, was unlucky enough to have the genetic abnormality involving the Philadelphia chromosome. The transmutation of this chromosome brings on CML. The young child's bad luck was further complicated by the fact that her malady had progressed to blast crisis after being treated. Based on what he was reading in Ari Spanos's progress notes, she did not have much time.

Empathy washed over Benedict. The pressure and stress that had been trapped inside seemed to lighten; a relief valve in him had been partially opened. He wasn't alone in his grief. In a twisted way, Lauren Blair's predicament assuaged his own. There was no greater bond than that between a mother and child. Lauren Blair was facing the incomprehensible promise of having to bury her own daughter.

His troubles, though daunting enough, seemed inconsequential, juxtaposed to hers. It also put his and Rose's situation into a different light.

Rose, at least, had lived enough years to qualify for a full life. She'd experienced the understanding of her parents love, the ecstasy and pain of love and marriage, the triumph of high school and college graduations. She had lived to adulthood and experienced a lot of what life had to give.

Angel Blair was not going to be so lucky.

The curtain hiding Rose's thinking had been pulled back, just a little. His focus had been on what he was losing. And though his loss was going to be gigantic, it was dwarfed by the anguish this woman was facing.

Tonight, he was supposed to be a clinician, impartial and unemotional. He was neither. He wanted to reach out and touch Lauren, to comfort her in some way. But he remained frozen in place.

After a minute, Lauren looked up, catching him watching her. Benedict removed a tissue from the wheeled tray at the foot of the bed and handed it to her.

"I'm sorry," she whispered.

"No need to be."

"You must see a lot of this kind of thing."

"Unfortunately, yes. It never gets easy, especially when it's someone so young."

"Do you have children?"

"No."

"You're pretty young. Planning any?"

"The answer to that is no, as well."

"You should," Lauren said. "They're wonderful."

Benedict forced a tight smile but remained silent. "So what are you going to do for Angel?"

"Dr. Spanos has ordered a strong antibiotic to quell the infection. As you know, she's on neutropenic fever precautions. The nurses and doctor will check her mouth, lungs and rectum for signs of bacterial and fungal infections. We're also giving her medications to fight the fever. I'm going to do some research to see if we can't conjure up a new treatment protocol." Both Benedict and Lauren were wearing face masks.

"I think we've been through it all," Lauren replied.

"I see from the chart that Dr. Spanos is still considering a bone marrow transplant from unrelated donors."

Angel stirred. Her head had been angled close to her teddy bear. Her eyes fluttered to alertness.

"Mommy, I'm thirsty."

Lauren Blair's fatigue disintegrated. She was on her feet, retrieving the cup and placing the bent straw to her daughter's lips. Angel took two long draws and lowered her head back onto the pillow.

The girl looked over at her mother. "Who's that?"

"Angel, this is Dr. Benedict. He's a pharmacist."

"What's a pharmacist?"

Benedict smiled and responded. "I know about medicines."

"Do you know about my medicines?"

"Yep, I do."

"I don't like medicines. They make me throw up."

"Some do. That's right." Angel's eyelids lowered in fatigue. Benedict tried to make conversation. "That's a good-looking bear. What's her name?"

"It's a he," Angel replied evenly. "He's Major Bear. He's my good luck charm."

"He brings you good luck?"

"Yep. Every time I hug him, he makes me feel better. Someday he's going to cure me."

Benedict smiled. "That's an interesting name. How did he come by that name?"

"My daddy was a Major and he gave him to me on my birthday."

"Your daddy was in the military? Army?"

Angel nodded and hugged the bear close. Benedict noticed the bear had been outfitted with an olive green uniform and epaulets.

Benedict looked at her mom. "Is your husband retired military?"

"No," Angel answered. "He's in heaven."

Benedict swallowed hard, recoiling inside. "Oh, I'm so sorry," he replied weakly. Benedict looked at Lauren for an explanation.

"Wyatt was killed in Afghanistan two years ago."

Benedict's measure of the woman's resolve and strength multiplied. She had suffered through the loss of her spouse, taken before his time in an endless war. And based on what he read in the chart, shortly thereafter her daughter was diagnosed with a terminal leukemia.

A length of awkward silence bounced between Lauren and Benedict. Angel seemed unaffected by the adult politics.

Another "I'm sorry" was all he could muster.

Benedict patted Angel's leg through the covers and said, "We're going to take good care of you, Angel."

"I know. Major Bear always cures me. You'll see. He'll cure me again. It happens every time."

CHAPTER 13

"Did you dispose of the body?"

"As you instructed," Ashan Habib replied. "It will never be found. The machine was washed and cleansed, and then sent to the crusher."

Kyle employed Habib, Timothy, and occasionally others, for the more unpleasant duties his project required.

Once he had inserted the rectal probe and applied the juice, it had taken only seconds for Katherine Diehl to scream out Alex Benedict's name. The woman then passed out. Kyle injected the "dog" mixture into her arm and she was dead in seconds. Habib had taken the body to a remote location in Williamsburg and pushed it into an industrial wood chipper. Kyle was impressed with the speed with which the electrified rectal probe had sucked the information out of the woman.

"Shall we now pick up Benedict the pharmacist and ply answers from him?"

"No, not yet," Kyle replied. "How much longer before the analysis of the contents of Margaret Queen's IV comes back?"

"We should have it in a few hours. What do you want me to do about the pharmacist?"

"Nothing yet. We need to find out what he knows. I want you to search Watson's house. See if you find anything. Tell Timothy to follow Benedict."

ΩΩΩ

Benedict woke in the semi-darkness of the hospital room beside Rose. His exhaustion caught up with him as soon as he sat down. He'd slept for almost three hours in the chair beside her bed.

She was in a two-room pod, the only one of its kind on the oncology unit. Both rooms were connected via a closet-like area for gowning and disinfecting. Cancer patients with depressed immune systems required special infection precautions. Nurses, doctors and visitors were required to wear gowns and masks.

Both rooms could also serve as overflow critical care rooms in the event the intensive care units were full. The common wall sported a large glass window so a nurse could monitor both patients, if needed. The curtain was drawn across the window at the moment. But Benedict could hear a conversation between a woman and a child coming through the disinfection room.

Benedict stretched, working the kinks out of his neck and back. The young girl was talking to her mother in the unabashed, honest way children speak.

"Dr. Ari is very nice. I like him," the child said. "Why did they move us into this room, Mommy?"

"I don't know, sweetie," the mother replied.

Undaunted, the girl continued. "I liked the other room better. So did Major Bear. That medicine made me feel a little better. Even Major Bear says so. When can I go home?"

Benedict had been listening to the innocent conversation with mild curiosity. Rose was asleep and he was somewhat refreshed by his nap. His head rested on the back of the chair and he was staring at the sterile ceiling. Rose's wall-mounted television was off, but the child's was on but muted. A cartoon of some sort was silently running.

Upon hearing the name of the teddy bear, Benedict sat up straight. Without giving a thought to his appearance or his circumstance, he stood and walked to the end of Rose's bed.

Not sure, he'd heard correctly, he sneaked around the common wall and spied Lauren Blair sitting on Angel's bed with her back to Benedict. She was holding her daughter's hand and listening. Over her shoulder, he caught a glimpse of Angel. Her color was lighter and sicklier than the last time he'd seen her.

Benedict retreated from the girl's room and called Spanos from Rose's room phone.

"How did you manage to get her moved up here? She should be in pediatrics."

"I wanted you to be able to keep an eye on her medications and consult without having to venture too far away from Rose," Spanos said.

"How did you pull those strings?"

"She works for Waldo Paige, remember? I asked the mother for his private number. I called him, explained the situation and asked him to call Ben Roberts. It works for all concerned. It also didn't hurt that the pediatric ward is currently full. By the way, Angel has two nurses, one on loan from pediatrics and one from oncology."

It was highly irregular to have a pediatric patient on an adult floor. Spanos had told him he would find a way for Benedict to be near his wife and still be able to monitor this sick child. This was Spanos's solution. He had made Rose and Angel Blair neighbors.

Benedict hung up with Spanos and returned to the child's room. Angel saw him, looking at her and turned her head. Lauren saw her daughter's distraction and pivoted on the bed. Benedict smiled. He noticed her eye's looking him up and down, not with any sense of contempt or uncertainty. Her reaction was one of surprise.

It was then that Benedict realized what he must have looked like. He smoothed his hair with a hand and shot a quick glance at his shirt, tie and trousers. His puffy eyes must have looked sinister over his mask, gown and gloves.

"Well, hello there," Lauren said.

Angel was much more direct. "It's the pharmacy man. Your hair is all messy." Angel studied his eyes. "Have you been crying?"

Lauren blushed. "Angel, that's not very polite." She turned back to Benedict. "I'm sorry."

Benedict checked on Rose by looking through the window. She was still asleep. He walked into Angel's room and into full view.

"It's quite alright," he replied. Benedict looked at Angel. "Yes, I have been crying."

"Why? Are you sad?"

Lauren's mouth formed a circle of recognition.

"Is someone you know a patient?"

Benedict nodded. "Yes, my wife. She's asleep in the next bed."

"Your wife is sick?" Angel asked.

Benedict nodded once more. "Yes, she is."

The second awkward silence fell between Benedict and Lauren Blair since they'd met. Angel lifted her teddy bear and began to adjust its buttons.

"Is there any coffee around here?" Lauren inquired.

"The first cup's on me. But I have to warn you it's pretty bad."

"That's okay. I need a boost. I don't think I've slept three hours in the last three days. I'll take anything I can get."

Benedict led her to the nurse's lounge. He poured two coffees into Styrofoam cups and pointed to the cream and sugar. Back in the hallway, Lauren and Benedict walked away from their loved ones's rooms.

"I need to take a walk. Will you join me?"

Benedict followed her to the solarium overlooking the great lawn bisected by Archer Boulevard.

"I'll review Angel's chart when we go back. But tell me how she's doing."

"Not good. Her white counts are through the roof and she's usually in a lot of pain. But, tonight's a good night for her." Lauren sipped her coffee. "How long has your wife been ill? What's her name?"

"Rose. She was diagnosed about eighteen months ago with ovarian cancer."

Lauren asked several gentle but probing questions. Benedict answered honestly and to the point.

"I caught a glimpse of her when they brought her in. She looks weak."

Benedict told Lauren about the seizure in the emergency room. They stood in silence for several minutes looking out over the lawn and sipping the bitter coffee as the sun began its descent behind the trees.

They chatted for a few minutes about Benedict's work as a pharmacist, his education and years of service at Tidewater.

"So how are you holding up?" Lauren asked,

"Okay, I guess. I hate the nights," Benedict said. "The nights are.... I can deal with it in the daylight but the darkness sends me to a bad place."

The light of Newport News twinkled in the expanding darkness. "It's amazing that you can know everything about all the drugs out there," she said.

"It's impossible to know everything. There are a lot of resources out there for us to use. I try to know all I can about the drugs I see in my practice."

Lauren nodded. "It's still impressive."

"So," Benedict said, changing the subject. "What's it like to work for Waldo Paige? Is he as much of an ass as he appears in his sound bites?"

Lauren smiled. "Senator Paige is a gentleman. He cares about his staff; he remembers everybody's name and is not afraid to ask our opinions. But when it comes to his political beliefs, he's ruthless. There's more to him than you see on television."

"Working in Washington sounds exciting."

"It is at times. But mostly it can be very cutthroat."

He turned to look at Lauren Blair. She was about five-four with large round caramel eyes set in a face that looked like it smiled easily in less difficult times. Her blue buttoned down oxford-cloth shirt was a size too small, accenting her curves, and tucked crisply into a pair of jeans.

"Can I ask you a personal question?"

"That depends on how personal it is."

"How did you cope with losing your husband?"

She raised her eyebrows in surprise. "Why do you ask?"

"Selfish reasons, actually. My wife has given up her treatments. She's going to die. So I was wondering what it was going to be like."

"I'm sorry. That can't be easy."

"I'm sorry I can't believe I just laid that on you with everything you're going through."

"No worries. Wyatt was a major in the Army. He was two months shy of coming home from Afghanistan when the truck he was in was hit by an RPG."

Benedict shook his head.

"The first couple of months I was numb. We had the burial at Arlington. I came home and immersed myself in my work and taking care of Angel. But, I found myself being very distracted, wandering around the house late at night after Angel was in bed. I couldn't lie down. I felt I had to get up and do something. But there was nothing to do. When Angel was awake, it was a lot easier. I had to be strong for her. It was a good distraction. Eventually, the pain subsided. It took awhile."

Benedict shoved his hands in his pockets and smiled tightly.

"Why," Lauren continued, "has your wife given up?"

"Rose is a very devout Catholic. She believes the Lord has spoken to her through a dream she's been having. Says she's tired of the treatments and is leaving it in His hands."

"Wow. That takes a lot of courage."

"Yeah, it does."

"She's not dead yet."

"I know, but I think it's only a matter of time." Benedict thought about Watson's Materia Prima and wondered if the claim he made was fact or fiction.

"You have one advantage that I didn't have. You know that she's leaving you. I did not have the chance to tell Wyatt good-bye. He was in danger, I know, but you never really think it will happen to you or someone you're close to. Inside, you think, it can't be him. It'll be someone else.

"Make sure you tell your wife how much she means to you, how much you love her and enjoy every minute you have left with her. You won't regret it. Don't worry about what happens when she's gone right now. Think about today, not tomorrow."

ΩΩΩ

"I think your pharmacist was quite a wacko," Spanos said. "A magic potion that cures disease? Check his boots for a clue? A scavenger hunt? This is insanity."

Benedict had just let his wife's oncologist listen to Watson's recording from his laptop. They were in the deserted physician's lounge with the door locked. *Better to let him hear it from the source*, Benedict told himself. *It might just convince him.*

"There are a few problems with your wacko theory," Benedict said.

"Such as?"

"A lot of the facts he cited are true. All the deaths occurred with the massive bruising and hemorrhaging; the fact that they were administering this potion in Nonarc IV bags. All those patients died. That's all true!"

"Do you actually believe this?"

Benedict shrugged. "I don't know."

"Alex, if you think what he says is true about the second dose being able to save Rose; I have to bring you back to earth. It's a wild goose chase."

"Will you humor me for a moment?"

"Go ahead," Spanos said in a mocking tone.

Benedict led his friend up to the oncology ward. The two men entered Margaret Queen's room and found the elderly woman sitting up in bed watching television.

"Miss Queen, I'm Dr. Benedict. This is Dr. Spanos. Do you mind if we ask you a few questions about your case?"

"Not at all, Sonny."

"You were very ill just last night. Now you seem to have made a miraculous recovery. Do you have any idea what happened?"

"It was my angel. I saw the light. The light came to me and I was cured."

"Do you remember anything else?"

"Isn't that enough?"

They retreated to the nurse's station. Spanos, with Benedict seated beside him, sat before a computer terminal reviewing Queen's case. The woman had been on death's doorstep, ready to step across. Benedict showed Spanos where a dose of Nonarc had been administered by Katherine Diehl the night before.

"And this Diehl woman is the one who gave you the CD?"

"This morning," Benedict replied nodding.

"I want to speak with her." They went to the nurse's station and asked when Diehl would be working again. The head nurse informed them that she had not showed up for work tonight and she wasn't answering their calls.

On the way back down on the elevator, Benedict said, "Ari, you know I'm sane. But I need to pursue this because if I don't and it turns out to be true I'll never forgive myself. Will you help me?"

"I can't believe that I'm agreeing to this. I'll go along for now. Word of Queen's recovery is all over the hospital. I called Queen's physician and asked him about what happened. He's stumped, too. He's ordered an MRI for today. I want to see the results. So for now you have a pass. What do you want me to do?"

CHAPTER 14

Benedict strode to the catafalque and looked down upon the dead man.

He had left Rose in Connie Steven's hands for a few hours to visit the funeral home.

Watson was laid out in full-view, head-to-toe; showing off the splendor of his re-enactor's rank and uniform. His deep blue Union General's uniform with the polished brass buttons, a wide black belt with "US" embossed across the gold buckle, a gold sash lay diagonally across his torso. His arms were folded across his chest and crisp white gloves pulled over his hands.

His trousers were lined with gold stripes and disappeared into the knee-high, spit-polished boots. A black Union officer's hat rested upon his chest, clasped in his hands.

He scrutinized Watson's head. A slight discolored area just behind the temple and under the hair was visible through the heavy makeup. If he hadn't known how the man died, Benedict would have assumed it was just a birth mark or a bruise.

Watson's face still held the tense, unsettling quality of despair. Benedict moved his eyes over the body and again stopped at the highly shined boots. He let his gaze linger there for a moment.

Check his boots.

Spanos had agreed to keep a close eye on Rose so Benedict could attend Michael Watson's viewing. Benedict had also made the physician promise to stay with her as much as possible until her father arrived from Florida. Spanos had agreed. But he had also mentioned he still thought this quest of Benedict's was a fairytale.

Benedict had responded to his friend by saying, "Maybe it is, but if I'm right Rose has a brand new future."

His trance was broken by the approach of a forty-something woman with streaks of gray in her thinning blonde hair. Her skin had begun the retreat to old age. Crow's feet and wrinkle lines spread out from the eyes and the edges of her mouth. Based on the resemblance, Benedict guessed it must be Watson's daughter.

"Hi, we haven't met?"

"Ah ... yes. I was Michael's supervisor at the hospital. I just wanted to pay my respects."

The woman extended a bony hand. "I'm Ruth Goodwin, Michael's daughter. Thanks for coming."

Benedict took the hand and held it for a moment. "I'm sorry for your loss."

"Thank you ..."

"Alex Benedict," he replied. "Michael was a good man and a good pharmacist."

"Thank you. He was a good father, too."

"Is there anything I can do?"

"I appreciate the offer. But we have things under control."

"He looks good in his uniform," Benedict said.

"Being a re-enactor was his whole life."

"I would have thought that his fellow re-enactors would have had a better showing tonight."

"They wanted to come. But most live quite a distance away. As a matter of fact, they will be gathering tomorrow just outside Richmond for the funeral."

"Richmond?"

"Michael will be buried just outside Richmond near one of the battlefields up there. We'll be transporting the body in the morning. His regiment will be giving him a full re-enactor military send off. Horse-drawn caisson, twenty-one gun salutes, the works. With the storm coming and all, it will be better. We need to get him in the ground quickly."

"I see. I was asked to apologize by Melissa Harrison, the Director of pharmacy. The hospital is undergoing a Joint Commission survey and she can't get away."

At the moment, Benedict guessed he was persona non grata in the pharmacy. Harrison wasn't pushing Benedict to come back to the office. She wanted him as far away from the surveyors as possible.

Benedict walked out into the foyer and stopped. He checked the windows and walls. What he saw, or the lack thereof, gave him hope that he might have a chance to get away with the crime he was contemplating.

Richmond was a good hour drive from Newport News. The fact Watson's body was leaving in the morning pushed up Benedict's timetable. They would be taking Watson early in the morning. He had to get back to Rose. But in the next twelve hours, he had to find away to get a look at Watson's boots.

ΩΩΩ

"When will the analysis be finished?" J. Edward Kyle asked his aide Ashan Habib.

"Six hours at the earliest," Habib replied. "The lab is one of the best in the state."

"We will attack this problem from all angles," Kyle said. "No option will be left unexplored."

"How?"

"The objective is to obtain the formula. We will accomplish that in any way possible. We could obtain a sample of Margaret Queen's blood, have it analyzed and try to decipher the correct proportion of ingredients. But the ingredients of the Materia are so many in number and comprised of the more common compounds found in the human body, it will be nearly impossible to decipher. There are two better ways.

"First, the IV bag," Kyle explained, "used to administer the dose of Materia Prima to Margaret Queen is in our possession thanks to Nurse Diehl. Despite the fact that Michael Watson has hidden the formula, we may be able to recreate it working backwards by analyzing the contents of the bag."

"Very good, Doctor."

"Did you obtain the listening devices?"

"Yes, Doctor," the Iranian replied. Habib handed him two small wafer-looking chips in plastic bags. "They have excellent sound quality. We will be able to hear everything that is said in the room through the receiver in your office."

Kyle took the bugs and placed them in a pocket. "Excellent work, ole chap. This is option two. We will let Alex Benedict recover the formula. Then we take it. Timothy will keep an eye on him and his friends. Because we cannot know which option will bear fruit, we will pursue both at the same time. While the analysis of the IV bag is underway, we will watch Alex Benedict and see what he can tell us."

"Most definitely."

"Did you have any trouble at the funeral parlor?" Kyle asked.

"No trouble. I followed Benedict. I have the items right here," Habib replied, holding up a large plastic bag.

"Good, we'll have a look in just a moment."

"Will there be anything else, Doctor?"

"Yes, tell your lab technician there's ten thousand dollars in it for him, if he gets the analysis to me in three hours instead of six."

ΩΩΩ

"Why am I here? It's almost one-thirty in the morning."

The question came from Tyrone Manville in the passenger seat of Benedict's Jaguar. Benedict did not look at the SEAL, but responded quickly.

"I told you I need your expertise."

"I'm a Navy SEAL," he shot back. "I kill people. I put them in funeral homes, Alex. I can't do anything for them once they're there."

"I need your ability to be stealthy. He's being moved to Richmond first thing in the morning. I have to get a look at Watson's body tonight."

"So you can look at a dead guy's boots?" The large black man said.

"Yup."

"You do realize what I'm risking if I get caught?"

"Are you forgetting about the night I kept you out of jail after you broke that guy's nose outside Manhattan's?"

Manville squirmed.

"He was an off-duty cop whose brother happens to be a friend of mine. If I hadn't convinced him that you were in the Navy, they would have hauled you off. It happened a week before you were supposed to go to SEAL training. If you got arrested, you'd never have become a SEAL. I guess you could say if it wasn't for me, you'd still be swabbing the decks. You owe me."

"Come on, man."

"Squid, it's a funeral home. Nobody's going to wake up yelling and screaming. We zip in, we zip out. We're in there, fifteen minutes max."

"What if there's an alarm system?"

"I already checked it out when I was in there today. Nothing I could see."

Benedict could hear the sharp intake of breath through Manville's nostrils.

"Okay, but this square's us. You got that?"

The D.P. Johnson and Son Funeral Home was a standalone building flanked by an old three door garage and a residence close by. The rear of the building was engulfed in darkness. Benedict approached a window with the Navy SEAL at his shoulder, and peered in, pressing a cupped hand to the glass.

"I didn't see an alarm control panel or any contact sensors on the windows. I think we're okay. The place looks empty."

"Except for the stiffs?"

Benedict ignored the comment and tried to lift the window. It wouldn't budge. "Let's try the door."

"Did you bring you're tools?" Benedict asked.

Manville removed a leather pouch from his rear pocket. "Get out of the way. I can't believe I'm doing this."

"Just remember, you're helping me solve a mystery that may involve the hospital's future and save patient lives. It's important. Watson—the dead guy—told me people were dying. There's a lot more at stake than you think."

"Yeah, right," Manville moaned as he opened the tool pouch on the doorstep. "Shine the light, right here."

Benedict produced a small key chain flashlight and watched him work.

"Did they teach you how to pick locks in SEAL training?"

"No, we just use a ram and knock the door in. This skill I learned working for my uncle back in Detroit."

"What kind of business was that?"

Manville paused then said, "He's a locksmith."

"Yeah, right," Benedict replied with a smile in his voice. "And I'm the Sultan of Brunei."

Inside, they navigated through the darkness using the small flashlight. Benedict quickly led Manville to the viewing parlor.

"Over here," Benedict said.

Together, they lifted the casket lid. Manville shown the small light at Watson's make-up coated face. He then moved the light along the length of Watson's body, stopping as the beam illuminated the feet.

"You gotta be shittin' me," Manville said.

"What's wrong?"

"Look at his feet."

Watson's right big toe protruded through a hole in his white stockings. Both boots were gone.

CHAPTER 15

Benedict patted Rose's forehead with a cold wash cloth in the dim light of the hospital room.

"It's hard to breathe," Rose said. "My chest hurts."

Her breaths were coming short and fast. She began to experience a coughing spasm that lasted for thirty seconds. Benedict held a napkin to her mouth and it came away tinged with blood. Her skin was hot and sweaty. She had spiked a temperature.

Spanos listened to her lungs and heard decreased breath sounds. "Start the pneumonia protocol," he commanded to Rose's nurse.

Spanos recited the orders from memory. "I'll fill out the form later. Get a CBC with differential; portable Chest X-ray AP; and get a sputum culture."

Spanos shot a glance at Benedict. "Okay, Pharmacy man, what drug does the protocol call for?"

Without hesitating, Benedict recited their options. "We'll have to consider it healthcare-acquired pneumonia. So we can start

Primaxin 500mg IV piggyback every six hours or Pip/Tazo 4.5gm every six hours."

"Let's go with Primaxin," Spanos said. "We'll see what the culture shows us. If we have to adjust the drug therapy later we will. I'm going to write up the orders. I'll be right back."

Rose gazed upon Benedict with rheumy eyes. "How's the Joint Commission thing going?"

"Everything's going fine," he lied. Rose had taken a turn for the worse while he was away. He was racked with guilt. He had to find the dose Watson had promised lay at the end of this journey.

"That's good," she said.

"Baby, I still have lots of work to do. I'm going to run down-stairs to grab some work and finish it up here in your room. I'll be right back."

Rose nodded, moving her head up and down once. "But I want you here before ... you know. Your face is the last thing I want to see."

"Please don't talk like that."

"Alex, promise me, you'll be here when it happens."

Benedict sighed as a shiver rippled down his spine.

"Say it," she persisted.

Benedict looked away.

"Alex!"

He turned his eyes to her once more.

"Say it!"

"Okay, I promise. I'll be here."

A spasm of watery coughs erupted from her chest again. She moved her bruised arm to her mouth. Benedict held out a tissue for her. When it passed, she lay back into the large pillow and smiled at him.

Connie Stevens, the neighbor, returned to the room with a large mug of coffee in her hand.

Benedict addressed her. "Connie, I'll be back in a few minutes to relieve you. I'll never be able to thank you for this. Call me.... if there are any changes."

Stevens hugged him and said, "I'll take good care of her."

Rose caressed his hand. Benedict swung back to face his wife. "Baby, will you call my father? He needs to fly up."

"I already did. He's on his way." He kissed the tips of his fingers through his mask and touched her warm, sweaty forehead.

ΩΩΩ

The man dressed in scrubs under a white lab coat stood in the doorway. The hospital room was dark. At this hour, it wasn't hard to make his way around the facility. He was a familiar figure to the nursing staff.

Both the patient, Rose Benedict, and her husband, Alex, were asleep. The husband's deep breathing was accompanied by the delicate whispers the wife's respirations. The soft bleep of the IV pump punctuated everything.

The man understood how fatigued Alex Benedict was. He'd been under tremendous strain of late. It was no wonder he had fallen asleep in the chair. The wife was probably drugged and out of it for different reasons.

The man turned to the nurses at the central nurse's station in the center of the circular patient floor. "I just want to check on Alex. I've been worried about him."

"No problem," one of the nurses replied.

The man moved into the room and slipped silently past the bed opposite where Benedict was sleeping. He stopped and checked on both people. Benedict stirred and rolled onto his side away from the man. Rose, the wife, did not move.

The man removed a small listening device from his lab coat pocket. Using a miniature flashlight, he placed it behind the bank of wall-mounted devices over the bed, right behind an electrical outlet.

The man moved back around the bed and quietly opened the bathroom door. He placed the second microphone on the wall behind the commode.

As silently as he arrived, the man slipped into the hallway.

"Thank you," he whispered to the nurses.

"No problem. Have a great night, Dr. Kyle," another nurse replied.

ΩΩΩ

Memories and visions filled his mind. The sentinel moments in his life with Rose surged forth like the tidal waters of the storm's surge: their first meeting at school, the first clumsy words he uttered to her in the library, sitting in the student lounge having coffee and her shy response to his request to take her to dinner.

He remembered with an out-of-body sensation as he recalled that first kiss outside her dorm room many years ago.

The soft, milky texture of her moist lips against his as her timid tongue caressed his. She pulled away slightly without losing contact as he gently thrust himself forward, trying to deepen the kiss.

Her inhibition yielded to desire. She pressed her lithe body against his. Benedict had become instantly hard and felt her reaction to his firmness as their hands began to explore each other in the dark hallway of the dormitory....

Benedict woke with a start. His breathing was rapid. For a moment, he did not know where he was.

"How is she?"

Benedict looked up at the hulking silhouette backlit by the light spilling in from the hallway. The man's hand was on his shoulder, gently shaking him.

"Alex, how is she doing?"

The ball cap and the outline of the face along with the familiar octaves of the gruff voice registered with the pharmacist.

"Grumps?" Benedict stood up and gave the old man a bear hug. "She's sleeping but doing better. They've given her two doses of antibiotic and her fever's come down a little."

Grumps looked at his stricken daughter. "How bad is it?"

ΩΩΩ

Benedict had never committed a crime in his life—until last night when he illegally entered the funeral home. Now he was about to add a second count to it. The back door to Michael Watson's place was locked. Benedict tried both windows. They, too, were locked.

The breeze began to intensify, swirling low and fast, picking up small papers and debris into its invisible vortex. Bits of dirt and dust pelted the house.

The one story neglected bungalow appeared empty. The white siding was caked with grime and black mold. The gray metal storm door did not close completely and vibrated in the growing breeze. The screens on the windows were dotted with holes.

Watson's place was on Deep Creek off Warwick Boulevard in a poorer area afforded by the lower classes and manual laborers that bore the brunt of the heavy lifting in today's economy. The houses were single-story affairs constructed in areas not defined by neighborhoods or city planning, ringed by rusted chain link fences and crowded with scattered bikes and toys. The depressed area, the approaching darkness and the black storm clouds pulled down his mood.

After finding the boots missing from Watson's feet, Manville had suggested that Benedict check his house. Maybe the family did not want him buried with his boots on. When Benedict asked the SEAL to join him, he begged off because he was on duty in Virginia Beach. But Benedict also sensed Manville did not want to press his luck.

Benedict didn't know much about Michael Watson's private life. What he did understand had been gleaned from an assortment of quick conversations and overheard comments over the years. Watson was divorced and had two children, a son and a daughter, both of whom had moved away from the area. The ex-wife still lived in the area, but he couldn't recall ever hearing her name. Watson's passion was re-enacting Civil War battles all over the South, from Antietam all the way to Vicksburg.

Benedict scanned the backyard and the house behind. Everything appeared quiet. No one was in sight. With his back to the window, Benedict rammed his elbow into the glass of the window beside the back door. His first blow was weak. He was afraid of making too much noise.

Cupping his fist in his hand for additional power, Benedict gave a second shot. This time the glass cracked. A third blow knocked a shard loose from the spider-webbed crack.

Benedict glanced around once more. A woman emerged from the house directly behind Watson's. She wore a long-sleeved men's denim shirt which was open and revealed a wife-beater's t-shirt beneath. She talked loudly on a cell phone while carrying a trash bag to the receptacle. Benedict froze in place and slowly dropped into a crouch, below the level of the banister.

The woman dropped the bag in the can, pivoted and returned into the house without ever glancing his way.

Benedict knocked out one of the loose pieces of glass and carefully picked away the rest creating a gap large enough for him to reach through. He unlocked the window, pushed it up and crawled through.

The back door opened into the kitchen. A light was on and the sink was full of dishes soaking in water that appeared to have been sitting for hours. A wrinkled newspaper sat on the dinette in the middle of the room. Benedict stepped slowly past the table, craning his neck to look down a short passageway towards the rest of the house.

A wave of guilt engulfed him as he walked deeper inside. At this very moment, Michael Watson's body was being transported to Richmond to be interred. And Benedict was breaking into the man's home.

Past the kitchen, Benedict found a good-sized living area with a leather sofa pushed against one wall and matching recliner angled nearby. A large, flat screen television was mounted on the wall across from the sofa. Watson had obviously invested more in furnishing his home than maintaining its exterior.

Floor-to-ceiling bookcases covered a third wall. Every inch was stuffed with pharmacy tomes many of which dealt with the art of pharmacy compounding, the nearly dead art of mixing and combining powders and liquids for use as remedies and cures. Thick, leather bound titles such as *Remington's Pharmaceutical Sciences* and the *United States Pharmacopoeia* were flanked by cases of journals and periodicals, newspapers and marbled composition books. Benedict leafed through several pages of handwritten notes. Then he spied two books, a leather-bound copy of the writings of H.P. Lovecraft and a biography of Union General Ethan Allen Hitchcock.

Remembering Watson's recording and the mention of both the writer's name and Hitchcock's, Benedict picked them up and carried them into the kitchen. He laid them on the table and returned back to the hallway and headed straight for Watson's bedroom.

He did not know who H.P. Lovecraft was. But, Watson had said it was important to deciphering the formulation.

He explored the room, checking under the bed and opening every drawer. His nerves were on fire. He found himself fingering the gold jet lighter with his other hand. He must have absent-mindedly removed it from his pocket.

Benedict stepped to the closet and flipped on the closet light. Standing in the narrow space between the hanging clothes and the wall was a life-size, faceless mannequin outfitted in the finery of a Confederate General. It was a gray full length coat trimmed in gold and brass with matching trousers hung from a mannequin. A long saber hung from a scabbard at the waist. To the right, hidden be-hind the sliding closet door was an identical, naked mannequin for Watson's Union uniform.

Watson's present day clothes hung from the rod behind the two mannequins. The floor of the closet was cluttered with an array of civil war era equipment: three pistols encased in open, velvet-lined boxes, a pair of wire-rimmed spectacles, and a pair of well-worn knee-high leather boots caked with dirt. The black leather was cracked and dirty, and folded over on itself. They could not have been the same boots Watson had on his feet at the funeral home. Benedict didn't know what happened to the polished pair of boots that adorned his feet at the viewing. This was the only remaining pair. A feeling of panic enveloped him.

What if whatever Watson wanted him to find was in the other pair of boots?

He pushed the negative thought from his head and dropped to his knees, grabbing the dirty boots. He checked the rest of the junk, making sure there were no other boots hiding on the floor or on the shelf above.

Convinced there were no others, he ran his hand along the in-terior of both boots. They were smooth and slick from years of use. But there was no message, no note or any other item that looked remotely like something Watson wanted to be found. He rifled through the pockets and sleeves of the uniform and came away empty again. The pistol cases also yielded nothing.

Stuffed into the back of the closet on the floor was a rumpled, brown grocery bag. Benedict pulled it out and found it filled with socks and underwear. He emptied these onto the floor and placed the boots in it. He returned through the kitchen, gathered up the tome of short stories and novellas by Lovecraft, the biography of Hitchcock and exited through the backdoor.

ΩΩΩ

"I've been over them five times," Ashan Habib said. "There's nothing here."

Kyle picked up one of the spit-polished boots by stuffing his hand into it. He felt around with his hand. He manipulated the heel and the sole to find a loose thread or hidden compartment. The boot—both boots—appeared to be brand new and in perfect condition.

"Are you sure the nurse told you it was the boots?" Ashan asked.

Kyle looked at his assistant as if he wanted to tear his head off. After Katherine Diehl had given them Alex Benedict's name, she revealed that she had listened to the recording she had given to Alex Benedict.

"Yes, I'm sure," Kyle seethed.

"I was just asking," the Iranian said.

Kyle's cell phone rang.

"It's Timothy," Kyle's aide said. "I'm tailing the pharmacist. He left Watson's house with a bag under his arm. He went back to his house and removed what was in the bag as he entered the house. He has a pair of boots. It looks like he's on the way back to the hospital. He has the boots with him. Do you want me to get them from him?"

Kyle thought for a moment. "No, just stay with him. Benedict will chase down the clues and riddles left by our dear departed Michael."

Kyle leafed through the pages on the desk. Each one had the name of each one of Benedict's friends printed in bold face at the top and outlined the lives and careers of Benedict's poker buddies.

Kyle spoke into his phone, but was talking to both Timothy and Ashan who was seated at the desk with the useless pair of boots.

"You have done your job well, Timothy. Both you and Ashan have. You both are to monitor the comings and goings of Alex Benedict. Keep an eye on who visits him and where they go and what they say in the hospital room. Benedict will utilize these people to help him find the clues. In fact, whenever possible, he will stay with his dying wife.

"Timothy," Kyle continued. "Call in your friend, Neville. We will need his services. I will pay him his usual rate. Make sure you stay on top of this. Alex Benedict will find the clues and when he does we will be there to take them from him."

Habib hung up his cell phone as Kyle ended his call.

He called over to his boss. "Doctor, the analysis of the IV bag is complete."

CHAPTER 16

Benedict watched from the hallway through the window of the hospital room as Grumps talked quietly with his daughter. He felt like an intruder. He couldn't hear the words. He didn't need to. The love and concern Grumps felt for Rose was communicated through the way he held her hand and looked upon his dying daughter. His eyes glowed above his face mask with a deep paternal love.

Rose looked better but still weak. Some of her color had returned. The bed was raised to allow her to sit up. Benedict did not want to interrupt the private moment. But Rose spotted him and waved. He put down the suitcase and the paper grocery bag and donned the mask and gown. When he was ready, he picked up his items and entered.

"There's my knight," Rose said with a crooked smile and slurred words.

"You're looking a little better. How are you feeling?" He kissed the top of her head through the mask.

Grumps answered for her. His mask puffed as he spoke. "Her fever's come down slightly. But she still has a pretty bad headache."

"What took you so long to get back?"

"I had to make a side trip," he replied.

"What's in the bag?" Grumps asked.

"I want to talk to both of you. Then I'll show you what's in the bag."

"We're listening," Rose said.

"I want you both of you to listen to what I'm about to tell you. And don't interrupt, no matter how crazy what I'm about to tell you sounds. Okay?"

"Agreed," Rose replied. Grumps simply nodded.

Benedict peered into Rose's green eyes. "What would you say if I told you I might have a way to make you better?"

ΩΩΩ

When he was finished, Benedict said, "That's it. Michael Watson has found the Materia Prima. I can find these clues and get the last remaining dose."

"Have you been drinking?" was the first utterance out of Grumps's mouth.

Before he began, Benedict had circled the room closing the blinds on the window to the hallway and the one with a view into the second room in which Angel Blair was a patient. Then he'd closed the door.

He had recounted the events in less than thirty minutes. Grumps tried to interrupt twice, but Benedict kept him at bay with a raised index finger. "You promised," Benedict chided both times. Spanos quietly slipped into Rose's room halfway through Benedict's speech. Benedict said, pointing to the Greek doctor. "He already knows. He's not quite convinced. But I'm working on him."

Rose and Grumps stared at Benedict with a mixture of bewilderment and pity.

"It's sweet, baby, that you want to go on this quest for me. I think you're under a lot of stress and it's affecting your sanity."

"I think he's been drinking, doctor," Grumps said, turning to Spanos. "Tell me you do not believe any of this."

"Mr. Blackmon," Spanos replied. "Words cannot convince anyone about what Alex is saying. Let us show you."

ΩΩΩ

"I'm a new woman!" Margaret Queen squealed.

They introduced Grumps to the old woman who was sitting on the edge of the bed. When Spanos described her miracle, Queen jumped to the floor and took Grumps by the arms and whirled him around the room in a clumsy waltz.

Queen's recovery had quickly spread among the hospital staff. She embraced the chance to discuss her good fortune. Rumor had it that her case would soon be written up in several medical journals.

"Come with me," Spanos said after the short romp around the room.

They retreated to the hallway and began walking to the elevator. Once in the car, Spanos removed a set of MRI images from his lab coat.

"I could get in a hell of a lot of trouble by showing these to you, Mr. Blackmon. So I'm trusting that this will remain between you, me and Alex."

"Don't worry, son. I can be trusted."

"The first image is Margaret Queen's MRI taken about two months ago. You see these lesions. Here, here and here. This is her cancer before she was admitted to the hospital. It's all over her body."

Spanos removed a second set of images.

"These are the MRI pictures taken just today. See any difference?"

"It's all gone."

"Exactly."

Grumps's eyes shifted back and forth between the doctor and the pharmacist. They stopped in the hallway halfway to Rose's room.

"So you're telling me that Margaret Queen was given this special formula and her cancer was cured?"

"Yes," Benedict replied.

"And you're also telling me that there is one last dose of the medicine out there somewhere and when you find it you will give it to my little girl and she will be cured, too?"

"We hope so," Spanos answered this time.

Benedict spoke to Spanos. "Are you completely convinced now?"

"Without a doubt."

Grumps closed his eyes. He opened them and looked at Benedict. "Then what the hell are you waiting for?"

ΩΩΩ

"Your pharmacist was definitely hiding something," Spanos said.

Benedict picked up the folded paper off the floor.

They were in the physicians' conference room. Grumps had returned to Rose's side. Spanos had found the hidden compartment in the heel of Watson's left boot from which the paper had fallen.

Nothing more than an average piece of lined notebook paper, with small, shredded rings running down the left hand side. Benedict unfolded it and a second, more colorful piece fell out. He flipped the notebook paper over, looking at both sides, before looking up at Spanos. Benedict retrieved the second piece of paper off the floor.

It was a bent, laminated strip. On one side was a photograph looking down an ornate arched hallway with a floor to ceiling perspective. The floor was an intricate tapestry of mosaic tiles patterned with repeating geometric designs, large circles inscribed with squares, followed by more squares and circles inscribed within each other. The walls were a combination of intricately carved Corinthian columns interspersed by what were apparently unseen windows shedding light onto the mosaic flooring. Each pair of columns supported an elaborately detailed arch whose soffits were adorned with coffers outlined with leaf and berry, filets, beads and reels and longer ornamental panels. From each arch hung a decorative lamp shining brilliantly for the photograph. The architectural photographer had blended the light from the windows and shimmering aspects of the hallway perfectly. Between the arches, Benedict could make out saucer domes empanelled with more coffers. He counted six pairs of arches and columns intermingled with five domes. The entire distance was bathed in the golden glow of marble and gold.

It was obviously a hallway in a very distinguished building, probably somewhere in Europe. It looked vaguely familiar. It could have been an elaborate hallway in any one of a hundred museums or government buildings.

The flip side was another photograph showing a portion of another expensively designed and adorned space. This was a close-up of a winged angel blowing a long trumpet set in a pendative between two arches. Benedict concluded it was in the same building since the photos were on the same bookmark. He flipped the bookmark over several times, checking to see if the winged angel appeared in the photo of the hallway. But it was not there. There were no words or descriptions on the marker describing where they were taken or what Benedict was looking at.

"What is it?" Spanos replied with frustration. He snapped the paper from Benedict's hand and scanned it himself.

"I don't know," Benedict spat. "Some kind of bookmark."

Spanos examined the bookmark as well. After a minute, he said, "What are these marks?"

He moved to the table and smoothed the crumpled bookmark under his hand. Benedict hadn't noticed them. Spanos
pointed to the hallway photo. Someone, probably Watson, had
traced lightly over a portion of the mosaic tile in the foreground
of the photo. It was barely noticeable, but it was obvious once
Spanos pointed it out. The mark was two lines at a right angle
over a section of tile beneath the first and leftmost Corinthian
column in the photo. Watson had traced over the lower left corner of a square:

L

"Then here." Spanos moved his finger over the bookmark to the next
tracing. "Get some paper and a pen."

Benedict returned with a yellow legal pad.

The second tracing followed a zigzag pattern along the edge of
the flooring in the next section of the hallway, under the first dome.
The pattern was a large square outlined on the floor with a circle
inside the square touching each side at its midpoint. The corners
of the square had been replaced by lines that zigzagged until they
connected with the next side. Watson had traced lightly over the
closest pattern:

M

The final tracing was in the same section of floor space. Inside
the large circle was a smaller concentric circle with a square whose
four corners intersected along the arc of the smaller circle. Inside
the square was a third circle. Watson had traced the left side of
the square, the smallest circle and the right side of the square to
create what appeared to be a three digit number. Benedict jotted
these onto his paper:

101

Benedict then wrote the symbols together in sequence:

LM101

"That mean anything to you?" Spanos asked.

Benedict shook his head.

The doctor flipped the bookmark over and pointed to an area just above the winged angel in the area of the dome. The dome sported a mural of some kind. The mural had been cropped out so as to focus on the angel. What appeared to be the artist's initials in the lower margins of the mural were visible. Benedict saw now that they did not belong in the photograph. They had been added by whoever had marked up the bookmark. They were a series of letters and number:

EAH C.13

"So we have a series of letters and numbers traced on a bookmark with photos of some fancy building," Benedict said.

He circled the symbols on the page.

LM101

EAH C.13

Benedict pushed away from the table. "I need to get back to Rose."

"What about these symbols?" Spanos followed Benedict.

"Ari, can you surf the net and see if you can find anything on this bookmark and what building it is and where it's located?"

ΩΩΩ

She still didn't feel quite right. Rose had all her faculties about her, but at the same time felt like she had a hellacious hangover. Her tongue was thick and her words felt like they were coming from her lips in slow motion. The fever had begun to come down, but breathing was still a chore.

Rose's self-pity had begun to mount since waking after her seizure. She'd begun to question her choice. Her decision to stop her medical treatment had hit home. Death and its permanence were a few steps away. At one point, she awoke alone. Alex had probably gone down to his office and her father had not yet arrived. A creeping loneliness consumed her that had swelled until the tears came. Since then, she began to realize how much these two men in her life loved her. As she lay here wasting away, they doted on her.

Lauren Blair's question, "Want to talk about it?" had surprised her. The woman had a disarming quality about her. Conversing with her was a welcome distraction. Her brown, curious eyes were distilled with the pain of loss. It touched Rose somewhere deep inside. But Rose had still responded with a simple quick shake of the head.

Lauren, clad in mask and gown, had relieved Grumps thirty minutes ago, sending him for a nap in the family lounge. Grumps and Lauren had been introduced earlier in the day and hit it off immediately, so he was comfortable leaving Rose in her hands.

Rose had told her she did not want to talk about anything. Tears had proceeded to spill from her eyes as she laid her head back and looked away.

"I understand," Lauren replied quickly and evenly.

At that point, a canyon of silence had spread between the two women. But Lauren had filled it, launching into an explanation of her daughter's condition, its history and the most recent symptoms that had lead to Angel's admission.

Rose had lived a relatively full life compared to that of the young girl in the room next to hers. And as Rose listened to Lauren rattle off the mind-numbing circumstances, she had begun to feel her depression lift if only slightly.

Rose interjected a few questions to keep her talking. And she learned that Lauren was the chief of staff for Virginia's senior senator, Waldo Paige. Lauren ferried back and forth from Washington on weekends. Angel stayed with Lauren's parents in lower Williamsburg during the week. But, at the moment, Lauren was on a leave of absence so she could care for her daughter. Rose learned that this domestic circumstance had been created by the death of Lauren's husband in Afghanistan.

"How do you do it?" Rose asked. She was immediately embarrassed by the fact that she had pointed out Lauren's pitiful circumstance.

"I don't know," Lauren replied with a smile and not one hint of felling self-pity. "I take one day at a time. It gets tough sometimes. But, you know who helps pick me up?"

Rose shook her head.

Lauren hefted her thumb over her shoulder towards her daughter. "She does. She's a real fighter like her father. No matter how bad her treatments are or the pain is she always manages to find a way to make me smile."

"She's beautiful," Rose said, glancing at Angel through the glass. She was busy toying with her military bear. Rose leaned in and said, "I'm sorry I lost it earlier."

"It's okay. I've cried many times." This time Lauren leaned in. "Can I tell you something?"

"Sure."

"But you have to promise not to get mad with your husband."

Alarm coursed through Rose's body. Her first thought was that Lauren was going to confess to having some sort of inappropriate relationship with her husband. "Okay?"

"Your husband told me that you have decided to stop your therapy."

Rose's concern melted away and swelled into relief and anger. Pissed that Alex had been discussing her decision with a total stranger, she was relieved that it was nothing more than talk.

"Did he now?" The consternation must have showed on her face.

Lauren nodded. "Please do not be angry with him. I see the anxiety in his eyes. He's very worried about losing you."

"Alex is a good man and a great husband. And he would have made a great father. I guess I should say someday he'll be a great father. It just won't be by me...." Her voice trailed off and her eyes looked toward the wall. But they were seeing the future, a future in which she would not be present.

"It's very courageous decision. I don't know if I'd have the *chutzpah* to do it."

"My body has been ravaged by the cancer and the chemo has taken its toll as well. I'm tired of all of it." Rose sighed. "You really want to know why I was crying earlier."

Lauren nodded.

"We had been planning to start a family. We'd been trying to get pregnant for a couple of months. I told Alex I'd gone to the doctor for a regular check-up. But I really was having problems with cramping and bleeding. That's when we found out I was sick. But there was something else the doctor told me. Something I never told my husband."

ΩΩΩ

Most nights, Ari Spanos would grab something to eat and scan a medical journal or two in bed. But tonight, he was too keyed up by the finding inside the boot to pick up a journal.

Spanos loved puzzles, mostly Suduko and crosswords when he found the time. Practicing medicine was deciphering a complicated human puzzle. As an oncologist, his patients looked to him to diagnose, treat and eradicate cancers. Patients arrived with signs and symptoms and Spanos had to figure out what was ailing them and then design a treatment plan to make it all go away, or at the very least shrink the tumors.

His field was slowly gaining ground in the fight. Three decades earlier, cancer more often than not was a death sentence, sometimes a slow, agonizing, fear-filled incarceration of pain and chemotherapy. But advances in diagnosis and treatments had leveled the playing field. Many times Spanos could eradicate a tumor or significantly extend a patient's life. But there were still instances where their cause was lost.

Rose Benedict's cancer was one of those cases. Treating ovarian cancer was like trying to kill a swarm of locusts with a fly swatter. Rose had decided to terminate the fight before her body was ravaged even more by the treatments and the disease. Though Spanos hated giving up the fight, it was not his decision to make and he respected it.

But Spanos had watched the toll it was talking on Alex Benedict, as well. His friend was struggling with her choice. Benedict's very nature could not understand it and the anguish he was feeling must have been gigantic. Benedict's situation reminded Spanos how important his job was as a doctor.

He would often deliver devastating news to a patient or family member then stuff the emotions away into a dark, recessed cubby hole in his mind. But he could not do that with Alex and Rose. They were constantly on his mind. There was little left for him to do medically except make her comfortable and console his friend. Spanos wanted to do something for Benedict, something that at least made him feel like he was making a contribution.

So Spanos had searched the Internet for three hours after coming home, looking for clues in which building the magnificent hallway was located. It might give them a clue as to what the dead pharmacist had been trying to tell Benedict.

His twenty-six year old daughter, Constance, a lawyer, who worked as a clerk at the Supreme Court, was home from Washington.

She padded past his bedroom on her way to the bathroom when she spotted him sitting in front of the computer.

"What are you doing, Dad?"

"I'm trying to help Alex find something out about the building in this picture."

Constance looked over her father's shoulder at the folded book-mark. "That's easy, Dad...."

CHAPTER 17

Kyle felt a surge of excitement course through him like none he'd ever felt in the past. The capuchin monkey covered with cancerous lesions lay unconscious on the metal table. With all the scrutiny going on at the hospital, he could not afford to take a chance testing the Materia on another patient. He would have to test it here.

He hung the IV bag on the pole and screwed the tubing into the permanent IV port in the monkey's belly. The animal had been sedated. Kyle was alone. He didn't need to be fighting with a restless primate. Habib was in Kyle's office monitoring the listening equipment, for any conversations going on in Benedict's wife's hospital room.

The solution looked like all the others he'd seen given. It was a deep green hue. Tiny specks of colloidal matter were suspended in the thick solution but they were dark. A nagging feeling crept into his mind.

Would this be any different than before?

In a few hours, he hoped to return and find the animal cured and healthy. And then the real work could begin.

It would work. Of course, it would, he convinced himself.

ΩΩΩ

"Mommy, when are you coming back to my bed?" Angel called out.

She looked through the window and held up a finger. Lauren smiled at Angel. "Soon, darling, I'm almost done."

"I really need to get back to her," Lauren said to Rose. "It would be great if we could continue this conversation."

"Maybe we can."

"What do you have in mind?"

Lauren went back to the room and returned with a pink device in her hand.

"What's that?"

"It's Angel's play walkie-talkie. She and I use it to talk when we're in different rooms at home. Here, you can meet my daughter."

Lauren returned to Angel's side and introduced her to Rose through the walkie-talkie.

"Are you sick, too?" Angel asked as Lauren moved around Angel's bed and brought a cup and straw to her lips.

"Yes, I am," Rose replied.

Angel sucked in a long sip. "What kind of sickness do you have?"

"I have ovarian cancer."

"What's that?"

"It's the part of a woman that makes babies."

"Are you going to die?"

Lauren's eyes widened at the question brought on by her daughter's childish innocence.

"Angel, sweetie," Lauren interjected, "we don't ask questions like that."

Lauren's eye caught Rose's, pleading for forgiveness. Rose lifted her weak right arm, telling her it was okay.

Rose responded with a question of her own. "We all are going to die someday, Angel." Rose looked to Lauren, suddenly uncomfortable that she was crossing into parental territory.

Lauren's gaze alternated between the woman in the bed and her daughter.

"But, you won't die for a long, long time."

"Are you afraid?" Angel asked.

"A little bit." Rose composed herself. "Do you believe in God, Angel?"

Angel nodded.

"Good. So do I. It's very important that you believe in God."

"Why?"

"So we can go to heaven and be with Him when we die. Your daddy died, didn't he?"

Angel nodded and hugged Major Bear tighter.

"He believed in God, right? Do you think your daddy is in heaven with God?"

"Yep," she replied, pointing to the ceiling.

"And do you think your daddy is happy right now?"

Angel nodded again.

"Well, I believe in God very deeply. And I know someday, hopefully, many days from now, I will be with God. But no matter when that happens, I know I will be with Him, and be very happy. It helps me to be brave."

Rose saw a relieved smile cross Lauren's lips. Rose smiled back. Lauren looked at her daughter.

"Your favorite show is coming on. Do you want to watch it?"

Angel nodded with a renewed sense of vigor. Lauren got her settled, fluffed her pillow, pulled her blankets higher on her chest and kissed her on the forehead. She crossed back to Rose's room.

Lauren placed her hand on Rose's arm and said, "You handled that very well. I'm sorry she's so direct."

"It's okay. I hope I didn't trample on your parental authority."

"It was perfect," Lauren said. She tightened her lips into a thin line. "You would have been a great mother."

Rose placed her hand over Lauren's. The tears clouded her vision. "Thank you. I almost was."

"You were pregnant?"

Rose nodded. "I was. When my cancer was diagnosed, I was about six weeks along."

"And you never told your husband. You never told, Alex?"

"No."

"Why?"

"It was the one thing he wanted more than anything. Everything he did from the day we got married was in preparation for us having babies. He's half Italian and wanted a lot of children. As practicing Catholics, we never used birth control. We were preparing for a large brood, maybe four or five.

"He drives that old beat up Jaguar. But we bought the Lincoln Navigator just for a family. We have a house with four bedrooms; one bedroom would be for the girls, another for the boys. We already had names picked out. Alex Jr. and Frances for a girl, after that we didn't have any idea."

Lauren stroked Rose's arm.

"So when I told him I had ovarian cancer, I couldn't bring myself to tell him I was pregnant. We had been trying to get pregnant for almost ten months. He thought it was his fault. I think he felt like he'd failed me as a man. That he couldn't get me pregnant. But that wasn't the case; he had done his fatherly job."

"But, you're not pregnant anymore." It was a statement, not a question.

"No, I'm not."

"What happened?"

CHAPTER 18

"The Library of Congress?" Benedict asked.

"Yep, Constance figured it out. She's works at the Supreme Court right next door. She and her co-workers use the Library all the time. Her office is steps away from the Library. She's also deciphered the markings, too."

"Well, don't keep me in suspense."

Spanos smiled as if he'd uncovered the secrets of the Oracle at Delphi. "The markings your pharmacist made on the bookmark coincide with a place inside the Library."

Spanos pulled the crumpled bookmark out of his back pocket and flattened it on the counter top. They were back in the hospital restaurant. It was packed with visitors and hospital employees.

He removed the scrap paper with the markings on which Benedict had scribbled the code and laid it before Benedict:

LM101

EAH C.13

The oncologist pulled out another paper. It was floor plan of some kind.

"She printed this off the website. It's The Library of Congress Floor Plan. The first line represents a room number. More specifically, a reading room."

"Keep going," Benedict urged.

"The Library of Congress is actually made up of three buildings. The most famous is the Jefferson Building. That's the one with the large reading room and the elaborate foyer. There are two other buildings, the Madison and Adams. The LM stands for Library Madison Building. The 1-0-1 is the room number in the Madison Building. It's the Manuscript Reading Room. Your pharmacist is pointing to a place. Whatever he hid is probably in that room."

"Yeah, but where?"

"I'm guessing that the second line tells us where," Spanos declared.

"Tell me your daughter figured that out, too."

"Sorry, buddy. She's good but she ain't that good. Did Watson tell you anything that might mean anything?"

Benedict sighed. "I don't think so. He just told me if anything happened to him to check in his boots. And we had to inspect the writings firsthand. You see Michael was a Civil War re-enactor. Those boots are his Civil War cavalry boots. He told me the guy's name he represents. It's some Northern general."

"The last name begins with an 'H.' He had three names. Was it Hancock? No, it wasn't Hancock, but it sounds like that. Hitchcock. That's it! Ethan Allen Hitchcock."

Benedict tapped the coded message on the crumpled page. "E A H stands for Ethan Allen Hitchcock!"

"Watson left his secret in the Library of Congress Manuscript Reading Room. And it has something to do with the General Hitchcock. Let's find out more about this guy." Spanos accessed the Internet from his cell phone and tapped the Google listing. "We'll start with Wikipedia."

Spanos scanned the document, reading out loud.

"Born in Vermont. Died and was buried at the West Point National Cemetery in New York, grandson of Revolutionary War hero Ethan Allen. Graduated from West Point. Rose to the rank of Brigadier General, then resigned for health reasons in 1855. When the Civil War started, he returned and was commissioned as a Major General and became adviser to the Secretary of War. From November 1862 to the end of the war he served as Commissioner for Prisoner of War Exchange."

"That doesn't tell us much."

"There's more. He collected music and played the flute."

"That doesn't sound too promising."

"There's a section here listed *Contributions to Alchemy and Jungian Psychology*. He was an avid reader of philosophy and a published scholar. He had amassed a large private library of philosophical texts including volumes on the subject of alchemy. It is regarded as one of the finest private holdings of rare alchemical works and is preserved at the University of Missouri-St. Louis. Through *Remarks upon Alchemy and the Alchemists*, Hitchcock argued that the alchemists were actually religious philosophers writing in symbolism."

Spanos looked up from his reading. "It says most of his collection of writings is in Missouri with a small collection in the Library of Congress."

"The answer is in Washington."

ΩΩΩ

"What do you have?" J. Edward Kyle barked into his cell phone.

Timothy was seated about twenty feet away from the doctor and the pharmacist in the restaurant. Kyle had provided him with a white lab coat and an old hospital ID. He had been aiming a long range listening device at the table. It was no larger than a ball point pen. A thin wire snaked from the pen in his hand to his right ear. The reception was excellent even in the noisy cafeteria. Timothy had jotted a page and a half of notes.

When talk shifted of a trip to Washington, D.C., Timothy called Kyle.

Timothy spoke softly but quickly. "They've found something in the second pair of boots. It's a clue. They're talking about going to Washington and the Library of Congress."

"Stay close to them and find out who's going and when they'll leave."

Kyle ended his call and turned to see Ashan Habib, standing in the doorway to Kyle's small subterranean apartment just off the main laboratory. The look on the swarthy man's face was one of sadness and horror.

"Ashan, what is wrong?"

The Iranian moved his right hand from his side. In it, Kyle thought he clutched a stuffed furry animal. As Ashan brought it up to the light, Kyle saw that it was too limp to be a doll. It had once been a living creature. Ashan turned the animal over.

The doctor recognized the distinctive markings around the head and face of the tufted capuchin. The sight of its deeply bruised torso and the dried blood which had leaked from its nose and mouth involuntarily made Kyle's hands clench into fists.

He let out guttural cry, lifted a lamp from the desk and flung it against the wall.

ΩΩΩ

"How long will you be gone?" Grumps asked.

Rose was asleep. Benedict had pulled Grumps away from the bed into a corner a few moments before and explained to him what they'd found in the boots and said, "I have to go to Washington, D.C."

"If I'm lucky, no more than six hours."

"It's a three hour drive from here. Up and back alone will take six hours."

"I have a friend who owns a plane. He's agreed to fly me up there. We can be there in just under an hour. Dr. Spanos is making rounds on his other patients. He will stay behind and check on both of you every few hours. Here's his cell phone number."

Grumps placed a heavy hand on Benedict's shoulder. "I admire what you're trying to do for my daughter."

"I hate having to leave her."

The large former banker pulled Benedict close and wrapped him in a tight bear hug and whispered in her ear. "I know. Just hurry back."

CHAPTER 19

Benedict pounded on the thick glass of the weathered bronze door of the Jefferson Building.

Devin McGuire, Benedict's friend and poker buddy, was a high-priced personal injury lawyer whose over-the-top television commercials made him a local icon. McGuire had flown them up to Washington, despite the fact that the plane still was not fully serviced. The technicians still had some minor maintenance to perform, but they had assured him it was flyable. They had hired a car at the airport. McGuire instructed the driver to return upon his call.

The door creaked open. A tall, thin black man with a graying, tightly-curled beard addressed Benedict and his lawyer pilot. The Library employee was dressed in a dark suit with a white bow tie.

"Which of you is Alex Benedict?"

Benedict lifted a hand. They followed him through dark foyer under the balcony into the bowels of the enormous library.

The Library of Congress's Jefferson Building sat behind the Capitol on Independence Avenue and to the right of the Supreme Court.

The most famous structure of the Library, it sported an elaborate foyer and the famous circular reading room. The building was dark, devoid of tourists and looked haunting in the early morning glow.

"How did you arrange for us to gain access to the Library before it opened?" McGuire asked.

"Ari's daughter clerks at the Court next door. She knows someone."

They turned left and right several times. Benedict quickly lost all orientation. In a few minutes, they were standing in the ornate hallway depicted on the bookmark. Benedict stood gazing down the elaborate corridor.

"We can admire this another time. Let's get where we need to be. I had my secretary clear my calendar today so I could bring you up here. I'd like to get back before dinner."

McGuire had peppered Benedict with questions on the flight. Ari Spanos had called McGuire asking that he fly Benedict to D.C. Spanos and Benedict had come up with a cover story that would leave magic potions and formula out of any explanation. When McGuire asked what the purpose of the trip was, Spanos had told him that they were going through Hitchcock's papers because he once made reference to the location of a series of medical documents that the physician needed for some research he was doing. Benedict managed to deflect McGuire's questions with enough skill to quiet his queries but not wipe the consternation from his expression.

The library employee led them through the Byzantine underground hallways lined with overhead conduits and pipes. The uninitiated would easily have become lost for days. Minutes later, they emerged into a gleaming white hallway.

"You're now in the Madison Building," the man said, pushing the elevator button. "You are currently on sublevel 2. Take that elevator up to the ground floor, turn right. Someone will be waiting for you in the Manuscript Reading Room."

ΩΩΩ

Timothy had watched the two men climb the steps and disappear into to the Library of Congress. He had commandeered a private jet at Kyle's expense and made up a great deal of time. The pilot initially balked at the late request. But a pistol aimed at one's chest tended to be very influential.

The lawyer had piloted his slower Cessna. Timothy's hired Gulfstream had landed only ten minutes after the Cessna touched down.

Timothy had dropped another hundred dollars on the tarmac attendant to tell him where the airport limo had taken them. With some creative driving, he'd arrived in time to watch Alex Benedict and the lawyer exiting the vehicle.

The place would open in less than thirty minutes. Timothy removed the Sig Sauer from his shoulder holster and placed it on the seat under a copy of the *Washington Post*.

ΩΩΩ

"We need to see all the writings you have on General Ethan Allen Hitchcock."

The woman punched her keyboard. "There are fifteen containers filled with his writings. Which one do you want?"

"All of them," Benedict replied.

"Since you don't have a Library card, please sign the register and show me your driver's license."

Benedict did.

"You are Alex Benedict?"

"Yes."

"I have something for you," the woman said. The docent placed a thick, manila envelope on the desk between them. Benedict's name was scrawled across it. "When Miss Spanos asked for your permission to be granted access to the Reading Room early, she also requested that we prepare photographed copies of General Hitchcock's papers. She said it would be a favor to the Clerk of the Court if we could rush it.

We are in the process of electronically archiving all the documents in the Manuscript Reading Room. We had not yet reached General Hitchcock's writing. I called in my best archivist and we moved him to the head of the line. Your woman friend has some pull."

Benedict opened the envelope and leafed through the contents. He recalled Watson's instructions on the recording.

"I appreciate all the effort. It certainly will save us a lot of time. But I need to inspect the storage containers personally."

The woman who still carried the air of someone dragged out of bed too early, made no attempt to hide her displeasure.

"Have a seat at one of those tables."

Five minutes later, she returned pushing a three shelf rolling cart holding the Library's collection of Ethan Allen Hitchcock's writings.

"Open one container at a time," she instructed. "Return all materials to each container before you open a new one. Needless to say, be gentle." The woman departed.

"Devin," Benedict said, "I'll need about thirty minutes. Why don't you get some coffee?"

The containers were blue archival rectangular boxes with metal beaver-tail handles. Benedict pulled one from the top shelf of the cart and slid it out.

He slowly opened the container as if he was unsealing King Tut's burial chamber. The stiff cardboard container creaked. Benedict peered inside and his eyes widened as he brought original American history into the present.

ΩΩΩ

Benedict was two-thirds through the fifteen containers. He had reviewed containers one through five and six through ten. The woman had placed the containers on the cart out of order. The final third of the numbered containers (numbers eleven through fifteen) was on the middle shelf instead of the bottom.

Benedict was amazed at the quantity of writings Hitchcock had amassed in his lifetime. Of course, he lived before the Internet, computers and Facebook. This was only a small portion compared to what must be housed in St. Louis. The penmanship was steady and elegant. It took Benedict sometime to adjust to reading cursive that had been penned more than a century and a half ago. He opened every journal and scanned every page.

Hitchcock had reduced his thoughts and opinions to the nineteenth century versions of bound leather journals and loose papers in letters and diaries. He was a man of eclectic tastes and thoughts. His imagination had been filled with ideas about alchemy, music and politics. Benedict focused on the alchemy.

From readings he'd devoured years ago, he remembered it as the science of turning base metals into precious ones, such as gold or silver. At first, Benedict thought Hitchcock was a crackpot. But, he was thinking about the man in terms of today's knowledge base. One hundred and fifty years ago, alchemy may have still been considered if not a reality, a possibility.

Questions assaulted him. *Was all this real? Would he find a dose of Materia Prima at the end of all this, one that would save his wife?*

Sitting here alone in the reading room, it seemed so crazy and irrational. *Was he on a fool's quest?* He needed to remind himself about the reason he was doing this. Benedict stepped out of the Reading room and called Rose. She answered on the third ring.

"Hey, baby!"

"How are you feeling?"

"I've been better, but, I'm okay. Daddy said you went to Washington. Are you there now?"

"Yeah, I'll be back soon."

ΩΩΩ

Timothy stood at the elevator extremely frustrated. He'd circled the same hallway looking for an elevator to the first floor. He was two levels underground and had passed the same point four times in the last twenty minutes. He'd checked the floor guide outside the elevator but it did not show any listing for Room 101 in the Madison Building.

He swore out loud.

A library employee passed and caught his outburst.

"Are you lost?"

Timothy regarded the woman for a moment. "Unfortunately," he said quickly. "It appears I am. I am looking for LM101, the Manuscript Reading Room."

"Ah," the woman smiled. "You can't get there from here. Follow me. I'll have you there in five minutes."

ΩΩΩ

Benedict had finished the top shelf. He replaced the container and scanned the boxes on the middle shelf of the rolling cart. He read the numbers of the last numbered containers: eleven thru fifteen.

That's when it hit him.

The notation "c.13" referred to Container Thirteen.

He opened the box and pulled out the journals and papers. He quickly leafed through them. There were personal letters to a family member and two volumes of journals. A small, worn, leather-encased box sat in the corner of the container. It was not a journal nor did it contain any writings.

Benedict cracked it open and looked inside. The cracked leather on the box was faded but the pen that lay inside was not of the nineteenth century. The box contained no papers so Benedict surmised that the archivist had left it alone when photographing the documents.

Benedict examined it. It was a thick, black pen tapering to a point at the business end. He twisted it and the ball point appeared. Then, Benedict re-twisted it going the opposite direction and it disappeared.

It certainly wasn't a feather or a fountain pen from the nineteenth century. The silver clip of the pen, held an inscription in very small writing. It read: *To Michael. Thanks for all your help.*

Benedict glanced at the docent at the desk. She was preoccupied with something on her computer. Benedict slipped the pen into his shirt pocket. He quickly scanned the remaining boxes, returning the delicate papers back to their storage place.

McGuire returned. "Are you done?"

"Yeah, let's get the hell out of here. I want to get back to Rose."

ΩΩΩ

Timothy peered through the glass door and into the Manuscript Reading Room. He saw the pharmacist, sitting at a table looking through boxes of old documents.

Kyle had him following this drug pusher around. It was getting old. The pharmacist and the lawyer had come to Washington in search of something Kyle needed. Timothy intended on retrieving it.

He had to leave his weapon in the car because of the metal detectors at the entrance. It was time to take the initiative. Sitting around waiting was insane. It was time to handle this matter.

He would wait for the right moment and seize it.

Timothy saw the two men making movements indicating they were finishing up. He hurried back down the hallway to the exit.

ΩΩΩ

Timothy sat in the rented Fiat. He was parked illegally on 1st Street, facing south, and pointed towards the Library. He watched the two men hurry down the front steps of the Jefferson Building and climb into the idling black SUV. The pharmacist was carrying a thick manila envelope under his arm. Timothy's eyes never left the package.

The vehicle hung a U-turn on 1st Street and queued at the light at the intersection of 1st and Independence. The SUV was in the right lane, preparing to turn. They were headed back to Ronald Reagan Washington National Airport.

Timothy pulled back the slide on his Sig Sauer, chambering a round, and placed it between his legs on the seat. He put the Fiat in gear and pulled up to the intersection, two cars behind Benedict.

ΩΩΩ

"Did you find what you were looking for?" McGuire asked Benedict as they sat an intersection on Independence Avenue.

Benedict was flipping through the photographs of Hitchcock's papers in the backseat. McGuire was riding shot gun.

"I don't know. I'll need time to look through these," Benedict replied. "I'll do it on the flight home."

The archival photographer had separated the papers into packets associated with each container. Benedict was focusing on the packet labeled as coming from Container Thirteen. The papers were various notes and letters about alchemy in general. There were no formulas or recipes of any kind. He would need to study them in greater depth, but he could see nothing of value.

Even more confusing was the pen. It was obviously Michael's. What value it brought to his quest, was a question Benedict could not answer.

"So what are you really looking for?" McGuire asked again.

"Jackleg," Benedict retorted, using the nickname Benedict and his cronies had given the lawyer, "if I told you I'm sure you'd try to sue somebody. So in the interest of preventing an unnecessary lawsuit, I'm going to take the Fifth."

ΩΩΩ

When the light turned the line of vehicles made the right turn and traveled west on Independence. The cars between them peeled away and Timothy closed the distance as they passed the House wing of the Capitol. Traffic was moderate but getting heavier.

They stopped at another light at Third Street. Timothy pulled along the driver's side, staying in the blind spot. He lowered the passenger side window and moved even with the SUV.

He lifted the gun and aimed it at the driver.

ΩΩΩ

The driver looked out his window and recoiled. He shouted, "Son of a Bitch!"

Benedict looked up at the driver and followed his turned head to the vehicle beside the SUV. He saw the glint of a barrel in broad daylight. McGuire dropped into the seat, out of sight as Benedict realized what was happening.

The man in the other vehicle shouted. "Get out of the car!"

"Go!" Benedict shouted. "Go now!"

The driver slammed the accelerator to the floor. Benedict could feel the rear tires spinning and burning over the pavement. The SUV fishtailed as it lurched into the intersection through the red light, narrowly avoiding a cab. The cab swerved to avoid the SUV and slammed head-on into an oncoming sedan.

The driver swung the wheel left and avoided the rear of the cab while cutting off the small foreign car and the man with the gun. A shot rang out and blew out the rear window, raining chunks of safety glass all over Benedict who was lying on the seat.

The SUV fishtailed in the other direction before the driver brought it under control and sped west along Independence. He careened down the wide Avenue, passing slower cars. At the Smithsonian Castle Building, the driver made a hard last second left onto Tenth Street heading toward L'Enfant Plaza.

The small foreign car was a heartbeat late making the turn, looped past the intersection, but re-corrected and doubled back to continue giving chase. By that time, the SUV was two hundred yards up the road. Benedict's driver had to hit the brakes because of traffic in front of the hotel.

The foreign car, which they had finally recognized as a Fiat, bore down on them with a high-pitched revving engine. Benedict's driver whipped the wheel and gunned the engine shooting through a gap in parked cars, up onto the sidewalk.

Pedestrians scattered as he navigated the narrow space between the Post Office Building and the parking meters. He tried to gain access back onto Tenth Street, but was blocked by more traffic. The Fiat found the same opening in the cars parked along the roadway and easily closed the distance, stopping a few feet behind the SUV.

Through the shattered rear window, Benedict could see the crazed, albeit determined, look in the man's eyes. Benedict was seated behind McGuire on the passenger side. He tried to open the door. It slammed into a five-foot cement pot holding a large tree and only opened about six inches. The driver was pinned by a parking meter, McGuire, by a large mailbox.

Benedict whipped his head around to watch the gunman approach the SUV. He raised his gun and pointed it at Benedict's face. Benedict dove below the seat back, gasping for breath.

The next moment the rear window on the driver's side shattered, sending more chunks of glass over the pharmacist. Benedict looked up into the mammoth barrel of a large handgun.

"The envelope, please," the gunman said with a thick Scottish accent.

Benedict alternated his focus on the barrel and the man's face. The man jabbed the barrel into Benedict's forehead.

"Unless, that is, you wish to die right here!"

Benedict slowly lifted the envelope up to the window. The gunman ripped it from his hands and walked back to his car. He backed the Fiat up to the opening, performed a skilled, high-speed turn back onto the street and sped away, passing the SUV, the stunned trio of men and a few gawking onlookers.

The wail of distant sirens began to get louder. Benedict brushed off the broken glass and issued a command to the driver. "Get the hell out of here! Now!"

CHAPTER 20

"Go thru these immediately," Dr. Kyle demanded. "Since we have them, we might as well see what's in them."

Neville, to whom the order was directed, bowed his head, and took the envelope to his desk and pulled out the photographs. "This will take me sometime," he announced. "There must be a hundred pages in here."

"Then get to it."

Kyle turned to Timothy who wore a smug look of satisfaction. Timothy was five inches taller and weighed fifty pounds more than the slight British physician. Kyle smiled. His lips were a thin, tense line.

He reached up and slapped Timothy. Timothy stood shocked, refusing to lift a hand to his face. His smile turned down and his countenance darkened.

"Did I not tell you, you bloody fool, to just follow them?"

Timothy stared back at his employer while Kyle continued his rant.

"Do you realize what you've done? Benedict now knows that we were following him. I gave specific instructions that he was *only* to be followed. When he recovered the formula, then we would take him and retrieve it."

Kyle turned away from Timothy.

Timothy tried to defend himself. "If we retrieve the first clue, then the pharmacist cannot possibly find it."

Kyle continued to face away from Timothy. He shook his head in an exaggerated fashion. "When I give an order, it is to be followed explicitly. We obtained information from Katherine the nurse. Did it ever occur to you Timothy, that maybe the nurse did not or could not give us all the information that was passed on to Alex Benedict. What if she left something out? What if Michael Watson decided to communicate something directly to Benedict? We would not know what it is. And our ability to find the formula would be compromised."

Timothy fidgeted. "I understand."

"Now, you see, my good man, I will have to alter my strategy. We will have to take Alex Benedict because you decided to be a hero."

"I'm sorry, Dr. Kyle. Next time...."

Kyle spun, interrupting Timothy. Kyle had produced a silenced weapon and leveled it at the man. "Next time?"

Kyle fired two rounds into the man's chest. Timothy dropped onto the cement floor of the underground lab. "Have Ashan dispose of this piece of trash!"

"Yes, sir," Neville replied.

"Neville, read over those writings of General Hitchcock. I want answers before tomorrow morning. Ashan, find Alex Benedict and bring him to me."

ΩΩΩ

"What's going on in there?" Benedict asked.

Through the common window of the two-room pod, Benedict could see two nurses and Dr. Spanos working on Angel Blair from behind masks, gloves and gowns.

"Angel's not doing well. Lauren said that she's spiked a tempera-ture. Like me, I think she's coming down with pneumonia."

One of the nurses was hanging a bag of intravenous fluids while the second was placing a green face mask over her face and fasten-ing it to Angel's head to provide oxygen. Benedict, who was already gowned and masked, entered Angel's room through the small con-necting nurse's station.

"Is there anything I can do?" he asked.

Angel was leaning forward and Spanos had the stethoscope to her back listening to her lungs. He looked over at Benedict and lifted a finger indicating for him to wait a moment. Angel's breaths were very rapid and she was struggling to suck in air. Spanos moved the bell of the stethoscope around Angel's back listening to various parts of both lungs. When he was done, he looped the stethoscope around his neck and spoke to Angel and Lauren.

"We're going to take good care of her. She's probably come down with pneumonia. We're giving her oxygen and going to draw some blood. And we will be starting antibiotics immediately." Spanos placed his hand on Lauren's arm. She was holding her daughter's hand.

Spanos walked to Benedict.

"Welcome back. You can fill me in later. But for right now, I need a pharmacy consult."

Spanos turned to the nurses and recited a litany of orders in-cluding blood work, chest films, sputum and blood cultures, urine tests and suctioning of the nose and throat if Angel was unable to clear her secretions.

When he was finished, Benedict recited from memory data from Angel's chart. He concluded by saying, "She's allergic to penicillin and it's healthcare associated pneumonia. We can't give her cipro-floxacin because of her age. Her renal function looks good based on the latest lab work. According to the pneumonia protocol, we'll have to go with a tobramycin and azithromycin combination. We'll dose the tobramycin traditionally because of her age, not with the extended interval dosing."

"I want the first dose given five minutes ago!" Spanos ordered.

ΩΩΩ

"The Joint Commission surveyors have been hounding us about you. I know you've been seeing to Rose. And I haven't seen you in the department in the last two days. That's fine, take all the time you need," Melissa Harrison demanded.

"I had to take care of something important."

"They want to talk to you about Nonarc and the deaths. We want to delay that as long as possible. We're going to tell them the truth. You're not available because you're tending to your wife. Make sure you stay out of their way."

"How did they find out about Nonarc and the deaths?"

"Someone tipped them off. We don't know who. They are asking a lot of questions during their tracer meetings about the drug administration. They want to see all our records on Nonarc for the last three months. They have someone in the pharmacy now going through records. They're going to cross reference those records with patient deaths."

"I don't think they're going to find much," Benedict replied. "I've checked all the Nonarc compounding records against the deaths. All the records show that the drug was mixed correctly. If anything happened, it happened after the IV bag of Nonarc left the pharmacy and went to the floor."

Benedict thought for a moment. "Where is the IV bag of Nonarc that I found in the trash can of Augustus Palladine's room?"

"I turned it over to administration," Harrison replied. "The lawyers and risk management have it by now. Why?"

"It needs to be analyzed to find out what was in it."

"That's not your concern, Alex."

"Mel, Tidewater has a big problem."

"Don't you think I know that?"

"I know what's been going on with Nonarc and why the patients were dying."

Benedict explained to his boss what had gone on with the formula Michael Watson and his employers were testing on cancer patients. He left out the part about the Materia Prima and the Philosopher's Stone.

"That's crazy."

"It's true."

"You can prove this?"

"What's in that IV bag will prove it. Someone, probably Michael Watson, added something else to the Nonarc IV bag. I have it on good authority that it was done multiple times. Three times, maybe more."

"Do you realize what you're telling me? That there's some sort of conspiracy to kill patients."

"Not kill, Mel. They were testing a new formula, some kind of drug. The deaths were a side effect."

"What does this drug do?" Harrison showed an increased level of stress and anxiety.

"I don't know," Benedict lied.

She patted her face with a tissue. "I have to make a phone call. Wait right here."

Benedict waited for a good five minutes. Harrison returned and looked only slightly better.

"We need to have the IV bag analyzed," Benedict said. *Perhaps,* he thought, *he could ascertain the recipe from the remnants of the IV bag.* General Hitchcock's documents had been stolen. Any clue in them was in the hands of those that were running this whole scheme. He did not have a chance to go thru the documents before they were stolen. For the moment, Benedict had reached a dead end.

Palladine's used IV bag might help in the search for the formula. Of course, Palladine had died after receiving it, so that particular version of the mixture was not the correct one. But it would give Benedict a starting point. The formula that had been administered to Palladine was the last incorrect dose given before Michael Watson had managed to discover the correct one.

"I'm sure the bag will be analyzed, Alex. But you and I will not be privy to that information. At least not right away."

He made a mental note to call the Manuscript Reading Room and ask for the documents to be e-mailed to him. Failing that, if he could obtain a list of contents in the bag, maybe he could reproduce the formula. That was the impetus for Benedict asking Harrison about the IV bag. But with the IV bag in the hands of the lawyers, it might as well have been on the moon.

The sinking feeling in Benedict's gut had been brought on by one other fact. If he could not find Watson's first clue, not only would he not be able to find the correct formula, but he would not be able to find the last good dose of the Materia Prima. The dose that could save Rose.

"You don't look so good," Harrison said. She stood up from behind her desk. "Follow me," she said.

Benedict followed Harrison in her Versace combination with matching shoes. He trailed her out of the pharmacy and down the basement corridor. About fifty yards away, two men in suits were headed their way. Benedict recognized one of them as the physician surveyor for the Joint Commission. He was walking with Ben Roberts, Tidewater's President.

"Mel, do you see what I see?"

Roberts spotted them and recognized Benedict. His eyes went wide. The physician surveyor was making a point in the conversation and did not see what was going on.

"Yes. Turn around," Harrison commanded. They pivoted and walked back from where they came. They reached a stairwell and both ducked inside. A tense, forty-five seconds elapsed until both men walked past the doorway.

They waited another minute and resumed their trek. They reached a side entrance to a parking lot. "We're going to my car," she replied. Harrison cursed. "I forgot my purse. Wait right here."

Benedict paced briefly in front of the door, waiting. Five minutes passed. A vehicle pulled up and parked in an open spot nearby. A dark-skinned man got out and walked towards the entrance. Benedict stepped out of his way to allow him to pass.

The man slowed. Benedict smiled at him, but the man's face remained a curtain of gloom. His hand moved from under his coat, revealing a handgun pointed at Benedict's gut.

"You have an appointment," the man said with a Middle Eastern accent. "One you will not miss."

CHAPTER 21

Benedict's captor rammed the pistol into the small of his back while propelling him forward. He had a firm grasp of Benedict's collar and punched Benedict in the neck when he moved too slowly, steering him as if he were a bridled horse. Benedict's hands were handcuffed in front of him. The edges of the storm had reached the area now. In the rain-soaked gales, they maneuvered towards the Great Lawn in the quad.

Benedict recognized his surroundings. The mammoth Georgian architecture of John Ratcliffe University dwarfed the two men. The dark-skinned man had parked the sedan in a lot beside the Haldan Student Union and Wingfield Hall, one of the dormitories.

The storm was growing closer. The school had been evacuated. Hurricane Lorraine would make landfall in about ten hours according to one of the forecasts Benedict had heard on the radio.

Under the columned portico of John Edward Kyle Hall, the university's science center, the man produced a set of keys, picked one and while still holding Benedict by the collar, unlocked the door.

They crossed through the granite and marble foyer and walked down the hallway to the left of the staircase. He found another key, inserted it, and punched the barrel of the weapon into Benedict's neck.

"Open it!"

When the light was flipped on, Benedict saw they were in a utility closet. The swarthy-skinned man closed the door and locked it behind him.

"On your face."

Benedict lay on his stomach. Ashan placed a firm foot on Benedict's back.

This is it, he thought. *I'm going to die!* He couldn't help but think of Rose who was in her hospital room, probably wondering where he was. He wouldn't be there for her because he would be dead before she was.

"Move and I'll send you to meet that false God of yours!"

Benedict's head almost touched the far wall. The man kept his knee planted on Benedict's back as he reached out and found a seam in that same wall. He pushed on the panel and the hidden door popped open.

"Through there," he said pointing with the gun. "Back in."

Benedict, on his handcuffed hands and knees, backed through the small opening. The gunman followed with the barrel of the weapon inches from Benedict's forehead.

They were in a very narrow corridor on a level landing. Naked incandescent bulbs hung from the sub-flooring above them. Ten feet in, it began a steep descent under the Kyle Science Building and into darkness.

"I bet the university would find your unauthorized use of their science building a bit troubling," Benedict deadpanned as the Middle Easterner secured the small hatch.

"Shut up!"

They walked down the cramped, sloped corridor towards the darkness beyond. The walls seemed to converge on them as they walked deeper. They reached the bottom of the ramp and the light of the last naked bulb was devoured by the darkness. Ashan flipped a switch and another set of naked bulbs came to life as the first string along the ramped corridor went dark. The sound of dripping water could be heard. The walls at this level were stained with moisture and a thin coating of water under their feet made their going slippery.

The corridor continued on a level path for about thirty feet before turning right. The walls, ceiling and floor were concrete and stained with water. They rounded the corner. Benedict stood before a large, steel door with a circular wheel mounted on it.

The man shoved him against the wall as he spun the wheel. He pulled the door open.

"Watch your step!"

Benedict stepped over the bulkhead into the next room.

Going from the rough, unfinished tunnel to the room beyond was like stepping into a new century. The equipment-filled room was perfectly round. Black granite counter tops and oak cabinetry circled the wall and was topped with expensive and daunting equipment: Bunsen burners heating round-bottomed flasks percolating fluids into beakers; clear tubing transported multicolored liquids bubbling along in a complex network of tubes and glassware. Several computer stations all guarded by four-drawer filing cabinets were interspersed along the perimeter of the circle between three other corridors. The three other corridors fed away from the circle to parts unknown. If Benedict was standing at due north, the additional corridors were at due east, west and south. An additional door sat in the five o'clock position.

If the subterranean laboratory had not been surprise enough for Benedict, standing in the center of the room was J. Edward Kyle, Tidewater's chief hospitalist and the man for whom the science building was named. His eyes held a vacant, desperate quality. He appeared quite agitated.

"You're behind all this?" Benedict whispered.

CHAPTER 22

"I wish I could say it was good to see you, Alex," Kyle said. "Your existence is an extreme pain in my ass. But you are in the unique position of being the only one who can help me achieve my goal."

"What is that, Dr. Kyle? Curing cancer?"

Kyle laughed. "If only it were that simple."

"Curing all disease?"

"You're getting warmer." Kyle looked at his employee. "You have met my most trusted aide, Ashan."

"What now? Are you going torture me to get what you want?"

Kyle ignored the comment. "You have what I have worked so hard to achieve. So Alex I'm going to try to appeal to your sense of compassion."

"I have compassion, Dr. Kyle, but not for the likes of you. You're a criminal. I'm going to make sure that you're prosecuted. I don't have what you're looking for. Give it up. The Joint Commission knows about Nonarc. It's only a matter of time before it all falls apart."

Kyle was unfazed. "Come with me."

Ashan shoved Benedict to where Kyle was standing in the center of the laboratory. Kyle led Benedict to the large iron door at the five o'clock position in the circular wall of the lab.

"How did all of this get here?" Benedict asked to the back of Kyle's head.

The metal on the wheel of the door was gray and shiny, not old and rusted like the door itself. Kyle spun the wheel and pushed open the door with a loud squeal. The low hum of sump pumps droned becoming louder as they walked.

The door opened into an earthen tunnel supported with thick timbers across the ceiling and down the walls. It was a wide tunnel that easily could have fit an automobile quite comfortably. Sitting there was a golf cart, facing the men but turned at an angle, ready to make its way back from whence it came.

"Do you recognize the tunnel?" Kyle asked.

He did. But his mind needed a moment to process the information. Benedict remembered the history of Tidewater Regional Medical Center and its humble origins as a Southern plantation owned by Rufus Archer. The tunnels had served as a means of escape for men and women in case Union troops made their way up the Peninsula. They had been sealed off for decades. At least so Benedict thought. Somehow, Kyle had gained access to the tunnels and was using them as a way of getting himself and God knew what else to and from this hidden laboratory.

"How did you get access?"

Kyle walked back to the lab, leading Ashan and Benedict. They entered his small apartment. It was nothing more than a one room studio with a bed, a desk and a fireplace in which a small fire burned.

The Iranian forced Benedict into a chair by the desk.

Kyle offered him "a spot of tea." Benedict refused. Kyle continued his lecture as he poured his own cup.

"The tunnels have been sealed off for more than fifteen years. Ever since that poor girl fell into one of them and died. This is one of the longest tunnels in the system. It's almost a half mile long and leads directly to Archer House. It has many hidden exit points along the way.

"I have been compensated very well over the years. I have dedicated my life and my vast resources to finding the answer to this dilemma. It was just a matter of greasing the right palms in order to get access to these caverns."

"Does Ben Roberts and Tidewater know?"

"Ben likes to think he knows everything. He doesn't have a clue."

"How about the university?"

"Of course not."

"So how did you build a whole lab under the science building?"

"This building was built right over the longest tunnel. When the science building was built the tunnel was reinforced in anticipation of making it an archeological sight. They completed the building right over the tunnel. The tunnel was excavated of its historical artifacts, many of which now reside in The Archer House Historical Museum. I know because I'm on the Board of Directors for both the museum and the hospital. In addition, I'm also on the Board of Regents for the University.

"That gives me unique access to the tunnels. It wasn't difficult to hire out-of town contractors to build the lab. The supplies and materiel were ferried through the tunnel from an access entrance in the wooded area near Lake Maury. The work was done around the clock out of view of everyone. It only took eight weeks. That was three years ago."

Benedict goaded him, "So you've done this in pursuit of a fairy tale?"

"It's hardly a fairy tale, Alex." Kyle smiled. "How much would a compound such as the Materia Prima be worth?"

"This is ridiculous," Benedict replied, pretending incredulity. "You're a fool."

"It goes by many names: Materia Prima, the Great Work, the Philosopher's Stone, and others. Humor me. How much do you think it would be worth?"

"I don't know. Billions?"

"Billions is what we spend on healthcare in the United States. How about around the world? Think about it. Trillions, maybe more?"

Kyle led him back into the lab and down the south corridor. It was a dead end with only one door at its terminus.

Kyle spun the wheel, looked at Benedict and pushed open the portal. "This was the real reason for starting my endeavor."

The two men stepped over the raised bulkhead.

Kyle walked and talked. "I hired Michael Watson to find the perfect ratios for the ingredients of the Materia Prima. But unfortunately he did not have the stomach to see it completed."

"You mean he didn't have the stomach to continue killing patients!"

"Every great endeavor has been paid for in lives and human blood."

The large square room was larger than the pharmacy department of Tidewater. It was huge. The space directly before Benedict was a gleaming polished tile floor. Benedict squinted under the bright light from the overhead lamps. His eyes followed the glint deeper into the room and moved a hand to shield his eyes.

The brightness lessened with every foot his gaze traveled. Halfway into the room, a wide hospital bed sat surrounded by a myriad of medical equipment. The patient was nothing more than a living skeleton.

"Sorry," Kyle said. "I should have warned you. " His voice carried a sincere apologetic tone Benedict had not ever detected before. "The light consists of intense, ultraviolet rays that kill germs. The air ducts are filtered as well. Every machine and person coming into this space is automatically disinfected by the light. It'll be years before it becomes common place in healthcare. Your eyes will adjust in a moment."

A nurse clad in white was bending over a catheter through which was flowing dark yellow urine into a half-filled collection tube fastened to the bed's side. She faced away from Benedict. His view was that of a pair of shapely legs in tight, white hose under a mid-thigh level nursing uniform that appeared to have been from the early fifties, not the bright colorful scrubs worn by most nurses today. The nurse sensed their approach and turned to face them.

Benedict recognized her. She worked on one of the nursing units at Tidewater.

"Hello," she said. "I'm Gretchen."

ΩΩΩ

"I'm afraid we can't produce him at the moment," Ben Roberts replied to the physician surveyor, Preston Mason.

Roberts, Mason, Melissa Harrison, the nurse surveyor and a hospital attorney were seated around Robert's desk.

"What do you mean you can't produce him? He was here just the day before yesterday," Mason said. "This wouldn't be an attempt to circumvent our investigation of this complaint, would it?"

"As you recall, Alex's wife is very ill, near death in fact. She could die at any minute. He's very distraught," Harrison offered.

Roberts jumped in. "No, sir, it is not an attempt to circumvent. We have provided you with all the records you requested to investigate this matter haven't we?"

"You have, President Roberts. Your staff has been very helpful. But we have an obligation to investigate an allegation that could require an Immediate Jeopardy Citation. Patient's lives could be in danger."

"And, if I may ask, what have you found thus far? Have you found any connection between the use of Nonarc, its preparation by our pharmacy staff, its administration by our nurses in the deaths cited in this complaint?"

"In all three deaths, the patients received Nonarc an hour to ninety minutes before they died."

"Dr. Mason, we've conducted our own investigation," Roberts said, looking to Harrison.

"We reviewed over ninety administrations of Nonarc to patients with varying diagnoses in this institution in the last month. Three deaths were reported. The ones cited in your complaint. In all the other eighty-seven incidents, the patients experienced no adverse outcome. In other words, they lived. So we believe the deaths of these three patients are coincidental."

Mason nodded solemnly. "That was our initial finding, as well."

"So what's the problem?" Roberts persisted.

"We are required to interview all parties involved," the nurse surveyor stated.

"I'm going to ask you to respect Alex Benedict's extremely difficult situation at the moment. We can produce him at a later date when he is less consumed by this grave situation."

Mason and the nurse stood to leave. "Very well," Mason said. "We will keep this case open and interview your pharmacist at a later date."

"Thank you." Roberts asked one final question. "Can you give us an idea as to your findings for the survey of our institution?"

"You will find out tomorrow during the Exit Conference."

ΩΩΩ

"This is Edgar, my only son," Kyle said, leading Benedict around the bed. "He is the reason for my quest. He's dying one of the slowest, most painful deaths imaginable. Amyotrophic lateral sclerosis—Lou Gehrig's disease. I am trying to save his life. That was the impetus for my research. But, we may be able to save many more. If you, Alex, cooperate."

"How did you pay for all this?"

"Unfortunately, I don't have all the funds necessary to finance such an endeavor. Many of my funds were invested in this project earlier. I have a silent partner who provides most of the funding, someone with a similar vision as me."

"Who is that?"

"Sorry, ole chap. You cannot be privy to everything."

Edgar Kyle probably weighed no more than eighty pounds. Benedict winced as he scanned the nearly naked patient. Every inch of his body was uncovered save for a white towel laid across his groin. Benedict's first thought was that he must be cold. It was then that he realized the room was warm with rich, moist, filtered air.

The bed was propped into a sitting position. Edgar Kyle's head remained motionless, never moving. But his eyes followed Benedict and his father's movement around the side of the bed. A small trickle of drool snaked its way down one side of his face and was about to drip onto his chest. His cheeks were sunken around the bone, craters of flesh. His green eyes were sunken into his skull. The tongue, visible through parted lips, was swollen and thick with a white crusty coating.

"I'm sorry," Benedict croaked weakly. "I never knew you had a son."

"He's my pride and joy. Right, Eddie?" Kyle reached over a put a hand on Edgar's bony cheek. Edgar did not smile though his eyes seemed to brighten. A hint of moisture filled the elder Kyle's eyes.

The sentiment dissolved and the steely icicle of a man returned. Kyle motioned for Gretchen to join him in the corner of the room. "You may join us, Alex."

"How has his day been?" Kyle asked.

Gretchen's eyes darted between Kyle and Benedict before she spoke. Her concern about revealing a patient's confidential information was second nature to the woman. "It's okay, Gretchen." Kyle turned to Benedict. "Gretchen is new to my staff. She replaced your nurse friend Katherine Diehl."

"Where is she?"

"Unfortunately," Kyle replied. "Katherine took leave of us. I don't know where she is."

Gretchen spent the next three minutes detailing the mundane vital signs and statistics that told Kyle his son was the same as he'd been for the last three weeks. She finished her short recitation and sneaked off, giving a quick, timid glance in Benedict's direction.

After, she departed, Benedict wasted no time in assailing Kyle. "I understand the desire to save your son, Dr. Kyle. But your *experiment,*" Benedict hissed the word "is costing other patients their lives. I know about three deaths. How many more are there?"

"You know the feeling, Alex. Don't you? Your wife is terminal. How does it feel to be on the brink of losing her? Knowing any day she will be gone forever."

"That's not the point!"

"It's exactly the point, young man. You're not seeing the big picture. When this experiment—as you so succinctly put it—is a success, no one will ever have to feel the way we do. No one will have to worry about losing a loved one to disease, to cancer, to any other affliction that eats away at human flesh unless they die in an accident, maybe not even then. Death will be eliminated. Don't you understand the consequences?"

"That's pretty short-sighted for a physician who's supposed to 'first, do no harm.'"

"Short-sighted? You are the short-sighted one. Think about the long-term goal. Hasn't medicine's goal since we crawled out of caves been to eliminate disease, to ease suffering? Besides, those deaths were unplanned. I had no knowledge that the adverse effect would be lethal until after the first one happened. Then it was too late."

"So that's it. You're innocent because you didn't know. Your involvement and the deaths are connected even if you had no knowledge that they would occur. You were conducting experiments on unwilling patients. You're no better than the Nazis."

"Don't lump me in with those monsters!"

They retreated out of the hospital room. Benedict glanced back at Gretchen who was looking at him with a pen poised above a chart.

Ashan had waited dutifully outside the door and took up a rear guard position as Kyle led Benedict back into the laboratory. They walked down the final corridor, the west one. Inside this final room was a quite comfortable studio apartment with a comfortable sofa, recliner, large screen television and a fireplace. A small kitchen with a small dinette set sat with newspapers and medical journals on it.

Kyle hefted a pipe from a pipe rack resting on the table beside his chair. "Would you like to join me in a smoke?"

Benedict declined.

Kyle jerked a thumb in the direction of the lab. "This is where your precious Michael worked on the formula he discovered and managed to hide from me before he killed himself."

"I have no formula. If Michael discovered it, he did not pass it on to me," Benedict pleaded.

"Don't play that game with me." Kyle removed a folded paper from his suit coat. "He left me this!"

Kyle held it out expecting Benedict to take it. Benedict was defiant and sat motionless. Kyle nodded to Ashan who unlocked the handcuffs.

Benedict studied the note.

Kyle:

The Materia Prima recipe is perfected. Unfortunately, I cannot let you continue. The cost of success is too high. The secret is safe. The world is not ready for the power it will unleash. I have left it for someone who will guard it wisely.

Michael

Kyle turned to take in Benedict's face. "It's written in his hand."

Benedict recognized the handwriting. Watson had most definitely penned the missive.

"So you see," Kyle added, "Michael's found the combination of ingredients that unleashes the awesome power of the Materia Prima."

"Maybe so," Benedict barked in a low, menacing voice. "But he did not give it to me."

"He says he did. You see in this experiment, we always retrieve the used IV bag. But in Augustus Palladine's case, you managed to find it in the trash because Katherine Diehl was careless. We also retrieved the IV bag from Margaret Queen. We both know that the formula works. She's living proof."

"I guess if Michael had wanted you to have it, he would have given it to you."

"I will still have it, trust me. I wouldn't bother with you if I didn't have to. You see, we tried to re-create the correct formula from the remnants of the fluid in it. I tested that re-created formula just a few hours ago."

"And?'

"And, it doesn't work."

"You killed another patient?"

"No, we tested it on a monkey."

"Better luck next time."

"So, Alex," Kyle continued, "this means that Michael did something to the ingredients in the formula. Something which cannot be recreated in a lab. He has given the formula and *all* of its secrets to you."

"There's nothing in his note that says he gave it to me."

"You're lying," Kyle said, sipping his Earl Gray.

"Your nurse friend, Katherine Diehl, was a friend of Michael's as well. She worked for me, caring for Edgar. Michael confided in her before his death. She was, let's say, persuaded, to tell us everything she knew. Michael left you an explanation on how to find the clues on a recording. The Materia recipe has been separated into three parts. A clue leads to each part. The final part has a second dose of the real formula. Katherine listened to the recording. She told us everything. It's why you went to Washington and the Library of Congress."

"Your assassin already confiscated the writings. So you have what you need. So I'll just be on my way, then."

"My assistant has reviewed those documents. There is nothing of value in them. Michael left you some other piece of information about the formula. What is it?"

"He didn't leave anything else for me."

"It's very unfortunate that you say that. Michael Watson's cowardly deed will destroy this project and condemn Edgar to death."

Kyle's hand swung quickly in a back-handed arc, connecting with the side of Benedict's face. The pharmacist dropped to the floor.

Ashan helped him up.

"Now tell me."

Benedict glared at Kyle for several moments. Then he said, "Screw you!"

Kyle removed a pistol from his suit and leveled it at the pharmacist and fired.

CHAPTER 23

The shot hit him in the left arm, near the shoulder. Pain seared up his shoulder and down his arm.

He landed in a heap face first on the floor. His jaw dug into the carpet-covered concrete, rattling his teeth. The pen he'd taken from the Ethan Allen Hitchcock's archival storage container in the Library of Congress hit the carpet and separated into two pieces.

The sight of the broken pen, lying in two pieces, triggered the epiphany. Michael Watson *had* given him the information to start him on the quest.

The wet sleeve had been punctured just below the shoulder. Blood flowered around the hole, mixing with his sweat and coating the rain-soaked shirt. Benedict had never felt anything so painful in his life. He rolled onto his back and watched Kyle step over to him.

The doctor aimed at his head. The weapon's barrel pointed between his eyes. "If I'd wanted you dead, you would be. Now tell me what I want to know or the next one will be fatal."

Benedict swallowed hard and spoke in gasps.

"You're a doctor. You've trained your whole life to heal people. You're not a killer. You don't have the balls to pull that trigger."

Kyle's lips spread slowly into a wide grin. He fired again. The round exploded into the carpeting beside Benedict's head. The muzzle flash lit the room and deafened Benedict.

"You can't do it, Dr. Kyle. You don't have it in you!"

Benedict knew he had him. Not because Kyle didn't have it in him, but because Kyle needed information from him. As long as that was the case, Benedict would be kept alive. He'd spent much of his career at Tidewater Regional in fear of this man. A powerful doctor connected to the hospital's administration and Ben Roberts like a Siamese twin. The medical rainmaker who got what he wanted whenever he wanted it, was at Benedict's mercy because the pharmacist had what Kyle craved. That fact became clear as the second shot erupted from Kyle's Walther.

Benedict had played the ace he'd had in his shirt pocket for the last ten hours.

"Okay," Benedict whispered. "You're right. I have what you're looking for. Michael did leave me his secret."

Kyle lowered the weapon just a bit. It was now aimed at his gut. But Kyle's eyes were on Benedict taking measure of the words.

Benedict continued. "But if you want it, it's going to cost you."

"Where is it?"

"It's close by."

"Where is it?" Kyle demanded again. "I want to see it." Kyle motioned for Ashan to search him.

The Iranian roughly patted down Benedict, including his wounded shoulder. Benedict let out a muffled cry.

Benedict shook his head and screwed up his lips. "I want the money up front."

"How much?"

"Five million in cash."

"The wise and just Alex Benedict is now willing part with his conscience for five million dollars?" Kyle eyes showed doubt. "I've known you for almost five years. In that time, I've never seen you show the least bit of temptation. Why now?"

Benedict propped himself up on his elbows. "You mind?" He asked, motioning that he wanted to stand.

Kyle backed up a few steps. Benedict struggled to his feet clumsily, grunting in agony. As he pushed himself up, Benedict glanced at the pen. His gaze lingered a moment too long. Kyle followed his eyes.

"What is that?" he asked.

"It's a pen. It fell out my pocket when you shot me."

Benedict moved to pick it up.

"Hold it!" Kyle pushed past Benedict, knocking him backwards. Benedict's foot caught on the chair and he toppled over it onto the floor.

Keeping the gun on Benedict, Kyle called to Ashan. The dutiful minion entered and the physician handed him the gun. "Make sure he doesn't move. Let's see what we have here."

Kyle moved to his small desk and sat before a large computer terminal. Ashan motioned for Benedict to take a seat. Benedict did and had a view of the screen over Kyle's s shoulder. His hopes sank as Kyle looked at the pen.

A USB flash drive was embedded in the pen's body.

Benedict had seen it as soon as the pen came apart. It was then that the realization struck him. Michael Watson *had* left him his secret in the form of a simple, elegant pen.

Dread filled Benedict as Kyle inserted the flash drive into a computer's USB port. His eyes alternated between Ashan and Kyle. The AutoPlay window appeared. Kyle double clicked on the prompt to open the folders and was rewarded with a listing of one file. A tinny version of the Civil War era, The Battle Hymn of the Republic began to play:

Mine eyes have seen the glory of the coming of the Lord....

Kyle turned around and smiled at Benedict. It was a proud, cocky, self-assured smile.

"I *always* get what I go after, young man!" He regarded his aide. "Ashan, it seems we are almost there." Kyle glanced at Benedict. "And you my friend are out five million. Not that you would have gotten a farthing's worth anyway."

Kyle clicked on the only file. A Word document appeared.

Kyle tensed as he read the first few lines. Benedict saw the anger mounting. He muttered something under his breath and slammed his open palm against the tabletop. Benedict could not repress a chuckle.

"What are you laughing at?"

"I don't know. But if it's pissing you off, it's good enough for me."

Kyle walked over and rammed a clenched fist into Benedict's face, snapping his head back. Kyle was a feeble old man. Nonetheless, the blow made Benedict wince.

Kyle said, "Tell me what it means."

Benedict spat in his face.

Kyle hit Benedict with the butt of the gun. The pharmacist crumpled to the floor as blood poured out of his nose.

"Get him up here!" Kyle commanded Ashan. Ashan picked Benedict off the floor with remarkable ease. Kyle backhanded Benedict across the face. "Look!"

Alex Benedict read Michael Watson's note to him:

I have left you the clue to the location of the first part of the recipe. Find it and you will find a second set of clues leading you to the second site which will unearth the third and final clue, leading you to the final piece of the recipe. Once the three pieces of the recipe have been rejoined, you will have at your finger tips the cursed power of the Materia Prima.

I have left you one final surprise. Use it wisely.

The first clue:

At Goodwin's behest, it was part of John D.'s gift
Where Spotswood was first and Jefferson was last.
Beyond the Portland Stone of the Lion and Unicorn
Behind Charlotte, you'll find your next clue and the first piece
of the recipe.

Through the pain, Benedict read the quatrain, fighting to concentrate. Benedict leaned back and sighed heavily. Kyle scribbled something on a piece of paper. Benedict closed his eyes absorbing the enormity of Watson's letter and the searing pain coursing through his body. When he'd memorized it, he quickly grabbed the pen from the port with his good hand and smashed it into the tabletop, bending the small rectangle at an acute angle. Then he tossed it into the fire in the fireplace.

Kyle lurched thinking Benedict was attacking him. When he realized what Benedict had done and saw the flash drive melting in the yellow flames, Kyle turned back to face Benedict with an incredulous look painted on his face. Benedict rammed his fist into the physician's face.

Kyle dropped to the floor. Ashan grabbed Benedict instantly. Benedict whirled and elbowed the Iranian in the nose. The Iranian also tumbled to the floor.

Benedict grabbed the laptop, ripping its cord from the wall. He grabbed a stapler from Kyle's desk and rammed it into the screen several times, darkening it. For good measure, he hit the power button and turned off the laptop.

Kyle's eyes widened then flashed with anger. He back-handed Benedict in the face with his gun hand, snapping the cartilage of Benedict's nose.

"You filthy bastard!" Kyle screamed.

Benedict ran the back of his hand across his mouth and nose, coming away with a smear of crimson.

"You will not leave this building alive!" Kyle seethed.

PART THREE

CHAPTER 24

"What's going on, Doc?" Grumps asked.

Ari Spanos did not respond immediately. He finished examining Rose, who was now flaccid and sweating.

Grumps had just finished calling Rose's sister to give her an update. Lily said she would fly out in the morning. That's when Grumps thought his daughter had been shivering. Sweat had been pouring off his daughter. He'd hit the call button. When the nurse saw her, she'd immediately paged the doctor and called another nurse to assist.

"She just had another seizure," Spanos said.

Seizure precautions had been in place since Rose's first seizure episode. Her room, as all the rooms were, was right beside the nurse's station. Rose's bed rails had been padded. Her bed had been lowered to its lowest possible position. And she had someone with her at all times, namely Grumps, Benedict or Connie Stevens.

"Check her vital signs every fifteen minutes until she comes around," Spanos instructed the nurse. "I'll call the neurologist." Spanos turned to Grumps. "Where's Alex?"

ΩΩΩ

Benedict did not respond to Kyle's promise that he would not leave the building alive. He could not even lift his head to look at this man.

Kyle studied Benedict for a full thirty seconds. His gaze shifted to Ashan, who stood unmoving with his hands clasped behind his back. Kyle began to pace.

His path was a five-foot line on either side of Benedict, who was still seated in the chair. Benedict was bent over. Blood dripped from his shattered nose and flowed from the gunshot wound that had torn through the muscle of his arm.

Kyle waved the Walther PPK about as he wrestled with the mental gymnastics of the situation. The doctor went to the desk and scribbled something on a piece of paper. Finally, he stopped in mid-stride and wheeled around.

He waved the paper in the air and held it before Benedict's face. "I have memorized the first clue. And now that you know of our plan and the existence of our lab and where it is, I'm afraid, the lab—and you—must be eliminated."

Before Benedict realized what was happening, Ashan had cuffed his hands behind the chair; sending white-hot pain through his shoulder and arm. A second set of cuffs fastened the first pair of cuffs to the chair. Then he wrapped his legs with duct tape, securing each to a leg of the chair.

Kyle whispered to Ashan and motioned with his head towards the wall.

Kyle moved back into Benedict's view and turned, but he was still speaking to Ashan. "Tell Ms. Gretchen to make preparations to move Edgar. She needs to have him ready to go in thirty minutes. Call Neville and tell him to have the truck at the ramp ready to go. We'll take my son to the mountains." Kyle shot a glance at Benedict. "Our quest is over—for now. We will find the formula and start again. I will set the timers. Forty-five minutes. Go!"

Ashan shuffled off to carry out his orders. Kyle turned back to Benedict who was sitting in the chair with his head all the way back. The blood coming from his nose seemed to have subsided. The wound in his arm burned but it, too, seemed to have stopped bleeding for the moment. Kyle raised the pistol and aimed at Benedict's chest. The pharmacist felt his chest heaving.

"When I had this place constructed, I knew that someday we would have to dispose of it." Kyle waved his hand around. "All this cost more than two million dollars to install and build. Its purpose was to bring the world the greatest medical discovery that man could imagine. It started as a labor of love and turned into a mission to save humankind from all the scourges ever devised by God. And it was all cocked up and has to be destroyed because of you.

"The ventilation system will push natural gas into every corner of the lab. A series of igniters will spark, igniting the gas, obliterating everything."

Kyle had relit his pipe as he spoke.

"I hope," he continued, "that you die believing your cause was worthwhile. You will die in obscurity. You, alone, are responsible for mankind's continuing pained and tortured existence in a world filled with death and disease."

"You're a murderer," Benedict said simply. "I will die with a clear conscience."

Kyle walked to the wall. On it was set a large, metal box. Kyle removed a key and opened it. He flipped several switches. The monotone beeping of numerals being entered from a keypad followed. Kyle swung the door fully open, letting Benedict see the timer.

"You have forty-five minutes left." Kyle then pressed a button and the readout began counting down. A soft chime bleeped from the panel. He turned and walked out.

Ashan gave the cuffs around Benedict's wrists a good tug. Benedict winced. Then Ashan came into Benedict's field of vision. He stank of acrid tobacco and cheap cologne.

Ashan jangled the key to the handcuffs on its chain in front of Benedict's face. He clutched it in his fist and walked to the center of the room. He stood over a drain pipe. Ashan knelt over it and forced the keys down into the drain. After a moment, a hollow metallic clank echoed from within the pipe.

Ashan returned and planted his shoe against Benedict's chest and kicked. The chair toppled backwards. He landed with a sickening thud and a wooden crack. The back of Benedict's head hit the hard floor.

A fast-paced collage of images raced through his mind, including Rose. His vision became clouded with tears. Benedict would break his promise to her and she would die without him by her side. His sight lines began to swim. Then everything went dark.

ΩΩΩ

"I don't know where he could be," Grumps said. "I've tried to call his cell phone about ten times. I've had the nurses page him at least five times. They're getting tired of me asking."

Spanos looked over Rose who was still groggy but awake. He checked her pulse and listened to her chest.

"Are you having any trouble breathing?" he asked her.

"It's not as bad as before. I feel like there's something stuck in my chest. It hurts a little."

"Okay, let the nurses know if it gets any worse."

Spanos draped his stethoscope around his neck and turned to Grumps.

"When was the last time you saw him or heard from him?" he asked.

"He was here this morning when he consulted with you about the little girl in the next room," Grumps explained.

"Hell, that was seven hours ago!"

Grumps pulled Spanos outside. "Do you think something's happened to him?"

Spanos turned to the nurse's at the station. "Get Dr. Nguyen on the phone," he barked. Spanos addressed the old man. "I'll have Dr. Nguyen watch over Rose while I'm gone. He's a good doctor and familiar with her case. He's one of my partners. Mr. Blackmon, I'll see if I can find your son-in-law."

ΩΩΩ

Benedict fluttered his eyelids and shook his head, trying to clear the fog in his brain. An intermittent buzzing noise filled his ears. In his ascent from the depths of unconsciousness, he realized it was his pager. Someone, probably Rose, Grumps or someone from the hospital was trying to locate him.

He squirmed against the restraints. The wound in his arm screamed. His mouth was coated with blood from his nose. The dried blood on his face cracked as he moved.

The bleeping timer shocked him back to reality. A turn of his head produced lightning bolts of pain. The numerals were moving, counting down the seconds.

18:28 ... 18:27 ... 18:26 ...

He'd been out nearly a half an hour. In less than twenty minutes, he would be incinerated. The pharmacist began to struggle against his restraints, checking for feeling and function in his legs, feet, arms and hands. The back of his head pounded where he'd hit it on the floor. The adrenaline surging through his veins blunted some of the agony. Benedict scanned the room, moving his eyes in a slow, pained arc, looking for anything he might use to free himself. The drain cover into which Ashan had stuffed the keys to the hand cuffs was a lost cause.

The sternly wound duct tape would not allow his legs to move. He pulled his right arm up fiercely—the left was too weak—trying to pluck his hand and wrist through the opening of the cuff.

The skin began to tear. Benedict screamed. After ten seconds, he released the tension in his body. Benedict's sucked in a lung-ful of air as he braced himself for another bout with the metal of the handcuffs. He scrunched his eyes closed and murmured the Lord's Prayer.

ΩΩΩ

Spanos had tried Benedict's cell three times using Rose's cell phone. But it rolled to voice mail immediately each time. He left an urgent message each time just in case. He also tried the pharmacist's pager with no success.

Spanos knew Benedict wouldn't ignore his calls. If he was not answering, it was for a good reason. But he guessed a call from his sick wife would give him more urgency to answer. Then a thought struck him.

He pulled up the GPS function on her phone and highlighted Alex's cell number. His phone was currently not on or not receiv-ing a signal. Spanos did see a history of where the phone had been. As early as five hours ago, it had been on the John Ratcliffe University campus.

ΩΩΩ

Tendons and sinew began to rip. A pop in his arm was followed almost instantly by the inside-out explosion of agony in his wrist. Pain shot up his right arm into his shoulder threatening to engulf him. Afraid he would pass out, Benedict relented.

He had been trying hard not to look at the timer. But he couldn't help himself. He was even more frustrated by the fact that his phone was vibrating and his pager was going off. And he was unable to answer either.

11:53 ...

Benedict closed his eyes, listening to the rhythmic bleeping, mocking him. In a panicked burst, he exerted all the force he could along all the pressure points holding him in place. He pushed his left leg forward against the thick, gray duct tape while pulling apart his arms, willing his battered hand through the ever so small opening ring of metal.

He felt his face reddening. The pressure in the veins of his face and neck multiplied. His leg and arm muscles burned hotter from the isometric forces he applied. It was then that he heard the crack.

He held his breath, anticipating the pain. He thought he'd fractured a bone in his hand. Maybe he would be able to tear a bloody stump through the opening.

But no additional pain came.

He flexed his hands. All his fingers moved. He could feel them. The skin of his hand had been torn away from his wrists and the meaty part of his thumb. All his digits and the bones in his hand appeared to be intact. Same with his arms, legs and feet.

Benedict clenched and exerted again. This time the crack was immediate and more discernible. He could feel it in his lower back and his butt. But it wasn't him.

It was the wooden chair. The seat had fractured.

Benedict flexed his left leg again. The left leg of the chair wobbled, moving in concert with the flexion of his leg. Benedict jerked it back and forth. It creaked, moving in a wider arc.

9:22 ... 9:21 ... 9:20 ...

If he could free his legs, he might be able to run. Benedict kicked again and the leg broke free from the seat. It was still securely fastened to Benedict's leg. But he was able to straighten his leg. The seat cracked even farther along the axis running under Benedict's crotch.

Next, he worked the right leg, flexing and working his lower leg back and forth. This right leg was more firmly seated in the chair. Benedict, for some reason, was not able to gain as much leverage. He was tiring. He furiously kicked. The arc of the leg increased until finally Benedict felt the right leg of the chair yielding.

On his back now, Benedict rocked back and forth. A human rocking chair trying to gain enough momentum to execute the maneuver he had in mind.

6:15 ... 6:14 ... 6:13 ...

Benedict rocked in a larger arc. More snaps and creaks, emanated from beneath him, not sure if he was hearing his own bones splintering or if it was what was left of the chair. He pushed his legs hard against the floor and in a great heave tried to roll over on his head, somersaulting backwards into a kneeling position. He rolled; his body paused. His legs reached the zenith of the arc, directly over him now as if he were going to do a head stand. The momentum was lost. He collapsed onto his left side in a rattle of wood, metal and flesh. His legs crashed to the floor. Benedict found himself in the same position as before, curled like a baby on his right side.

4:08 ... 4:07 ... 4:06 ...

Exhausted, he lay, catching his breath. Summoning a reserve strength ignited by a surge of adrenaline, he rolled onto his back again and scooted himself closer to the wall. His head bumped the wall. Benedict swiveled his body one hundred and eighty degrees so his feet were planted against the wall. This time he pushed himself all the way over. As he rolled, his chin planted against his chest.

In an excruciating stretch of his dorsal neck muscles, his head was free as his torso rotated over. He balanced on one knee almost tilting back over. He re-centered his weight and crashed down on the other knee. He lay spent with his face against the floor and both his knees forming a human tripod. He looked to see how much time he had left

2:56 ...

Benedict lifted himself up to a kneeling position. Slowly and carefully, he raised his right leg putting the foot on the floor. Then fearing too much haste would cause him to topple over again, he, slowly stood up.

With the broken chair legs clanking along the floor and the chains binding him rattling, he felt like a hobbled Frankenstein quick-stepping to the exit of the small apartment. He stepped back into the center of the circular laboratory. In the office, the timer continued to beep its warning. Another digital readout in the Main Lab read the time remaining in Benedict's life if he did not escape.

1:42 ...

All five doors were closed and sealed. Benedict turned around, raised up to grab the wheel as high as he could along the side with his cuffed hands. He gained a purchase on the large wheel awkwardly with both hands and bent his knees allowing gravity and his body weight to spin the wheel. But it would not budge.

The timer was down to one minute fifteen seconds.

Benedict scanned the room. He needed to find something long and sturdy that he could slip through the spokes of the door's wheel to use as a lever. A sturdy rod of some sort.

He hobbled among the counters, equipment and chairs. A large distillation apparatus sat on one of the center counters, its glass tubing dripping a clear liquid into a large beaker. The tubing was supported by metal bars and clamps. Near the distillation contraption, a glass beaker sat on a metal ring. A Bunsen burner's flame licked its base. The liquid inside simmered; large bubbles percolating to the surface.

The counter was waist high. Benedict hopped on one leg and kicked the burner away, sending the beaker to the floor and disintegrating into a shower of liquid and glass. He then kicked at the other beaker, knocking the liquid out of the way.

Balancing on one leg, Benedict raised one foot and gently pushed the metal scaffolding to the opposite side of the bench, to within an inch of the edge. He raced around the bench to the opposite side, backed into it and grabbed hold. He began working the clamps, trying to loosen their grip on one of the metal bars.

1:01 ... 1:00 ... 0:59 ...

The piece he was working on slipped towards the floor. Benedict quickly leaned back against the counter, trapping the metal rod against his back and the work bench. Benedict let out a shaky breath. If the rod had fallen to the floor, there would be no time for him to recover it and still open the door.

The rod was a half inch of solid metal. He thought it might be aluminum. If it was, he feared, it would bend under the pressure. But he was out of options.

He backed the rod into the wheel, inserting one end under the far spoke of door's wheel and setting the opposite end above one of the nearer spokes. Twelve inches of rod extended beyond the wheel itself.

0:29 ... 0:28 ... 0:27 ...

Benedict rose up and took hold of those twelve inches, placing all of his weight on his hands and the rod. He balanced there for a moment.

Then he felt his body sinking towards the floor. A surge of elation engulfed him. It was quickly washed away when he realized the rod had bent.

"Shit!" This was followed by a longer string of more potent expletives.

He rotated the bent bar, turning the bend upward. He tried again, forcing the bar down with all his weight. After a moment of hesitation, his body sank once again, this time falling all the way to the floor. His heart sank and Benedict prepared himself to hear the hiss of forced gas from the vents.

Then the bent rod slipped from the framework of the wheel and clanged to the floor. He pivoted and saw that the spoke of the wheel on which he'd been applying pressure was not horizontal any longer but vertical. The wheel had turned.

He stood up awkwardly. Grasping the wheel again with his hands still bound behind him, Benedict worked his knees and his legs so his torso rose and sank like a piston as he worked the wheel counterclockwise, hoping to disengage the pins sealing the door. His progress was measured in inches along the arc of the wheel as the timer beeped down its final seconds.

0:06 ... 0:05 ... 0:04 ...

Benedict continued working the wheel, rotating then pulling to see if it was free. He spun it one more time, and then pulled. It did not budge.

The timer hit all zeros and a loud klaxon sounded.

CHAPTER 25

The vents hissed. Benedict could smell the sulphur-like gas filling the room.

Benedict worked harder and faster, spinning the wheel and tugging at the door. He began to choke and gag on fumes.

It took every ounce of conscious effort to override the impulse to breathe. He was afraid, he would lose consciousness and it would be all over.

He rotated the wheel a few more inches and yanked, bracing his feet against the door frame and grunting with all his might. The door moved and Benedict fell forward into the lab, releasing the wheel.

He opened his eyes and caught a glimpse of the open door before he had to slam them shut. The gas burned his eyes. With his eyes closed, he aimed for where he remembered the opening would be and launched himself horizontally at it. He tripped over the bulkhead and fell into the darkened hallway.

He gulped in large quantities of stale, dank air. The storm above ground and its wind-swept torrents fed a steady stream of running water down the slanted corridor. A rivulet collected at his feet. He stood; hands still bound behind him, and trudged up the slope in a darkness that became more complete as he separated himself from the light spilling from the open laboratory door.

Not knowing how much time he had, Benedict retraced the steps he'd made with the Iranian. When he found the horizontal landing, the darkness was absolute. He walked forward, counting the steps until he bumped into the wall with the small panel in it. He dropped to his knees and tried to spy cracks of light along the perimeter where it met the casing. Nothing. He turned around and used his blood-stained fingers to feel for the outline of the rectangular hatch. With a mental outline formed in his mind and memorized in relation to the height of his body, Benedict walked back along the landing.

He would have one chance to do what he was about to do. If he missed, he would probably break his neck or back or render himself unconscious. Because of the imminent explosion, all three scenarios equated to a death sentence.

The pharmacist retraced his steps, counting backward using smaller steps so he wouldn't accidentally hit the slope. He toed the floor until he found the ridge where the floor sloped away. He moved as close as possible and spun. Drawing in several deep, quick breaths of air, Benedict prepared himself.

A loud rumble rocked the dark corridor almost knocking him off balance. A second explosion followed the first. He glanced over his shoulder. A large orange fireball filled the tunnel advancing up the slope, hurtling towards him.

The fireball sucked the oxygen out of the air. Benedict turned and bolted. The glow illuminated the wall and the opening for which he was aiming. He launched himself low, knee high, tucking his head into his shoulder, preparing for the collision.

He hit the rectangular access panel and felt it flex. But it did not open. A fraction of a second later, the concussive blast hit him, blowing the small door open and thrusting Benedict through milliseconds before the wall of fire was upon him.

He was catapulted over the polished floor of the utility closet, propelled by the escaping gases and slammed into the door of the opposite wall while in mid-air. The water soaking his clothes and dripping from his face evaporated before he hit the floor. Benedict lay on the floor, stunned. The closet door had been blown open. His ears hummed and his head felt like it was inside a large cast iron bell that rung non-stop. Smoke and gas billowed from the open doorway, filtering up to the perfectly white wall until it hit the ceiling where it mushroomed along the flat surface.

Benedict lay dazed and deaf on his back. The floor shook as pieces of ceiling plaster rained down around him. A fist-sized fissure snaked up the wall above the hidden doorway through the cloud of smoke and mist. Another rumbling shook him. Larger pieces of the building began to shower him. If he didn't move now, he would be crushed by huge chunks of debris.

Shell-shocked and confused, he flipped to his belly and awkwardly scrambled to his feet. Pieces of wall and ceiling rained down around him, hitting him in the head and shoulders as he limped through the main foyer. He rammed the glass doors at a full run, rebounding off the safety glass. They were locked.

A second try produced the same result. On the third try, the floor lurched. A diagonal crack appeared in the marble. Benedict leapt over it as he charged. The shifting floor separated the doors a second before Benedict hit. They blasted apart under his body weight. And Benedict tumbled out under the columned portico, rolling into the open where wind-swept water ravaged the campus.

Not bothering to get to his feet, Benedict simply rolled away from the building. He stopped, lying face up in pool of water in the Great Lawn of the quad, letting the rain soak him. An over-coated figure walked to him and looked down at him. Benedict stared up into the soggy face of Ari Spanos.

The earth shook again and another explosion rocked the J. Edward Kyle Science Building. Spanos shifted his gaze towards the sound.

Benedict turned to see what Spanos was looking at. The ground shuddered again and the entire middle of the building collapsed onto itself. The ends of the structure remained upright, creating a huge U-shaped valley in the center. The huff of dust and brick particles was quickly drowned in the downpour.

Spanos looked back at Benedict who met his gaze. Spanos's lips moved. He was shouting something. But Benedict could not make out his words. Spanos repeated them, shouting louder.

"Let's get the hell out of here and get you to a hospital."

ΩΩΩ

J. Edward Kyle sat in the back of the medical transport van, talking softly to his son, Edgar, who was covered in gray blankets and strapped into the gurney. The van was parked a mile up the street from the university in the parking lot at the local high school football field, Todd Stadium. Gretchen and Ashan had moved the essential medical equipment into the van along with their patient. They'd wheeled him through one of the tunnels to an access point behind the JRU campus. Then they drove to the football field to await their orders.

Kyle arrived several minutes later and handed to Gretchen the name and address of the facility where they were to take their human cargo.

"Gretchen will stay with you," he said. "I've hired a driver to take you to the mountains. You will be well taken care of, Edgar. I will stay behind and finish up my business here. Then I will join you."

Edgar Kyle moved his eyes back and forth to communicate with his father. The senior Kyle counted the number of times his son's eyes moved back and forth.

"... Seven ... Eight ... Eight times, Edgar. That's the letter 'H.' Is that correct?"

Edgar blinked once indicating yes.

The son then moved his eyes back and forth fifteen times. "That's O?"

One blink again.

"H-O," Kyle said. "Are you spelling 'How'?"

Edgar blinked again.

This process was repeated until Edgar managed to ask his question.

"How long?"

"Tomorrow. After I have obtained what I need to help you." Kyle patted Edgar's head. "You must stay strong. When I have the formula and we are able to release it to the world, I will name the company after you. We will call it Edgar Pharmaceuticals. We will only make one product. For it will be the only product the world will need."

In the distance, Kyle heard a low rumble and two explosions. In seconds, thick columns of black smoke became visible over the low buildings to the east, pushed by the strong winds into one large curtain. Kyle smiled and continued.

"We will call the formula, Edgar's Potion. And when you are healthy again, I will be President and you will be Chief Executive Officer. The world will most definitely beat a path to our door, my son."

ΩΩΩ

"The bullet passed through the outer aspect of the deltoid," the emergency room doctor said as he sutured the bullet wound. "You're pretty lucky. It missed the humerus by millimeters. We've hung some Ancef to prevent any infection. Your nose is probably broken. We won't be able to tell until the swelling goes down. I'll refer you to an ear, nose and throat guy. A friend of mine, Joe Wilson, is one of the best. He'll probably put a splint on it."

His nose had been packed with gauze. Benedict, sitting upright on the stretcher, was holding an ice pack on the bridge with his good arm. Spanos had left a few minutes ago to inform Rose that her husband was okay and his wounds weren't life threatening.

"How did you get shot?" the physician asked.

"It's a long story."

"And the handcuffs?" he persisted.

The handcuffs had been cut off his wrists using a pair of industrial metal snips obtained from the maintenance department. They lay on the stretcher beside Benedict whose left hand and wrist were wrapped in gauze and elastic bandages.

"When can I go?" Benedict asked.

"We're going to admit you for at least one night. We have to notify the police about the gunshot wound. They are on the way to take your statement."

Benedict thought for a moment.

"I need a piece of paper and a pen," Benedict said. "And I have to pee."

The doctor finished off the last of the twenty-five sutures and called for the nurse to bring the requested items.

"I'll be right back," the doctor said.

The side rails were in the up position. Benedict scooted to the end of the stretcher and hopped off. He grabbed his phone and his lighter from his clothes piled on the chair. A nurse helped him off the stretcher and guided him to the bathroom as Benedict toted the IV bag and tubing inserted into his arm.

"You've lost some blood," she instructed him. "So I want you to pee sitting down. No falls tonight."

Alex sat on the commode as the nurse waited with her back turned. He didn't have to relieve himself. He scratched the four line clue from memory onto the paper. Then he tried to think of a way to keep from being questioned by the police.

ΩΩΩ

"Where's the GSW?" the Newport News detective said.

"He's in bed eight. But Sally took him to the john. He should be right back," the doctor replied. He turned to another nurse. "Go see what's taking them so long."

The nurse walked around the corner towards the bathroom. She returned a minute later.

"I don't see Sally and the patient is gone!"

CHAPTER 26

"What happened to you? Why aren't you in the ER?" Grumps demanded.

Spanos had explained to Grumps that Benedict had been abducted and shot in the arm. He left out most of the other details.

Benedict was standing in the doorway to Rose's room. He was barefooted and holding the back side of the gown closed with his good hand. His note was wrapped in the fist of his wounded arm. He didn't want to enter because he wasn't properly gowned up.

Spanos appeared from down the hall. "What the hell are you doing?"

Benedict pulled him aside and whispered. "I'll be just a minute, Rose." Benedict stepped away from the door and addressed Spanos. "The cops are in the emergency room here to question me about the shooting?"

"So?"

"I can't tell them what's going on. They'll ask me where it happened. I can't make up a story. They'll know I'm lying. They'll detain me because I was in the building just before it blew up. They'll think I had something to do with it. You know how suspicious cops are. If they detain me, I won't be able to find the ... you know."

"You didn't do yourself any favors by taking off. How did you manage to get out of there?"

Once Benedict was on the toilet and he'd finished making his notes, he lied to the nurse. He'd left the pen on the stretcher and asked if she'd retrieve it for him. He needed to write something down before he forgot, he'd said.

The nurse named Sally told him she would as long as he promised not to try getting up until she returned. When she turned the corner, Benedict had removed the IV line and discarded it. Then he stood up and walked out, heading in the opposite direction. He exited into the main hallway and slipped into the elevators in his thin hospital gown.

"Okay. Stay here." Spanos left and returned a minute later with some scrubs. "Put these on. I'll get you a mask and gown."

"How's she doing?"

Spanos patted him on the shoulder. "She's going downhill," he said.

ΩΩΩ

"She's had a relapse," Grumps said. "The fever's come back. The doctor changed antibiotics." Grumps stroked his daughter's hand. His mask puffed in and out as he spoke. His eyes were moist and rimmed in red. "Rose is delirious. She goes in and out. They drew blood. The doctor said something about sepsis."

Spanos explained. "We'll start the sepsis protocol. We're not going to move her. Rose stated with her father as a witness that we are to perform supportive measures only. So we'll do as much as we can."

Benedict walked around the side of the bed and took his wife's other hand. He leaned in close and whispered in her ear.

"I love you, baby."

Rose mumbled incoherently. Her skin was hot and clammy. Her breaths came in short, rapid spasms.

Benedict felt the tears welling in his eyes. He looked over at Grumps. The pained look in the man's eyes was too much for Benedict to handle. He wiped his eyes with his sleeve.

"I don't know what to do, Grumps. I don't want to leave her."

"If you're going to find this potion, you'd better hurry," he said.

Benedict looked at Spanos who watched the scene from behind a curtain of worry.

"I'll call the guys and tell them to meet us here," the doctor said.

ΩΩΩ

"What's all the brouhaha?" Gregor Jablonski, the tobacco shop owner said.

The large glass windows of the first floor conference room in the hospital had been boarded with thick plywood. Water cascaded down the large window-walls between the wood and the glass. Hurricane force winds buffeted the plywood which in turn rattled the panes of glass.

"What the hell happened to you?" Tyrone Manville, the Navy SEAL asked, noting Benedict's wounds.

"I promise to tell all of you at our next poker game," Benedict said. "But right now time is of the essence."

"What are you looking for?" Devin McGuire, the lawyer asked.

"I'm trying to find something that may save my wife's life. Unfortunately, it's been hidden. The final piece of the puzzle has with it a dose of medication that might save Rose. I have the first clue, right here."

"I like this cloak and dagger shit," Joseph Bellini, the tow truck driver said.

"How is she doing?"

"If we don't do something soon, it won't be long."

"Who's the sick twisted bastard that managed to put you in this spot?"

"Let's just say, it's a group of people."

Benedict hated not being completely honest with his friends, but he didn't want the nature of the Materia Prima getting out. "I need your help in figuring out what it means. The storm has knocked out the phone lines. We can't get Internet access."

"We should call the police," Ulysses Lee, the private investigator said. Lee was a balding, barrel-chested, cigar-chomping, retired cop with three decades of police work under his belt. He occasionally made appearances at the weekly poker game.

"There's no time. They're probably dealing with the evacuation because of the storm and the explosion over at the University. I need the collective brain power of everyone in this room to get the answer."

"We're all in," Manville said.

"Alex, read the clue," Spanos ordered.

Benedict read from his notes. "At Goodwin's behest, it was part of John D.'s gift/ Where Spotswood was first and Jefferson was last/ Beyond the Portland Stone of the Lion and Unicorn ... The clue is hidden behind Charlotte." Benedict had jotted down the passage from memory.

Benedict did not read the passage about formula. "Does anyone have any idea what it means?"

The lawyer spoke up. "We need to break it down, piece by piece. Read it again."

Benedict did.

"Who were Goodwin and John D.?" Manville asked.

McGuire said, "I don't know." As the rest of them shook their heads.

"I know what Portland Stone is!" Joseph Bellini spoke up. "It's a limestone used for buildings in England, most notably Buckingham

Palace. It's quarried on Portland Isle in the English Channel, south of Weymouth."

All heads turned towards the Italian man.

"Who are you and what did you do with our tow truck driver?" the lawyer said.

"I watch a lot of History Channel," Bellini said, smiling.

"That makes sense," Manville chimed in. "Aren't the Lion and the Unicorn two of the symbols in the Royal Crest of the United Kingdom? So he's talking about England."

The lawyer shook his head then put his hand over his eyes. "That's good, Squid," Benedict said using Manville's nickname.

"You learn a lot traveling the world. I've been stationed all over," Manville replied.

"It says, 'beyond the Portland Stone of the Lion and Unicorn'. So what does he mean by that?"

"Maybe he's saying it's behind the gate at Buckingham Palace?" the lawyer asked.

Benedict shook his head. "I don't think so. Michael Watson, the man who left these clues, wouldn't have had time to travel to England to leave a clue. Plus how would he leave a clue inside Buckingham Place. I'm sure it's heavily guarded. Michael left these clues before he died. He had not been on vacation or leave. It means something else. Probably more local. Nice try, though."

Jablonski chimed in. "So we're talking about England, but locally. There's got to be a hundred places like that. Hell, it's our history."

"What about the part about Spotswood being first and Jefferson being last?" Benedict challenged them.

They all slowly shook their heads or shrugged.

"They're obviously people, he's talking about. Good ole, Tommy Jeff. Wasn't he the fourth President?" Manville asked.

"Try the third," McGuire retorted.

Manville said, "He's obviously talking about some famous people. Or, at least locally, famous. It would have to be people a lot of folks would know."

"That's right," Spanos joined in. "So who are some famous people we would know named, Goodwin, John D., Spotswood. We all know who Thomas Jefferson was."

"John Goodwin, the actor!" Bellini shouted.

"That's Goodman! John Goodman."

"Guys," Benedict said, raising his voice. "They need to have local connections."

McGuire smiled. "I just remembered. I know someone famous with the name, John D," the lawyer said, pausing as if making a point to a jury.

"Well, don't keep us in suspense."

"That would be John D. Rockefeller."

"Didn't you listen," Lee, the cop-turned-private investigator said. "It has to be someone with a local connection."

"John D. Rockefeller has a local connection," McGuire persisted.

"He does?" Lee asked.

"Yep, he donated a lot of money to help build Colonial Williamsburg."

"That's right," Jablonski agreed.

"That would mean Goodwin would be Reverend Goodwin," Bellini added. "He was rector of Bruton Parish Church. He convinced Rockefeller to fund the cause back in the early twentieth century."

"More History Channel?" McGuire asked.

"No, I've taken the tour up there."

"This is good," Benedict said. "So he was talking about Bruton Parish Church in CW?"

"Does that have a Royal Coat of Arms out front?"

"I don't know."

A wide smile lit up Benedict's face.

"I don't like it when you get that shit-eating grin on your face," Spanos said.

"What's it mean when he smiles like that?" Bellini asked.

"It means you guys are going to Colonial Williamsburg," Benedict said.

CHAPTER 27

"He's alive," Ashan said weakly. The Iranian thought about the way Timothy had died. He hoped the news he'd just delivered did not result in a bullet being fired into his chest.

"Who's alive?" Kyle demanded.

"The pharmacist, Benedict."

"Impossible. He was chained. The doors were sealed shut."

Habib pressed a button on the laptop in Kyle's home office. The screen filled with the oscillating waves of three recorded voices, Alex Benedict's, his father in-law's and the oncologist's.

"I don't know what to do, Grumps. I don't want to leave her."

"If you're going to find this potion, you'd better hurry."

"I'll call the guys and tell them to meet us here. They'll help," the doctor said.

Habib had been right. The sound quality was excellent. So much so that it served to irritate Kyle on a much deeper level, making it somehow more real.

Kyle pounded the desk with a fist. "We have not had time to decipher that first clue. They are a step ahead of us. How did he escape?"

"The pharmacist is very resourceful," Ashan said.

"Get Neville on the phone!"

$$\Omega\Omega\Omega$$

On a good day with no traffic, the drive to Colonial Williamsburg would take thirty minutes. Tonight with Hurricane Lorraine, a category three storm on top of them, there was no traffic but the deteriorating weather kept their speed to twenty miles per hour. It took almost ninety minutes traveling up the winding, tree-lined Colonial Parkway.

Bellini had made the call that they should use the Parkway. Interstate 64 was jammed with cars stuffed with passengers and belongings heading inland to Richmond and points west. The hurricane gates on the exits had been put into use, allowing traffic to head west on both sides of the highway. The extra lanes did little to speed up the evacuation. Westbound traffic was backed up all along the interstate to the Hampton Roads Bridge Tunnel and the Monitor-Merrimac Bridge Tunnel. The flood gates had been closed on both tunnels hours ago. Those foolhardy enough not to evacuate from the Virginia Beach, Norfolk and Chesapeake areas were trapped.

Ulysses Lee and Devin McGuire rode in McGuire's Mercedes. Joseph Bellini, Gregor Jablonski and Tyrone Manville were crammed into the front bench seat of Bellini's tow truck.

The Parkway was relatively open. Downed trees and debris littered the roadway. They had to stop twice to remove large limbs stretched across the roadway using the winch on the wrecker.

Bellini pulled to a stop at the corner of South Henry and Duke of Gloucester Streets, at the tip of the historic area. Merchant's Square was immediately to their left with the College of William and Mary beyond. McGuire pulled his sedan beside the truck. They talked quickly through open windows and rain.

"We have to go on foot from here. Can't get onto DoG Street with the cars," Jackleg said. DoG Street meant Duke of Gloucester Street.

"*Idiota*," Bellini shot back. "I ain't walking a mile in this weather. You're taking your life into your hands."

"Vehicles aren't allowed in the Historic Area."

"Who's going to stop us?"

Bellini did not wait for a reply. He raised his window and navigated the tow truck onto the brick sidewalk to the right of the permanent barricade. The opening between it and a lamp pole was not wide enough. He gunned the engine and crumpled the street lamp.

The two vehicles bumped over the downed pole and proceeded down the wind-swept street littered with branches, leaves and wooden shingles. Bruton Parish Episcopal Church appeared on their left. Bellini braked. The church had no lion or unicorn anywhere on it.

"Now what?" Jablonski asked Bellini.

"Roll down your window," Bellini instructed Manville. Bellini shouted to McGuire in the other vehicle. "We have to find a lion and a unicorn."

"I know exactly where to go now," McGuire shouted back over the wind.

ΩΩΩ

Three minutes later, the two vehicles sidled next to each other facing in opposite directions in front of The Governor's Palace. The Palace was a short drive along Palace Green from the church. Bellini conducted an impromptu history lesson through the open driver's side window of the tow truck.

"It's coming back to me now," Bellini began. "The Governor's Palace was the home to the Royal Governors designated by King

George during the British rule over the Colonies. Lieutenant Governor Spotswood was the first royal representative to inhabit the original building. He served under George Hamilton, the First Earl of Orkney who was the absentee governor. Patrick Henry was the first post-colonial Governor and Thomas Jefferson was the last man to inhabit this building after the Colonies won their independence. The Capitol was then moved to Richmond. Check out the pillars!" Bellini continued.

Battered by the weather and illuminated by the peripheral wash of the headlights, the gate stood as a portal to the walled grounds of the palace. Two large towers of red brick supported a white wrought iron gate fifteen feet high. Standing atop each brick pillar were carved, stone statues. On the left pillar was a lion and on the right a unicorn.

"The clue is hidden inside the Governor's Palace!" Jablonski shouted. "How do we get in?"

ΩΩΩ

Bellini approached the three-story, hip-roofed English Georgian palace followed by Manville and Lee, the private investigator. The lawyer and the tobacco shop owner stayed outside the wall to keep watch. Though Bellini wasn't sure what they needed to watch for, since only the craziest and most desperate people were out on a night like tonight. On either side of the gate cut into the grass were two areas where benches must have rested. They had probably been removed in preparation for the storm. Jablonski and McGuire had hoisted Lee, Bellini and Manville over the seven foot brick wall.

The mansion was flanked by two outbuildings. The front door of the palace was ten foot high and constructed of solid wood. The eight-foot rectangular windows were their best bet. Bellini moved to his right in front of the first window and shone a flashlight produced from his glove box. The window was situated just to the right of the door and over the marble steps making access easy. It was shuttered from inside against the storm. The irregular panes had been hand-blown.

Bellini looked at the SEAL and the investigator. "I hate to do this."

He turned around and cocking his left elbow, he rammed the lower left pane, cracking the glass. Two more blows were required to break it. Unlike today's windows which were one large sheet of glass set below the false cross-hatching, this re-created window was constructed of small individual panes.

"This is going to take forever," Bellini complained.

Manville grabbed the flashlight from Bellini, smashing panes with the handle. "No time to be timid," he said.

He smashed out six panes, the bottom two rows. Bellini pushed on the interior shutters, but they did not budge. "They must be nailed shut."

Bellini ran to the wall and shouted to the three men on the other side. Inside of a minute, he was handed a large, oversized wrench. All the men were drenched at this point, and shivering against the cold rain.

Bellini handed the wrench to Manville.

Bellini and Lee backed away. Manville rammed the massive metal wrench into the finely polished black walnut shutters. Three blows later, the wood splintered and they swung open.

"Someone's going to have to climb through," he wheezed.

"I'm small enough," Bellini replied. Without delay, Bellini hoisted himself through the window.

"We're going to jail," Manville said watching the two of them.

A minute later, Bellini swung open the mansion's door.

The former cop and SEAL entered and both shrugged off as much water as possible, stamping their feet on the black and white marble floor. Bellini swung the flashlight about in the Entrance Hall. The space was an oval with black walnut paneled walls covered by an impressive display of swords, muskets and eighteenth century weaponry. Above them more bayoneted-muskets were arranged in a decorative oval with the bayonet blades pointing to a gold-plated medallion in the center of the ceiling.

"I just broke into a national treasure by breaking the window and you guys are trying not to track water into the place. I'm sure the King would be appreciative."

Manville ignored the comment. "Does the clue say where inside the mansion he hid whatever it is you're looking for?"

Lee removed a page of soaked notes from his pants pocket. "It's in the clue."

"Something about Charlotte, right?" Bellini said.

"That right," Lee responded "How do you know all this stuff?"

"It doesn't take brains to drive a tow truck. Not many people know this, but I have a Master's degree in United States history."

Manville cocked his head at him. "I never knew that."

"And if either of you tell anyone, I'll tow your cars above the Arctic Circle."

"I'd like to hear how you ended up driving a tow truck for a living."

"I have other sources of income. But that's a story for another day. What does the rest of your clue say?"

"It says, 'Behind Charlotte, you'll find the next clue and the first piece of the recipe.'"

"He must mean the Ballroom. Follow me!"

They moved slowly through the hall under an arch to another walnut-paneled room. A set of stairs bedecked with more weapons led to the second floor. Bellini ignored the steps and proceeded straight. He swung open a set of double doors, revealing a large rectangular room painted in a royal blue with virginal white trim. The floor was true to Colonial form and made of pine planks. Three chandeliers hung from the domed ceiling. Bellini aimed the beam along the far wall.

"There she is!"

ΩΩΩ

At the far end of the ballroom on either side of a second set of doors hung two life-sized oil portraits set in gilded frames. Bellini aimed the beam at the eighteenth English man whose image hung on the left.

"That is King George III," he explained. Then he swung it to the woman's on the right. "That is his wife, Queen Charlotte."

They moved to the frame and Bellini pulled the base slightly away from the wall. "I'm going to need your help here, guys."

Lee and Manville slid a chest and two chairs sitting against the wainscoting toward the center of the room. They took up positions under the frame.

"Lift it up then away from the wall. This sucker's heavy," Bellini commanded. "Ready, on three."

They pushed the frame up, freeing it from its hangers. They tried to balance it as they moved backwards. The top-heavy portrait slammed back into the wall with a crack.

"Try again!"

On three again, they lifted the frame away from the wall. In unison, they backed slowly from the wall, balancing the frame vertically. Manville's foot hit one of the chairs they'd moved earlier. He stumbled backward, losing his balance and kicking the chair along the pine floor. As he fell, Manville instinctively clutched the frame tighter attempting to stop his fall. Doing this caused the portrait to waver in the other's hands. Manville tumbled on his backside, finally releasing the portrait a moment before he hit the floor in a wet flourish.

Lee and Bellini tried to blunt the picture's momentum, but it was too late. The top heavy frame listed and began to tip. They attempted to stop its fall, but the queen slipped through their wet hands.

Manville rolled out of the way a split second before the framed canvas crashed into one of the chairs and the chest. The frame bent, cracking at one of the corners.

"Nice job, guys," Bellini chided.

"Oops," Manville said. "That's not good."

"We broke the frame," Bellini said.

Manville scrambled to his feet as Lee explained. "It's worse than that. Look!"

Bellini retrieved one of the flashlights they'd laid on the floor and pointed it where Manville was pointing. He quickly made the sign of the cross. "You guys killed her!"

A corner of the chest had poked through the canvas, tearing a triangular hole in the center of the canvas.

As Lee and Bellini sparred verbally back and forth over the hole in the portrait, Manville moved to the lower part of the portrait. There he found a manila envelope taped to the back of the canvas.

"Here's the next clue," he said softly.

Lee and Bellini stopped arguing and turned to Manville. He tore it away from the canvas and ripped into it. He removed a single sheet of white paper. The next clue was typed near the top of the page. A list of ingredients and instructions was typed near the bottom.

"What's it say?" Lee demanded.

Bellini grabbed the paper and read it.

"It says 'it's time to get the hell out of here.'"

CHAPTER 28

The huffing and hissing of the storm rattled the plywood over the windows and rivulets of water streamed down the glass of the hospital conference room. The group collectively waited for Benedict to turn away from the window, thinking he was devising a plan. In fact, he was simply trying to keep it together.

Spanos had remained at Rose's side while Benedict went downstairs to meet with the team.

Manville approached Benedict. "You're ready to do this?"

"Yeah," Benedict said. "What's the second paper say?"

"Before we go there, Alex," Jablonski began, "I have a question. What are the items listed at the bottom of this clue we took from the Governor's Palace? It looks like a formula of some kind."

"Guys, it's a long story. I promise I'll tell you. But right now we have no time to lose."

"We're gonna hold you to that, Drug Man," Manville threatened.

Benedict opened the manila folder that had been taped to the back of the Queen's portrait. He read Watson's words:

A Union stronghold in Confederate Virginny throughout the War of Northern Aggression,
Commanded by Eustis, Bernard's design became Butler's Great Contraband Camp later known as Slabtown.
The second piece of the recipe along with the next clue is hidden in the president's pillow.

All eyes were automatically set upon Bellini.

"What?"

"You had all the answers the first time," the lawyer teased.

Bellini shrugged. "Read it again."

Benedict did.

"Well, let's take the part about Eustis. He must be talking about General Abraham Eustis. He was an artillery expert. So maybe he's talking about Fort Eustis," Bellini explained.

"Negative," McGuire added. "I was in the Army before I became an attorney. I know the history of Eustis. General Eustis never commanded Fort Eustis."

"What did he command?" Jablonski asked.

"I'm trying to recall," McGuire replied. "I remember reading about it at Fort Eustis. General Eustis commanded another facility on the Peninsula before the Civil War."

"What other military facilities are there the Peninsula?" Bellini added.

"Let's see," Jablonski began. "There's Yorktown Naval Weapons Station."

"That's not old enough. It can't be that," Benedict said.

"What about Fort Monroe?" Manville asked.

"That's it," Jablonski shouted. "That's what he's talking about. General Eustis was the first commander of Fort Monroe in the eighteen thirties. I don't know who Bernard was. Butler must be referring to Benjamin Butler. He commanded Fort Monroe during the Civil War."

"I remember now," McGuire chimed in. "President Obama made Fort Monroe a National Historic Monument through the Antiquities Act. The National Park Service administers it now. The head honcho over there came and spoke to our Rotary Club. She told us the story."

"That's right," Bellini chimed in. "Fort Monroe and the island it sits on at Old Point Comfort, were the only part of Virginia not to fall into Confederate hands during the Civil War. Benjamin Butler commanded it.

"Three slaves escaped from Norfolk on a skiff and sought asylum at Fort Monroe. A Confederate Major, demanded the return of his 'property'. Butler was a lawyer by profession and an opponent of slavery. He refused to return the slaves citing that the South considered them property. So they were classified as contraband of war and thus not entitled to be returned.

"Word quickly spread through the slave community. Slaves escaped and came to Fort Monroe under Butler's Contraband Ruling. It formed the Great Contraband Camp and was moved nearby where Hampton now sits."

"Alex," Jablonski continued. "It appears that he's talking about Fort Monroe."

"Okay, now we're getting somewhere. What about the President's pillow?"

"Fort Monroe is named after President James Monroe," Bellini said. "Is it that president?"

Everyone shook their heads and shrugged in unison.

"Lincoln stayed in one of the houses over there during the siege of Norfolk," Bellini stated. "Is there a museum there or something with one of his pillows?"

"Wrecker, what did you just say?" Benedict demanded.

The driver repeated himself.

"It's not Lincoln's pillow. I know what Michael was talking about. You all have to get on Fort Monroe!"

CHAPTER 29

Manville exited Jablonski's Ford crossover vehicle and raised his collar against the storm. The walkway leading from the curb to the entrance of the Casemate Museum was fifty feet away.

Fort Monroe is a six-sided stone fort with diamond-shaped bastions jutting from each point. The entire installation was surrounded by a wide moat. The bastions allowed for excellent, criss-crossing fields of fire upon enemies approaching from the lower Chesapeake Bay. Three narrow gates allowed entry. Each one is fed by a slightly wider, two lane bridge spanning the watery ditch. Only one vehicle could pass at a time. A signal light on either side of the gate regulated traffic. Drivers had to wait until oncoming traffic cleared and the light turned green before proceeding. Tonight, that was not a problem.

It had been decided that there only a need for two people to chase down the second clue. Five men and two vehicles was overkill. The storm was growing in its intensity, pouring more precipitation and pushing stronger gales over the area. Manville and Jablonski had volunteered for this next assignment. Manville was single and Jablonski had been divorced for almost ten years. They had already made themselves and their homes ready for the storm. Bellini, McGuire and Lee stayed behind to assist their families in their evacuation, but promised to check back in a few hours.

Manville walked/ran passed a Civil War-era cannon on his left and a concrete set of steps leading to the top of the fort's wall on the right. When he arrived at the entrance, he was drenched.

The Casemate Museum was housed in the hollow casemate of the southwest wall of the fort. Its notoriety was derived from its most famous prisoner. Jefferson Davis, the former President of the Confederacy, had been held in the casemate for four months after being captured by Union forces.

Manville surveyed the entrance. A large white metal door similar to what might be found on a private residence was nestled beneath an arch-shaped window. The portal was flanked by two full-length, double-sash windows. He moved to the right window and without hesitating smashed the lower window with a tire iron taken from the Ford.

He cleared the shards of broken glass and crawled through. Taking in what little his eyes could make out. The security lighting didn't provide much help. Again, he waited, expecting an alarm to sound but none did.

Manville was about to step into the room when he stopped. A figure stood beside a low archway leading to the next room. He crouched, waiting for the man to move. His eyes adjusted to the relative darkness and realized it was a wax figure of a soldier, standing beside the arch and a life-size diorama.

He took two steps into the room along the uneven bricks. A light began flashing and a muted alarm began to sound. He looked to the source over the doorway and spied two motion detectors whose red indicator lights were blinking angrily. The emergency beacon between them was flashing.

Manville raced under the first arch into the next stone and brick-lined area, past a white stone bust encased in glass, somebody named Bernard. Trained to absorb every detail, Manville's eyes scanned everything along the way. Having never been to the museum, the SEAL was not sure where he would find what he was looking for. He darted from section to section under the archways, scanning the walls, searching the room in which the next clue lay.

Through a doorway into another square area, under several more low arches and past the displays and exhibits which took on an eerie mood in the flashing light, he noticed a placard on the wall outlining the service of Edgar Allen Poe at the Fort during the writer's military career.

Keep moving!

He moved through another curved, low-ceiling arch and came to a display bearing the image of a black woman. Harriet Tubman.

He made another right and saw what he was looking for. The cube of glass sat on a pedestal. The signage proclaimed: Jefferson Davis Exhibit. The case held an ornate smoking pipe. Its bowl clutched in the claw of an eagle. Manville surveyed the room and found the former president's cell.

Without hesitating, he bounded through the doorway with the klaxon bellowing out of sync with the flashing lights. Half the room was roped off. Beyond the rope lay a simple bed and a desk sitting in front of a brick-lined window. On the desk rested an oil lamp, a water pitcher, a glass, a letter opener, and a Bible. An aged wooden chair was tucked neatly into the desk. The emergency lighting did not penetrate into this cell. Manville flipped open his phone to provide some light. He stepped over the rope and moved to the bed. The striped pillow was stiff and faded. He mashed it between his fingers feeling for the clue. Towards one corner, he felt unnatural stiffness and heard the crinkle of paper.

He moved to the simple desk and retrieved the letter opener. He manipulated it into the seam and jerked it, breaking the blade. The seam separated easily. Stuffing seeped out as Manville removed the envelope from Jefferson Davis's pillow. He turned and raced back to the entrance.

ΩΩΩ

Gregor Jablonski had left his Ford running. He heard the sirens before he saw the lights. In his rear-view mirror, he spied the pulsating beams emanating from the light bars atop the cruisers reflecting off the brick masonry of the fort's walls.

The police had entered through the West Gate and Ruckman Road. They swung right. He killed the headlights.

When the cruisers turned into the fort, circling along Bernard, Jablonski knew they were headed towards the museum. He checked the museum entrance for any sign of Manville, and saw nothing but the intermittent blip of yellow lighting inside.

Jablonski waited another five seconds then he depressed the accelerator, keeping the headlights dark. If he was lucky, he could make the East Gate and find the agreed upon rendezvous point.

ΩΩΩ

When Manville reached the broken window he'd used to gain access, he peeked out. Jablonski and the Ford were gone. The beam of a flashlight arcing back and forth caught his eye. Manville backed up inside.

He found an alcove to the left of the doorway. The flashlight beacon moved closer outside the window. Manville stuffed the manila envelope under his shirt as the cop came through the window with a gun drawn. Manville squeezed up against the aging brick of the casemate.

The crouched officer moved into the museum through the window. A gut-twisting fear gripped the SEAL as his eyes followed the trail of watery footprints from the window to his current position.

The beam of light swept the space illuminating the pulsing shadows caused the by alarm. It arced towards Manville, hitting the wall support behind which he was hiding, a portion stopped by the support, the remainder slipping in front of the Navy man illuminating the space to Manville's right. He held his breath.

Just as quickly as it appeared, the light swung away.

Manville hazarded a look. The cop was moving away from his position, his flashlight aimed at the footprints leading towards Jefferson Davis's prison cell. In a moment, the cop's silhouette turned a corner and was out of sight.

Manville slipped along the wall back to the window. The flashing blue lights of two police cars careened off the trees and brickwork. Manville knelt and stuck his head out into the rain, checking along a one hundred and eighty degree arc.

Despite the lights, there was no sign of other cops.

He sucked in a deep breath and stuck one leg under the bottom half of the window, followed by his torso. As he pulled his second leg through, his momentum carried him forward. His wet pant leg caught on a shard of glass protruding from the window frame. He stumbled and crashed to the wet brick outside the window.

A moment later, a beam of light at the corner of the building swung in his direction. Manville stared into it. He wriggled his leg free with a crackle of glass, scrambled to his feet and darted for a set of stairs scaling the parade wall of the rampart to the terreplein.

"Freeze!"

He was at full speed instantly. The oscillating beam of light created a moving shadow of his form along the wet concrete. He reached the top of the stairs and turned left, glancing over his shoulder to check on his pursuer.

The cop was half-way up the stairs. "He's up on the wall!" the cop shouted.

The flat terreplein atop the rampart was blanketed with soggy grass. As it neared the outer edge of the rampart, the inclined banquette crested and fell away to the wall's edge. Manville glimpsed snapshots of the scene ahead of him in lightning filled air. Grass and granite walls dotted with lines of rusted iron gun emplacements. Curved iron rails set in granite. The SEAL zigzagged to get out of the flashlight beam's path, changing direction several times, all the while trying to avoid tripping over the aging gun emplacements. In the distance, an increasing number of the blue lights seemed to light up the interior of the Fort.

Manville ran at full speed for a full minute. He reached a bastion at the corner formed by two ramparts. In it, a large flag pole spiked through the dark night. An inclined walkway led back down to the interior of the fort. Manville started down the incline. Before he'd taken five steps, two police cruisers one from each direction skidded to a halt at the base of the walkway.

"He's on the Flag Staff Bastion!" an unseen cop hollered.

Manville slid to a stop and pivoted. His footing gave way. He fell face first. He pushed himself up and climbed back up the incline. He reached the flag staff again and continued left just as the officer following him along the rampart reached the flag pole. The man grabbed at Manville's jacket, clutching at the shoulder. The SEAL flailed an elbow, knocking the arm free.

The cop stumbled and fell. Manville leapt onto a small retaining wall and continued his escape along the angular ramparts of Fort Monroe, multiple beams of light following his path. He spied three more police cars on Bernard Road inside the fort, following from below.

Manville checked both ways along the top of the wall. Cops were a hundred yards or so to his right from the direction in which he'd just come. To his left, where he was headed, three hundred yards away, more flashlight beams danced in the distance, waving about along the rampart. He was trapped. He looked over the edge of the wall to the interior of the fort. It was a twenty-foot drop in the darkness. There was no way he could judge his landing. A broken leg or ankle was a good bet.

He ran to his left and reached the third bastion, looking out over the blackness of the wide moat. Rain assaulted his head and face. In the chase, Manville had lost all frames of reference. He was not that familiar with Fort Monroe to begin with. But the rain, the chase and the adrenaline had short-circuited his internal compass.

A police cruiser skidded to a halt just below him. He was flanked on both sides by cops closing in on him on the wall and another squad beneath him inside the fort.

He moved up the slope of grass and crested the hill of the parapet. He toed his way down the outside slope towards the moat. The cops to his left were fifty yards away.

"You, there! Freeze! On your knees!"

Manville glanced quickly in the direction of the beam, blinded by it.

"I said, 'On your knees!'"

He sucked in a lungful of air and leapt.

CHAPTER 30

All sound and light were replaced by the sensation of plummeting. The cool rush of wet night air disappeared, gobbled up by the electricity in his gut. He hit the water feet first. The concussion jolted him, thrusting him forward slightly causing his face to slam into the icy water. Water gushed into his nostrils, threatening to force his eyes out of his head. He pushed the fear and pain somewhere deep and swam beneath the surface, breast stroking, not towards the opposite wall but back to the wall from which he'd jumped. He found the slimy granite and moved laterally along the wall. He opened his eyes underwater and saw the wavy beam of light above him, bent by the water and joined by more beams searching for him.

He needed air. But he held himself under pushing up on the slime covered wall. Against all human instincts, he pushed the air from his lungs and his buoyancy decreased and he sank several feet.

He pulled himself along the wall past the point in the bastion and finally allowed himself to surface. Gasping, he quietly sucked in air, trying to stay as silent as possible. But his breaths came hard and fast sounding in his head like they could be heard for miles.

He peeked around the point of the battery, watching the white circles in the water. They moved towards the far wall of the moat looking for him.

Manville had seen an iron rung ladder in the stone of the outer wall. The kind of ladder in which each rung was a rectangle of rusted metal drilled into the stone. Several police officers on the opposite shore of the moat stood over the section of wall above the ladder, shining their lights into the water around the ladder, waiting for him to surface.

Now what?

ΩΩΩ

Manville continued ducking under the water's surface to avoid the searching beams, playing a game of cheater's Marco Polo with his pursuers. Eventually, they moved on. His limbs were numb and he was shivering constantly. His teeth rattled in his skull. The weight of his water soaked clothes threatening to pull him under.

The first vestiges of daylight crept above the tree line, mixing with the storm as low, dark clouds raced by. His precarious foothold on the underwater crevices of the stone wall became harder to maintain. His muscles were burning and his coordination was beginning to fail.

In the faint light, Manville could once again make out the iron rung ladder on the outer wall of the moat. Out of options and his body screaming for warmth and relief, he pushed away from the wall and breast-stroked towards the ladder. The trip took longer than expected because his body was not cooperating.

On the opposite side, he took hold of the lowest rung. He turned to look back across to the bastion and the grassy embankment. The police were out of sight. But he could make out the flash of blue lights against the low ceiling of clouds.

He took one rung at a time, finally pushing himself over the top. He lay sprawled on his back. Manville turned and duck walked his way away, retreating from the fort. He stopped at a roadway, crouching by a wide oak tree. The sound of a revving engine intensified to his right.

Jablonski's Ford came into view.

"Get in!"

CHAPTER 31

"I'm beginning to hate this pharmacist of yours," Manville said, referring to Watson, as he looked over the message. The SEAL had changed clothes and was now wearing a pair of jeans and a t-shirt taken from the suitcase Benedict had previously brought to the hospital. A steaming Styrofoam cup of coffee sat before him.

Benedict, Manville, Jablonski and Spanos, who had left Rose in the care of her nurse and Grumps, were looking at the pieced together clue back in the hospital conference room. The envelope and white page it contained had been completely soaked. Benedict had cut the envelope away and torn the white page as he separated it from the manila envelope.

Benedict had already given them an update on Rose's condition. She was still weak and delirious. They were pumping her full of fluids. Her lucidity came and went frequently.

"We're getting there," Manville said. "Two more clues to go. We'll get it done."

"Thanks, Tyrone," Benedict said.

"You can call me Squid."

Benedict read over the clue. "Okay, anybody got any ideas?" Benedict, as he had done with the first two clues had photographed the pages with his cell phone.

Originally German Flats, its residents include The Boy General and Old Fuss and Feathers, and the Builder of the Great Canal and Sumter's Commander.

The second piece of the recipe and the final clue will be found at the right hand of my namesake who also resides here.

"Where are the German Flats?" Manville asked.

"You mean, 'Where were the German Flats?'" Jablonski corrected. "It says it was originally German Flats. It alludes to the fact that it has been renamed."

"Okay, smart ass," Manville protested. "Where were the German Flats?"

"I've lived here my whole life," Jablonski explained. "I've never heard of anything called German Flats."

"Well probably because its name's been changed—and a long time ago at that," Spanos added.

"There are four other men mentioned in the message. They appear to be more people or their nicknames. Who are they?"

"Sumter's Commander is easy. That was Major Robert Anderson," Bellini stated as he approached the table.

"Wrecker," Manville said. "Did you get your family squared away?"

"Yep, they're in a hotel in New Kent."

"Where's Sumter?" Manville asked changing his focus back to the problem at hand.

"It's the Fort in South Carolina where the Civil War began."

"Good," Benedict said. "The Builder of the Great Canal. The Great Canal has to be Panama. Who built that?"

"Probably about fifty thousand men," Jablonski joked.

"Someone had to be in charge," Benedict replied

"I don't remember his name. But he was in the military," Bellini replied.

"Are you sure?" Jablonski asked.

"As sure as I can be."

"Okay," Benedict said, "so maybe there's a theme here. Two military guys. The Boy General obviously is talking about another military man. What about Old Fuss and Feathers?"

"Wasn't that Patton's nickname?" Jablonski asked.

"That was Old Blood and Guts," Manville added.

"Does it really matter who it is? That sounds like the nickname of a military chap. So we're dealing with military commanders, right?"

"There is a fifth person," Spanos added. "Your pharmacist says the clue is 'at the right hand of my namesake.' That's a person, too. But who?"

"Michael Watson was a Civil War re-enactor," Benedict stated. "He played Ethan Allen Hitchcock, he was a Union general. But he never saw much action. Among other things he was an aide to Lincoln."

"So he's dead?"

"I'd say all these guys are," Jablonski said.

"What are you getting at?" Benedict asked Jablonski.

"If he's dead, then he must be buried. If he's buried, your pharmacist is talking about a cemetery. These guys are all probably buried in the same place."

"Okay, so what military cemeteries are there around here?" Benedict demanded.

"There's one in Hampton," Squid noted.

"Yeah, but none of these guys are buried there. Don't you think we'd know if the Builder of the Panama Canal and the Commander of Fort Sumter were buried there? It would be a tourist attraction. We'd all have heard about it."

"True. So maybe he's talking about Arlington," Bellini said

"It's possible," Manville noted. "But we can't drive all the way to D.C. on a hunch."

"We need to find out who each of these guys is? We've got Anderson and Hitchcock. Who are the other three? The key lies with who they are?"

"Who was The Boy General?" Manville demanded of Bellini. "What Generals have been really young? You're the one with the degree in US history."

"Really, Wrecker? You have a degree in US History," Jablonski said. "After all these years? And you never told us?"

Bellini shot the Navy man a look of disdain. "Thanks, Tyrone."

"What's the big deal anyway?"

"The big deal is I didn't want anyone to know."

"And I thought you were just some lowly working stiff. There's actually a brain in that head?" Jablonski chided.

"So why do you drive a tow truck?" Manville inquired.

"That's a story for another day."

"Back to the question. Do you know any young generals?"

"Sure," Bellini said. "Galusha Pennypacker enlisted when he was sixteen during the Civil War. He rose quickly to the rank of brigadier general, supposedly when he was twenty years old. But there are some doubts as to his actual date of birth. But I doubt your Michael Watson is talking about him."

"Well, who then?" Benedict asked.

"It's most likely Custer. He became a general at twenty-three. That's documented. And his nickname was The Boy General."

"Were you going to volunteer this information? If we hadn't asked, would you have told us all this?"

"I was getting around to it."

"This is not the time for keeping secrets."

Bellini nodded. "Point taken." His face flushed with embarrassment. But Benedict saved him.

"Okay, so we think it's Custer. That leaves Old Fuss and Feathers and the Panama Canal guy."

"We all agree we're looking for a cemetery, right?"

Everyone nodded.

"Then let's find out where this Hitchcock guy is buried. That's all we need to know. It says the information is at his right hand."

"We don't have Internet access," Jablonski declared. "And unless Wrecker is holding out on us again, I don't think anyone knows where he's buried."

Manville eyed Bellini. "Do you know?"

Bellini shook his head. "No."

"Maybe," Manville continued, "there's something at this pharmacist's house that'll tell us where he's buried. Some papers maybe."

Benedict shook his head slowly. It was the kind of movement men make when they realize the answer has been staring them in the face. "Of course," he said slowly.

"What is it?"

"McGuire and I went to D.C. to look at this guy's writings and papers. They're stored in the Library of Congress. At least some of them are. There might be something in there."

"I thought one of Kyle's men stole those from you," Spanos asked.

"He did," Benedict replied. "But the photographs of the papers were digital photos. I had the docent in the Manuscript Reading Room send me them in a zip file. It's an attachment to an e-mail on my laptop at home. You can also get two books I took from Michael's house. One is a biography of the man."

"Can't you access your web mail account from here?" Jablonski asked.

"No Internet, remember? Can someone go to my house and bring my laptop here?" Benedict slipped his house key off the ring and held it out for the first person to take it.

ΩΩΩ

"We're chasing the fountain of youth?" Manville asked. "You've got us running all over the place looking for a magic formula?"

Benedict had spent fifteen minutes outlining the events leading up to this moment after Manville, Lee and Bellini insisted they be brought into the know. McGuire had shown up rounding out the group. Benedict didn't have a mutiny on his hands. But, doubt was creeping in. These men had broken the law and put themselves in jeopardy for a friend, trusting that the help they were providing was for a good cause. They were experiencing the same doubt Benedict had experienced just days ago. But Benedict had a lot more skin in the game than they did. They were risking more than Benedict had a right to ask.

"I don't know. I can only hope," Benedict replied. "That's what Kyle and Watson think. They tested this formula on several patients and they all died. Kyle claims that he's found—or that Michael Watson, my pharmacist—found the correct formulation. They tried that recipe on the last patient at the hospital and she made a miraculous recovery. Kyle is after that formula. He will not rest until he has it. If I can get the formula which Michael has dispersed among these clues, then I can keep Kyle from doing any more damage. I have to find it before he does. Since you guys have been able to find the first clue, we've neutralized Kyle. He can't make the Materia Prima without the whole recipe. So even if this is all a hoax, you've managed to stop the deaths. For that, I—and the hospital—can only thank you."

"This sounds all too incredible," McGuire added. "It's make-believe."

Bellini, Jablonski and Lee were all shaking their heads.

"No, it's not. Ari can vouch for it. He validated the woman made the recovery. He's seen it with his own eyes. So have I. The woman was on her death bed. Now, she's cancer free."

They looked to the doctor. "What Alex says is true."

"You believe all this, doc?"

"I don't know what to believe at this point," he replied. "Watson claims to have left one last life-saving dose of the correct formula. If you'd seen what we've seen and you had a chance to save your wife, what would all of you do?"

The group contemplated that question for a moment. Then Benedict spoke. "What you've done so far has been above and beyond what one friend should ask another. But I have to see this through. I don't know if we will be able to find the rest of the clues in time. Rose is very sick." Benedict's voice clogged with emotion. "I made a promise to stay with Rose, to be with her at the end. That time is close. So I will stay here and Ari, as her doctor, will, too. We will make her as comfortable as possible. If Rose is going to have a life, it will be because you five gave it to her."

"Where is Kyle now? Is this man dangerous?" Bellini asked.

"I don't know where he is," Benedict replied. "After he left me to die under the Science Building, I haven't seen him. He also has the first clue. We obviously got there before he did. He must not have figured it out in time. The man is relentless. I don't know when or how, but I assure you he will make himself known. He's already responsible for at least three hospital deaths and the murder of one, maybe two, nurses. He won't hesitate to kill to get this formula."

"I'm asking for you guys to finish this for Rose. You've already done enough. But if you choose not to, I understand."

Jablonski cleared his throat as did Manville. The rest of them stared at the floor. Manville finally stood up and smiled. "Well, Alex, when you put it that way how can we say no, right?" he said, nudging Bellini.

"I'm in," Bellini said. "We all are. But, from now on, whenever I raise you at the poker table, you better fold."

"I can't believe you blew up the Science Building at JRU," Lee said.

"I didn't blow it up. I just happened to be in it at the time. He wanted to blow me up with it."

"What did you find out from Hitchcock's papers?" Jablonski asked.

"Nothing," Benedict replied. "But the biography on him says he's buried at the West Point Military Academy. I guess all of the guys named in the clue are there."

"What was the part about the German Flats?"

"The cemetery is on an area formally known as the German Flats."

"So now we're going to West Point. That's a fifteen hour drive."

Spanos looked towards Devin McGuire who had been silent for the entire meeting. "Devin, you can fly them up there."

"He can't fly in this crap," Jablonski said.

McGuire walked to the large glass window. The storm had let up momentarily. But the sky was still ominous. "The rain's let up. Hurricanes rotate counter clockwise. If we fly to the east and then head north, we would have tail winds."

"Devin, as a lawyer you have to be a smart man, but if you do this, you're an idiot. You'll get yourself killed."

"Not just me, but anyone with me," he teased.

McGuire remained with his back to his friends as he spoke. "This is important stuff we're chasing down. I've been flying for twenty-five years. If the next clue is in New York, we're going up there to find it—or die trying."

"We're wasting time," Bellini urged. "If you're going to fly to New York, you better get going."

"Joe's right," McGuire said. "We'll fly up and find Hitchcock's grave, get the clue and come right back."

"What if the next clue leads you to Ohio or Canada? Then you won't be right back," Jablonski pointed out.

"It's possible he could lead you somewhere farther away," Benedict said. "But I'm guessing he'll bring us back to this area. Michael was not a worldly man. He was local, with local roots. He didn't travel much except to attend Civil War re-enactments. My guess is he went to Hitchcock's gravesite and placed the clue there because of its symbolism. The next clue should come back to this area. If not, we'll deal with it then."

"If you say so," Jablonski replied.

"I say so," Benedict replied smiling.

"Okay then, it's settled," Spanos interjected. "Who will go?"

ΩΩΩ

"They're headed to New York," Neville said.

"New York's a big state," Kyle replied. "Is that the best you can do?"

"They're going to the West Point Military Academy. They're in a conference room with the door closed. I was in a small side room. I could only hear parts of the conversation."

"Where is the next clue?"

"Somewhere in the cemetery. That's all I can tell you. What do you want me to do?"

"Timothy followed him to New York," Ashan interjected. "Too bad he's dead."

Kyle squinted at the Iranian.

"Alex Benedict." Kyle began, "already has the first part of the formula. If we can get the next piece of it, we can keep him from retrieving the final clue. We will have the clue to the third and final part of the formula. We will have two parts of the formula. When we can take the first one from Alex Benedict, we will have what we need.

"Neville, I want you to fly up there and wait for them. Get the second part of the formula!"

CHAPTER 32

"What are you going to do when you have all the clues?" Rose asked.

Benedict had pulled a chair to the bedside and was resting his arms on the mattress. Rose was doing better at the moment. She was coherent. But Benedict expected that to change any minute.

Grumps had decided to get some sleep in the waiting area after Benedict had convinced him that he was here for the night. The old man had been at the hospital since arriving straight from the airport.

The flight to New York would take the three men at least four hours direct. But they would have to land somewhere between Newport News and New York. McGuire's Cessna did not have the necessary range. Benedict figured with a stop for gas both ways and another hour before they secured whatever Michael Watson had buried there, meant it would be a good ten hours before they returned home. But Benedict would have the clue in half that time if they called from New York.

He grasped her hand. "Absolutely nothing."

Benedict was as relaxed and as content as he'd been in the last few months. There was nothing he could do for the moment except enjoy his wife's company. He'd spent so much time chasing down his investigation and worrying about Rose, he'd not taken time to appreciate the life he'd had with this incredible woman.

"All this running around and when you find the answers, you're going to do nothing with it? What about the Materia Prima?"

"I have two goals, Rose. First, we have to make sure the Materia formula stays out of Dr. Kyle's hands. If Michael is true to his word, when we find the last clue we will find the last dose of the real formula. If we're lucky, we will be able to give it to you."

"Baby, do you really think it's real?"

"I've seen its benefits, Rose. It's real. You'll have tomorrow back. You'll have a whole bunch of tomorrow's back."

Rose nodded. "I'd never take another day for granted. That would be heavenly."

"Yes, it would," Benedict agreed.

"If you did release it to the world, how would you do it?"

"I don't know. But, just imagine how different the world would be if we could. No more sickness, no more disease. Michael was right about its power though. It has to be tested and released in the right way."

"You may have convinced Daddy. But you have to be realistic. It's probably not real. I don't want you getting your hopes up."

"You're wrong, it is real. I'm going to see this through."

Rose smiled at him. It appeared to consume all the energy she possessed.

"I need to sleep."

"Me, too, baby. I'm exhausted."

Benedict put his head onto the mattress beside Rose's hand and closed his eyes.

ΩΩΩ

"How the hell are we going to find this guy's headstone?" Manville asked.

The West Point Military Cemetery was sandwiched between a ribbon of pavement called Washington Road and the Hudson River just north of the Military Academy, nestled at the foot of several mountains. A slight breeze whisked in over the mountain tops with an unseasonable spring like warmth.

They'd landed at Stewart International Airport in Newburgh. McGuire, accompanied by Bellini and Manville drove the rented Chevy Malibu south on Washington Road to the entrance of the cemetery.

The cemetery was closed. Operating hours were from nine to sunset each day. The gates were locked and a seven foot high black wrought iron fence ringed the property. They were parked across the street from the main gate. While the Military Academy itself was heavily guarded against unauthorized entry, the cemetery did not appear to be.

"Give me your iPhone, Joe," McGuire commanded. "We're going to find this gravesite."

McGuire pulled up the website and found a .pdf file, a map, of famous people who'd been buried here. Ethan Allen Hitchcock was number twenty-one on the list.

"We'll have to climb the fence and stay out of sight," McGuire said.

ΩΩΩ

Neville knelt just inside the tree line on the cemetery grounds. He'd been in place for two hours when the car pulled to a stop outside the locked gate. The view was blocked by a thick copse of trees. He heard the voices but could not make out the words

Neville circled around for a better view and listening post. He carefully stepped through the trees watching every footfall before it touched the ground. It was difficult making out potential noisemakers, such as dried leaves or branches, through the dark shadows created by the weak moonlight.

He halted about thirty yards from the roadway with a clear line of sight. He leaned in trying to hear what was being said by the large black man, the Italian and the Irish lawyer.

He pressed his foot onto a bed of leaves carefully, finally applying his full weight. A branch or twig must have been buried beneath the leaves. It snapped in the clear night like a bone breaking.

Shit!

ΩΩΩ

"What the hell was that?" Manville whispered, whipping his head in the direction of the sound.

"What's what?" McGuire said.

"Someone's out there in the shadows."

Bellini watched with wide eyes as the SEAL withdrew a massive handgun holstered inside his coat. "Pretend you didn't hear anything. You guys keep looking for the grave. I'll go check it out."

Manville moved across the street and inside the tree line and took up a position against a large oak. Someone or something was moving around to his left, north of McGuire and Wrecker's position. The cemetery at West Point was heavily wooded along the outer edges. From what he'd been able to see from the circular driveway, even the gravesites were dotted with clusters of trees. It provided excellent cover from detection which worked both in his favor and against him. Manville leaned close to the tree and slowly pulled back on the slide of his weapon, silently chambering a round.

Seeing no movement or strange shadows, he motioned for Bellini and McGuire to approach.

ΩΩΩ

"Okay, now we're talking. It's this way. Follow me," McGuire said, referring to the map on the phone's display.

From the trees, Manville was alternately watching the area from which the last sound had emanated and where the silhouettes of his friends mingled with the rented car. Nothing had happened for nearly five minutes. Occasionally, he could make out the muffled, unintelligible sounds coming from whatever conversation the two men were having by the car.

Manville met them at the locked gate, helped both of them over and scaled the fence with ease himself. Once inside, McGuire, with Bellini in tow, moved off into the cemetery. Manville stayed five paces behind and turned his attention to where he thought the stalker would be, creeping closer, using the cover of an adjacent tree. He saw a shadow begin to move in a line parallel to his friends.

ΩΩΩ

The glow of morning was beginning to take hold over the treetops. The cemetery would open in a few hours. McGuire checked the sky and noticed the lack of cloud cover. The promise of a gorgeous day loomed. The breeze slapped him in the face and was almost cold, a welcome change to the thick winds of the hurricane ravaging Tidewater. But the lawyer took no notice. He was more interested in finding the grave. He was three paces ahead of Wrecker making a line for the gravesite.

The cemetery's epicenter was a circular plot of land bisected by two paths dividing it into quarters.

McGuire recited the names of some of the more famous residents from the map which included a short synopsis of their achievements. "The list is impressive: General William Westmoreland, Lieutenant Colonel Ed White, one of the astronauts killed in the Apollo I fire in January 1967, Brigadier General John Thompson, the inventor of the Thompson submachine gun and, among others, the five famous residents referred to by pharmacist Michael Watson: Hitchcock, George Armstrong Custer, Major General Robert Anderson, the commander of Fort Sumter during the first battle of the Civil War, George Washington Goethals, the builder of the Panama Canal and Old Fuss and Feathers, General Winfield Scott...."

"Can we just get to the grave and get the hell out of here," Bellini said with irritation. "I don't like this place."

They circled the general area, searching for the grave as the morning fog hugged the terrain. The heavy dew on the grass soaked their shoes and the cuffs of their trousers as they whooshed around in smaller and smaller circles.

McGuire located it as the first spikes of sunlight penetrated the sky over the trees.

"Here it is," he said barely above a whisper. "Not a bad spot for a final resting place."

The headstone was a simple, white marble slab, rounded at the top, sitting beneath a copse of shade trees and engraved with an even simpler epitaph:

Ethan
Allen
Hitchcock
Maj General
2 Infantry
August 5 1870
Class of 1817

The tow trucker moved to his side, still checking over his shoulder for any sign of Manville or the ghost in the forest. He removed a folded sheet of paper on which he'd scribbled the clue from the soaked paper taken from the Casemate Museum. Bellini had scribbled the names of the answers to Watson's clues along the margin. Now he was focused on the final sentence:

The second piece of the recipe and the final clue will be found at the right hand of my namesake who also resides here.

"Look for a place of disturbed earth, where someone may have dug up the ground," McGuire instructed.

Hitchcock's headstone was flanked on the right by a grave bordered by a low concrete curb. Just inside the curb, Bellini spotted an indentation inside the curb, almost under the concrete itself.

"Here," Bellini announced.

He stepped over the concrete and knelt to examine it when he heard a noise behind him. He turned and let out a shrill shriek.

ΩΩΩ

"Don't move," the stranger said as he placed the barrel of the handgun directly between Bellini's eyes. "If I shoot you, you won't have far to go."

The gunman produced a second weapon and pointed it at McGuire who was standing outside the concrete rectangle and had begun to step in the direction of the headstone.

"Just stay still and no one will get hurt. Both of you on the ground. Now!"

The two men lay on their stomachs. The man stepped around Bellini to face the tree line.

"Tell the Neanderthal following me in the trees to show himself. Or I'll kill *Guido*." The gunman took up cover behind a tree but maintained a bead on both prostrate men.

McGuire turned his head towards the forest. "Squid, come on out," he said, using Manville's nickname.

There was no response.

"I mean it," the man repeated, kneeling now. "He has five seconds to save your friend." The man was shouting now towards Manville. He crouched and pressed the barrel into Bellini's skull.

"Five ... four ... three ..."

The sound of rustling branches and forest debris snapping preceded Manville's appearance from the brush twenty feet from Hitchcock's grave.

"Just take it easy," the SEAL said calmly. "I'm right here."

"Throw down the weapon! Toss it into the trees."

Bellini managed a glance back at Manville. The handgun was in his right hand at his thigh. The SEAL stood unmoving. The expression on his face told the tow truck driver that giving up a weapon was something a SEAL had never been trained to do.

"Do it now!"

Manville flicked his wrist and the weapon flew ten feet from him and away from Wrecker and the gunman.

"On your face!"

Tyrone Manville's eyes darted about, taking in every piece of information. Using the barrel of the weapon against the back of his head, the gunman pushed Bellini's face, into the soft ground. Bellini let out a muffled cry.

"Now!"

Manville dropped to his knees and then with agonizing slowness lowered his torso onto the wet grass, all the while keeping his eyes on the stranger. The stranger instructed both McGuire and Manville to stretch their arms out from their sides. When they had complied, he stepped back from Bellini, but kept the weapon trained on his head.

"Dig it up."

"I don't know what you're talking about," Bellini lied.

The stranger's left boot connected with the left side of Wrecker's head, snapping his head to one side. He groaned, clutching his face with both hands.

The stranger shoved him to the side with another kick. "Get the hell out of the way."

The man knelt at the curb and began scratching at the soft, green turf. He looked up at Manville, then McGuire who were both still prostrate, whipsawing the gun between the two of them.

He clawed away the grass easily and moved the loose earth beneath it. A large manila envelope in a plastic bag caked with dirt was removed from under the concrete. He stuffed the envelope into his trousers and yanked Bellini by the collar.

"Get up!"

When he had Bellini on his feet and in a choke hold, he said, "Guido is coming with me. You two stay put." He backed Bellini out of the curbed area onto the paved footpath.

CHAPTER 33

Manville strained his neck trying to keep the two men in his vision. The gunman was dragging Bellini backwards away from Hitchcock's headstone. Manville was still on his stomach with his chin resting on the grass and his eyes taking in all of it.

Manville had gradually moved his right arm down to his side, keeping the left extended. While the gunman had been preoccupied with digging up the envelope, the SEAL had positioned himself to retrieve the second weapon holstered in the small of his back.

His chance came a few seconds later.

Bellini, blood streaming down his face and his left eye swelling from the kick to the head, stumbled as he was pulled backwards. Both his hands were grasping the forearm around his throat and when he lost his balance, his weight pulled the larger man to the side. The gunman was unprepared for the shift in weight and Bellini fell to the ground, landing on his butt.

The gunman let out a groan, trying to yank him up by the collar again. But Bellini was dead weight.

Manville pulled out his second weapon and leveled it at the now-exposed gunman, pulling off two shots. The reports cracked through the fog-encased silence of the dead.

The stranger was hit by at least one round. He spun around as if jerked by a chain, staggered but did not fall, now facing away from Manville. The wounded man began to clumsily step away.

Manville watched as Bellini reached out with one hand to grab one of the man's feet. He missed but his arm found the space between the man's legs, tripping him. The stranger plummeted face first into a headstone of an adjacent grave, hitting his head and face.

Manville was on his feet and at Bellini's side instantly, his weapon leveled at the fallen man.

Manville moved to him and picked up the handgun. He frisked him and found no other weapons. The envelope and plastic bag lay at his side. McGuire, who had approached more cautiously, picked it up, moving back to his fallen friend. "You okay?" he asked Bellini.

"Better now."

"We need to get the hell out of here," Squid commanded. "Those shots won't go unnoticed."

"Check his wound, Tyrone," McGuire said.

Manville tore open the bloody shirt at the impact point and quickly examined the entry wound. He rolled him over slightly and checked the exit wound. "Geez, Squid. What the hell did you shoot him with—a cannon?"

"Pretty much. Forty-four Magnum. Dirty Harry was right, most powerful hand gun in the world."

"He's bleeding bad," Manville said. "Help me get him up."

The three men lifted the wounded man off the ground. Manville folded him over his shoulder and carried him, battlefield style, in a direct path to the gate.

"The gate's locked. How are we going to get him over it?" Bellini asked.

"I'll shoot the lock off," Manville replied. "We need to get him to a hospital. We need to get out of here before the cemetery opens."

ΩΩΩ

"She's taken another turn, Alex," Spanos told his friend.

"What is it now?"

Spanos was reading a printout of lab values from her most recent blood work. "She's septic, and it's getting worse. Her heart rate is still above ninety-five, temperature is 101.5 and her respirations are too fast. Blood pressure is falling."

Benedict could see Rose's chest rising and falling weakly but rapidly.

"Based on this lab work, her kidneys appear to be failing. BUN is up and her urine output has dropped off. She still has decreased breath sounds on the left side. We're not winning the battle."

"She's going into severe septic shock," Benedict said.

"I'm afraid so," Spanos replied. "You should go wake up her father."

ΩΩΩ

"Where the hell have you been?" Lee demanded.

"Have you seen the roads?" Jablonski shot back. "In case you haven't noticed, we are in the middle of a hurricane."

Jablonski drove ten miles per hour under the speed limit. The vehicle was buffeted by crosswinds, making it hard to maintain a straight line. It would take longer to get back to Tidewater Regional Medical Center, not only because of the storm, but because both sides of Interstate 64 were being used for the evacuation and the traffic was spilling onto J. Clyde Morris Boulevard.

When the SEAL, the lawyer and the tow truck driver had left for New York, these two had taken the break to attend to their interests. They were coming from the Coventry subdivision in lower York County, driving south, taking J. Clyde Morris Boulevard which was also Route 17. Jablonski pulled to the intersection of Coventry Boulevard and J. Clyde. Jablonski had picked up Lee just minutes earlier to make the return trip to the hospital.

The traffic lights were out. He turned left onto J. Clyde Morris when a blinding shock of white lit the intersection. Sparks showered above them as power lines snapped and dropped around the vehicle.

A sharp gale rocked the crossover vehicle as a loud, squealing crack sliced through air.

"Watch it!" Lee shouted.

A large power pole, topped with a transformer, toppled like a giant oak. Jablonski saw what was happening and gunned the engine to get past the pole before it hit. His tires spun. The vehicle fishtailed into the median and found the muddy earth.

Jablonski and Lee both covered their faces as the pole crushed the front half of the roof and windshield.

ΩΩΩ

The phone on the bedside table rang once. Benedict picked it preventing a second ring.

"Yeah?"

"We've got it," McGuire voice on the other end said.

Benedict heard a loud droning in the background. "Where are you?"

"We're in the air headed back. We landed and refueled at Teeterboro about ninety minutes ago."

"How are you calling me on a cell phone from a plane?"

"I'm on a satellite phone," McGuire said.

"What took you so long? I was expecting your call about two hours ago."

"Let's just say we ran into some trouble."

"What kind of trouble?"

"Manville had to shoot someone."

Benedict sucked in a lungful of air and expelled it slowly. "Wonderful. Is he dead?"

"Who, Manville?"

"No, the guy he shot."

"I don't think so. We took him to a hospital."

"That was generous of you."

"Do you want to know what this clue says?"

Benedict studied his wife who was drowning in pillows and blankets. Lauren Blair, seated on Angel's bed, saw Benedict through the glass as he spoke into the phone. Benedict smiled and gave a short wave. Grumps was placing a cool cloth over Rose's forehead.

"Go ahead," Benedict said.

"You're on speaker. Bellini's going to read the clue."

"Hey, Alex," Bellini announced. "Here it is: '*Sitting between the towers, it's served both nations with distinction. It sits at the head of its namesake boulevard near the junction of Robert Rich's boulevard and the avenue of one of the builders of a former wonder of the world. Find what you're looking for beneath Rufus himself.*' It goes on to give you the final part of the recipe ...'"

"We don't need to worry about the recipe right now," Benedict replied. "Read it again."

Bellini read the passage one more time.

"There's a truckload of questions in that clue," Benedict observed.

"Let's break it up again," McGuire said.

"Who's Robert Rich? Is there a street named after Robert Rich in the area?" Benedict asked. He'd lowered his voice to a whisper.

"None that I know of," Bellini replied. "Are we sure that Watson is talking about someplace in Tidewater?"

"I can't be one hundred percent sure," Benedict replied. "But again, I don't think Michael would have sent us all over the country looking for clues."

"So what is a 'former wonder of the world' in our area that he's referring to?" Squid chimed in.

"I don't know. Throw out some ideas of things that might have been considered wonders of the world," said McGuire.

"How about Norfolk Naval Base?" Manville's voice said in the background. "It is the world's largest naval base."

"But was it a 'wonder of the world'?" Benedict scribbled Norfolk Naval on a note pad by the bed.

"How about Waterside?" Bellini added.

"Nice try, Joe. I don't think that would make the list," McGuire said.

"How about the shipyard?"

Bellini was referring to the Penrose Gatling Shipyard, the only builder of aircraft carriers in the United States.

"Where are you now?" Benedict asked.

McGuire replied. "We're over Northern Virginia at the moment."

"Can one of you get on the Internet?"

"Yeah, I can use the sat phone as a wi-fi hot spot."

"Doing it now," Bellini replied. "I'll Google 'Wonders of the World'."

There was a moment of silence then Bellini spoke again.

"The Wonders of the World, according to Wikipedia, are comprised of several lists which are updated periodically. They include natural wonders and man-made structures. There are the Seven Wonders of the Ancient World, Seven Wonders of the Modern World. There are dozens of these lists."

"It's not going to involve the ancient world," Benedict said. "Try the Modern World list."

"Hold on."

"There's nothing on that list about anything in our area."

"The clue said something about a former wonder of the world," McGuire observed. "Does it have something about past wonders?"

Except the sound of the engines, there was more silence.

"They have lists going back fifty years," Wrecker said. "I'm checking to see if there's anything that fits."

Several eternal minutes passed. McGuire asked about Rose's condition. It was a depressing conversation that ended with Benedict stating: "It's almost over, Devin. I can't believe I'm saying this. It's almost over."

"I think I found something," Bellini announced. "After it was built in 1964, the Chesapeake Bay Bridge Tunnel was named one of the Seven Engineering Wonders of the Modern World."

"That's got to be it," Benedict agreed. "The clue talks about an avenue of one of the builders. The CBBT must have a website. Check the history."

"I'm on it," Bellini said.

"Hold on guys. It's going to get rough. We're on the outer edges of the storm ..."

Static interrupted the line for a moment.

"McGuire, are you there? Can you hear me?"

"Yeah, we're here.... Can you hear...."

"Barely," Benedict said.

"He's got something," McGuire said. The connection was much clearer now. "I've turned away from the storm until we can get the message to you. I can't do it for long. Fuel is a factor. I should have enough. But I can't take too many detours."

"What's he found?"

"The first executive Director of the Chesapeake Bay Bridge Tunnel District was none other than J. Clyde Morris. It's the Chesapeake Bay Bridge Tunnel complex that connects Virginia Beach with the Delmarva Peninsula. J. Clyde Morris was the only city manager of the city of Warwick before it merged with Newport News. Morris had also been the first executive director of the Chesapeake Bay Bridge and Tunnel District. The Boulevard named in his honor was the section of US Route 17 traversing through Newport News."

"As in J. Clyde Morris Boulevard?"

"One and the same."

"The clue says the piece sits at the junction of Robert Rich's boulevard and J. Clyde Morris Boulevard. What other boulevard intersects with J. Clyde?"

"Lots of streets intersect J. Clyde," said McGuire.

"Yeah, but not boulevards," Benedict replied.

"Then there's only one boulevard I can think of," McGuire said.

Bellini, Benedict and McGuire all spoke at the same time. "Warwick Boulevard."

"That makes sense," Bellini continued. "That's who Robert Rich is."

"Go on," Benedict said.

"Robert Rich was the second Earl of Warwick back in England and a member of the Virginia Company of London. J. Clyde Morris Boulevard intersects Warwick Boulevard which is named for Robert Rich."

"Excellent! Hold on a minute," Benedict said.

Rose began coughing, slow and soft at first. Then the spasms intensified in both depth and volume into watery, painful choking sounds. He stroked her scarf-covered head. Her eyes were shut and she was shivering when she was finished. Benedict pulled the blankets higher.

He sighed and placed the phone back to his ear.

"Okay, so the clue is near the intersection of Warwick and J. Clyde Boulevard."

"That's near the hospital and John Ratcliffe University," McGuire said.

"Let's hope Michael didn't place the clue in the Science Building."

Tyrone Manville finally chimed in. "The clue says something about 'between the towers'. Doesn't your hospital have two towers?"

"It sits at the head of its namesake boulevard between the two towers. That's it," Benedict said. "I know where the final clue is. I have to go find Gregor and Ulysses. They can retrieve the last clue."

Before he ended the call, Benedict heard an ominous beeping sound coming over the static on the line.

"What's that?" he asked.

"I've got a warning light. We're losing oil pressure. I've got to get this bird on the ground. We have to find a place to land. We're going to have to terminate the conversation."

CHAPTER 34

"They're not in the conference room. I had them paged but there's no answer," Spanos told Benedict.

Benedict paged Spanos after he ended the call with the guys on the plane. Benedict had asked his friend to find Ulysses Lee and Gregor Jablonski. They had promised to return to the hospital to help with the search for the remaining clue. Spanos had checked the conference room, the cafeteria and the patient lounges on the first floor and had not found them. He'd even overhead paged them through the hospital's intercom system.

"We can't wait any longer," Benedict said.

"I'm on my way back up there," Spanos said. Ten minutes later, Spanos donned his gown and mask, and entered the room.

"I'm going to have to find the last clue," Benedict said to both Grumps and Spanos. "We can't wait any longer. She could die any minute."

"Where is the clue?" Grumps asked.

"On the hospital grounds."

"I'll go," Grumps said. "Just tell me where."

"No," Benedict replied. "I know exactly where to go."

ΩΩΩ

Benedict looked up at the two-story plantation known as Archer House with its ornate balustrades and columned balcony. The words of Michael Watson's final clue came to him in the form of Joseph Bellini's words over the static-filled radio connection from the aircraft:

Sitting between the towers, it's served both nations with distinction. It sits at the head of its namesake boulevard near the junction of Robert Rich's boulevard and the avenue of one of the builders of a former wonder of the world.

Archer House sat at the head of the boulevard named for Rufus Archer, the original owner. It served both nations as a military hospital. First, the Confederacy then the Union after falling into Northern hands during the siege of the Peninsula. Michael Watson had placed the final piece of the recipe inside Rufus Archer's plantation house within sniffing distance of J. Edward Kyle and the hospital where all the trouble began.

The house, now a museum, was dark and locked. Benedict, clad in scrubs and now completely drenched, walked to a first floor window and kicked out the glass. The glass shattered and he battered it again and they fell into the house. He crawled through.

The interior space had been restored to its Civil War-era adornments. A large wide staircase led to the second floor. On either side of the stairs were large, spacious rooms. To the right was a drawing room with a roll top desk and sitting area. To the left was a large dining room set with ten elegant places beneath a brass and crystal chandelier. The walls were adorned with blow-ups of photographs from the hospital archives: female slaves carrying buckets of water and wood, weary and bandaged soldiers, physicians in blood-stained aprons and landscapes of the surrounding acreage.

Benedict stood in the foyer at the foot of the grand staircase. The clue instructed him to find "what he was looking for beneath Rufus himself." He scanned the rooms, thinking for a moment.

He guessed it might be hidden behind a photograph as Watson had hidden the first clue behind the portrait of Queen Charlotte. Beginning in the dining room, he scanned the life-size photos. Two contained images of Rufus Archer. In one, he was standing in what was the very same dining room, between two wounded soldiers. The caption beneath the image indicated that the soldier to Archer's right was a Union private. His left arm had been amputated. The soldier to Archer's left was a Confederate corporal with a dirty, blood soaked bandage wrapped diagonally around his head covering one eye. His chest was bare save for another larger bandage which looked more like a bed sheet. It, too, was tinged with blood.

Archer was looking directly into the lens as if staring into hell itself.

Benedict grabbed the plain, wooden frame and lifted it away from the wall, inspecting the back of the photo and the wall. It was bare except for a rectangle of grime outlining the clean wall. He repeated the process with the second photo of Archer, standing with an unnamed Confederate officer as they stood on the front porch of the home. Again, he found nothing.

Benedict moved to the opposite end of the house and entered the drawing room. He spotted movement outside one of the windows. A large shadow appeared across the walls. The figure was silhouetted against the emergency-powered lighting from outside. The shadow moved onto the porch towards the front door. Benedict waited, hoping the figure would move away.

ΩΩΩ

The plane's engine took on a different pitch. Its drone mixed with a soft whine. Bellini was seated beside McGuire up front. Manville was looking out the window into the darkness. Several warning lights were illuminated on the cockpit panel and the bleep of an alarm filled the headsets.

"This is Cessna Corvalis November Zero Two Four Zero Tango Tango, calling Washington Center. We have an emergency and request immediate landing. Come in. Over."

The radio responded with static and an occasional obscured word.

"Say again, Washington Center. This is Cessna November Zero Two Four Zero Tango Tango We need to land immediately. Over."

The lawyer banked the plane to the west in the general direction of the landing field he'd used on three previous occasions.

"Washington Center, do you read?"

More static.

"How far is it to the airport?" Manville asked.

"About twenty minutes," McGuire replied.

"Will we make it?" Bellini asked.

"That depends," McGuire replied calmly.

"On what?"

"On the engine."

McGuire had just leveled out of his turn when the whining of the Cessna's engine climbed in pitch. Two loud thunks shook the fuselage. The propeller on the front of the fuselage seized, locking in place at an angle.

"Oh, *merda*," Bellini squealed. He made the sign of the cross and began praying in Italian.

"Look for a place for me to put down. A roadway, an open field. Anything!"

"It don't look good, boss. It's pretty dark. It looks like forest down there."

ΩΩΩ

Benedict moved through the museum towards the rear, staying in the shadow. He circled back to the drawing room and crawled to the roll top desk. The desk's roll top was closed and locked. Benedict tried the drawers. They were locked, as well.

He'd thought the figure outside the window had moved off. Footfalls on the front porch told him he was wrong. Benedict balled himself up, wrapping his arms around his knees hiding on the far side of the desk. Peering over the desktop, he saw the silhouette peering in through the shattered glass of the window, followed by a series of rapid hand signals.

Benedict held his breaths, squeezing backwards as the gunman passed through the open window turning from a silhouette to a well-detailed threat. He recognized the Middle Eastern associate of J. Edward Kyle.

Once inside, his weapon was leveled in one hand. In his other hand was a large flashlight. A tiny glint moved along the barrel as he slowly swept the gun in a horizontal arc.

The Iranian noticed the wet outline of Benedict's shoes on the aged, polished planks of the floor. Carefully, he stepped towards the dining room, following the path.

When he was out of the line of sight, Benedict crept deeper into the museum towards an open door off the drawing room. The doorway had no door. Benedict crept into a modern looking room with a large, desk and the accoutrements of modern business: a cordless phone, computer monitor, combination fax and printer. It was the museum director's office.

He checked the floor in the hallway. Wet footprints traced his path into the carpeted office, giving him away. Benedict stuck his head into the door opening and listened for the Iranian's progress. The creak of floor boards in the dining room told him where he was.

Benedict stepped out of the office, carefully, re-tracing his path over the wet tracks he'd created going into the room. Back in the drawing room beside the desk, he stepped onto the woven rug centered in the drawing room. He took three measured steps across the carpet and halted.

Mounted on the far wall opposite the desk, Benedict spied where Watson had hidden the final clue and hopefully the one and only remaining dose of Materia Prima.

CHAPTER 35

The plane descended at an awkward angle. The two passengers and the pilot, McGuire, leaned as far back in their seats as they could with the feet braced against the floor boards.

"When I get down to the treetops, I'm going to try and level out, skimming along the top of the forest," McGuire was shouting into his headset. The first sign of fear crept into his voice. The rushing air screamed past the windshield and the silence of the engine.

"We'll be there in about twenty seconds! Are there any roads?"

Neither Manville nor Bellini responded.

Fifteen seconds later, McGuire shouted, "Hold on!"

ΩΩΩ

The porcelain urn sat on a shelf enclosed in glass.

It contained the ashes of Rufus Archer. Benedict remembered the brief tour he received when he began his employment at Tidewater. Archer died in late 1889 and asked that his remains be cremated. His sons complied with his request and kept the urn on the mantel above the fireplace and beneath Archer's full length portrait.

Benedict rose up on tip-toes to look inside the glass box. The urn sat in the center surrounded by various personal items that once belonged to Archer: a ring, a pocket watch and his favorite pearl-handled revolver.

Another wooden creak warned Benedict of his pursuer's approach. The shadow appeared before the Iranian did. The silhouette crept along the hallway under the staircase, connecting the drawing room, dining room and the back of the house.

The gun came into view along with a flashlight lighting the way. Benedict stopped breathing, frozen like a mannequin. If Benedict moved he would be detected. If the Iranian rotated the beam, Benedict would be detected.

A wretched anticipation filled him. The only sound was the soft squish of wet footfalls on one of the wooden floorboards. The gunman slipped towards the director's office. Benedict hazarded a careful glance over his shoulder and watched him enter the director's office.

Benedict, forgetting the clue for the moment, moved around the wall and back into the dining room, pressing himself against the wall. As he stood there trying to control his breathing, another movement caught his eye. Another form had moved into view through one of the windows in the dining room. The man's eyes locked onto Benedict's. Benedict recognized him. It was J. Edward Kyle. He raised a weapon a degree or two to take aim.

"I've got him, Ashan," Kyle hollered from beyond the window. "First floor in the Dining room! I want him alive!"

$$\Omega\Omega\Omega$$

Benedict leapt away from the wall, turned the corner and darted back into the drawing room. He located the glass-encased urn and lifted the whole case slightly. Beneath it laid the last manila envelope. The envelope would not slide out from under the case. It was caught on something. Benedict yanked on it and the entire glass case moved toward him, nearly falling from the shelf. The urn inside teetered for a second then toppled over. It crashed to the floor of the case, but did not break. The lid fell open and the gray, dusty remnants of Rufus Archer slid out.

Kyle fired three shots through the open window. The slugs whizzed past a recoiling Benedict.

The manila envelope was not flat. Something else had been placed in it. Something bulky. Watson had placed the flat part of the envelope under the glass case, leaving the protruded section between the case and the wall.

Kyle outside was trying to gain access to the museum through the locked door, not realizing a window had been broken. The large door popped and shook in its frame every time his foot crashed into it. Then two shots rang out splintering the door near the lock.

Benedict saw the beam of the flashlight from the director's office swinging his way. He slid the envelope out from the side of the case and bolted from the drawing room. Kyle's henchman rounded the corner. A rough hand clasped at Benedict's collar.

Benedict shrugged and whipped an elbow in the direction of the man's head, connecting with his temple, dislodging the hand. He bolted up the stairs. Another hand clutched at his ankle. He kicked the Iranian in the face away as the museum door arced open, crashing against the fallen man.

Benedict was at the top of the stairs, darting to his right toward a line of bedrooms when Kyle entered. Two more shots rang out imbedding in the upstairs wall. Benedict ran to the large bedroom at the end of the hallway and closed the door. Benedict heard the creaks of the weary hardwood floor on the stairs, then in the hallway as Kyle and his accomplice checked each bedroom. His freedom and probably his life could be measured in seconds. Benedict pulled a dresser in front of the door.

ΩΩΩ

Both men took the stairs two at a time, turning right. They checked each room, plunging weapons inside as their eyes scanned the space, repeating the procedure with each room until reaching a door that was closed. The Iranian tried the old knob. The door opened but was stopped by something large.

He backed up and launched a kick to the door just above the door knob. The door arced open, slamming against the dresser. A third blow knocked over the wardrobe. They pushed the door open. They leveled weapons and scanned the room.

"Where'd he go?" Kyle asked.

The bedroom was empty. The windows were all closed and intact. A partial wet foot print lay at his feet where the suspect had entered the room. But that trail ended when he'd stepped onto the carpet.

"I'll be damned," Kyle seethed.

ΩΩΩ

Benedict moved carefully along the tunnel, holding the crumpled manila envelope in one hand and the lighter Rose had given him in the other, using it as a torch, lighting his way through the darkness.

Musty, stale air filled his nostrils. His escape had been razor thin. The door smashed into the dresser just as Benedict had closed the panel concealing the secret staircase.

Years ago, during his tour of the Archer House, the docent had revealed the existence of the passageway Archer had used to escape Federal troops during June of 1862 as they stormed their way along the Peninsula. The docent's description had flashed into his mind as he reached the top of the stairs.

Benedict wasted little time in descending the narrow wooden staircase. It would only be a matter of time before they discovered his escape route. The steps led into the shallow basement of the home, a rarity even in today's building market. The water in the basement was knee deep and rivulets of water were pouring into the space.

The water level shallowed as he made his way out of the basement and along the escape tunnel. The tunnel was four feet wide and no more than five feet high causing him to crouch. He'd dropped to his hands and knees, sloshing water with the unlit lighter in his mouth. After kicking out a rusted grate, the tunnel finally deposited him from a tall knoll through what looked like a small square cave.

He ran back to a rear entrance of the Archer Tower, opened the door and stepped out of the rain. Inside, he found a dark conference room. Dripping wet, he tore open the envelope.

CHAPTER 36

Benedict removed the white page from the manila envelope. It was soaked along the edges. His hands began to shake as he read Watson's final words to him:

Alex,

You now have in your possession the formula for the Materia Prima. That's what it has been called down through the ages. The quest for the Philosopher's Stone—the elixir of life—the Materia Prima has been completed.

Please guard these clues. If the world is careless with this formula, the consequences would be enormous and too devastating to contemplate. All the steps of the formula are in your possession. But in order for the formula to work, remember Rubedo and Lovecraft.

All samples of the Materia Prima have been destroyed save one. It works. Remember the last patient. Hopefully, you have seen its power.

I have left you the one and only remaining dose. Your loved one is dying.
I have given you the ability to save your wife.
Thanks for the kindness you provided an old man.

Michael Watson

PS. Give Rose the contents of the entire vial (10ml) in a mini bag of 100ml of saline. It is the universal dose.

Benedict pulled out the one remaining item from the wet envelope. He lit his lighter and examined it. He tilted the vial at varying degrees, holding it up to the flame of his lighter. The liquid within was not like any other solution he'd ever seen. Its viscosity was thicker than water, yet more fluid than syrup. The fluid resisted the pull of gravity as Benedict tilted and swirled the vial, leaving a faint residue along the inner aspect of the glass vial. Its hue was leprechaun green and suspended within it were golden particles of solid matter.

Unlike a suspension, the solid particles did not settle to the bottom of the vial when he stopped moving it around. They hung suspended. But another quality of these particles captured Benedict's attention.

They held the light. Benedict released the igniter of his lighter, casting the conference room into darkness. The tiny particulate matter glowed for several seconds before the light they held faded. Benedict lit the flame for a few more seconds, and then extinguished it. He saw the same effect. The particles glowed then slowly faded as the light slipped away. He repeated this two more times with the same result.

Did this small amount of liquid possess the power Watson claimed?

As he held the vial inside the golden circle of light created by the flame, urgency imbued with hope and desperation filled him. Benedict closed his eyes.

When he opened them, beads of sweat appeared on his forehead. He became dizzy with elation. The hands of his internal clock began to turn in super fast motion.

Move, he thought.

Before going back to Rose, he had one more stop to make, a stop, as pharmacist, as a healthcare professional and as a scientist he had to make. Benedict sprinted for the stairs.

ΩΩΩ

The small, elderly woman lay propped up by pillows. The tray table was pulled in front of her loaded with a spread of food. A medium sized steak flanked by a mound of mashed potatoes cratered by a thick, juicy pool of sweet gravy and plump peas topped with a pat of butter. A second plate filled by a wedge of strawberry shortcake and large glass of chocolate milk. The whole ensemble was set on fancy china and flanked by a cloth napkin and silver flatware.

Benedict approached the bed in fast but respectful step. A young couple seated on the sofa beside the bed looked up at him and smiled. Margaret Queen was too busy cutting her steak and wolfing down two quick cubes of meat to notice.

"Grandma," the younger woman said, nodding to Benedict.

Margaret swiveled her head and took in Benedict's curt smile.

"Would you like some?" she asked. Queen nodded towards the young woman and the man. "Chelsea and Curt ordered it from Outback and snuck it in here. You won't tell, will you?"

Benedict smiled. "Your secret is safe with me."

"You sure you don't want any?"

"Thanks, I'm good."

"Good. 'Cause this dinner is history."

"Miss Queen," Benedict said, turning serious. "I won't take up much of your time so you can get back to your meal. I wanted to ask you a question."

Margaret nodded. "When are they going to let me go home? I feel wonderful."

"Grandma, the doctor said he wanted run some more tests just to make sure."

Benedict interrupted. "I was curious as to what happened. I mean to not put too fine a point on it. One minute you're close to death. Then the next day you seem to have made a miraculous recovery. Do you remember what happened that night?"

"Sonny," Queen replied. "It was a miracle. Plain and simple." Margaret scooped a dollop of cream from between the layers of shortcake and licked it from her bony finger. "I was visited by an angel."

"An angel?"

"That's right."

"Did this angel say anything to you?"

"No, not that I remember."

"Do you remember anything that happened that evening?"

"Why are you so interested young man?"

"Miss Queen, I apologize, but time is critical for another patient. Anything you could tell me might help someone else. Did you hear anything or see anything?"

"I remember lying in the bed. My children and grandchildren were all around the bed, crying and praying. I was in a lot of pain and was having trouble breathing. Then I must have fallen asleep until the angel arrived."

"Did anyone enter your room?"

Margaret shook her head. Benedict looked to the young couple on the couch. "Do either of you remember anything?"

"One of us was in the room all time. Nothing happened, except the nurse that came in to give Grandma her medication. She asked us to leave for a moment. So we did."

Benedict turned back to Margaret. "Did this angel speak to you? Could the angel have been a nurse?"

"Perhaps. I do remember a light, a glowing light, now that you mention it. I thought it was the Lord coming to take me."

Benedict moved to the head of the bed, reached up and switched off the fluorescent light on the wall over the bed. The room turned dark except for the wash of light from the hall and the crack in the curtain.

"What are you doing?" Queen asked.

Benedict turned away from Margaret Queen and her visitors. He removed the vial from his pocket and used his body to shield their view. He lit the lighter and held it up to the vial for five seconds.

He clicked off the lighter and turned around, holding the vial up in the relative darkness of the room.

"Is this what the light looked like, Margaret?"

Margaret Queen's eyes grew wide. She had just spooned herself a mouthful of mashed potatoes. Some if it slipped over her lip and onto her hospital gown.

"Praise the Lord," she whispered. Margaret Queen bowed her head and began mouthing a silent prayer.

ΩΩΩ

The oncology unit occupied the entire third floor of the Archer Tower. Twenty patient rooms ringed the outer perimeter of the circular floor plan, except for the area occupied by the elevator shafts and stairwells. Nurse's stations, offices, a nurse's lounge, patient waiting areas and storage facilities filled the center nucleus of the unit.

Margaret Queen's room was on the opposite side of the circle from Rose's. In fact, it was room 303 which was as far away from

Rose's room as it could be. Benedict could have chosen to go left or right from the room and he would have traveled the same distance, not that his mind was in any shape to calculate such things. As it was, he made a fateful choice and chose right.

Benedict's momentum carried him towards the inner wall of the corridor. He braced himself with a stiff arm against it. He passed the elevator when the stairwell door just in front of him swung open. Benedict caught the movement of the door and a figure coming at him. Before he could react, the long muzzle of a silenced handgun angled at his face stopped him.

"You are a very resourceful man, Alex," Melissa Harrison whispered. "Come with me," she commanded. She stayed several feet away from Benedict and motioned with the gun for him to enter the stairwell.

"Mel, what the hell are you doing?"

"Unfortunately, Dr. Kyle and his associates have failed. So it is up to me to handle the situation."

"What are you talking about?"

"Give me the formula ... the last dose of the Materia Prima. I know you have it. Michael Watson left it for you. We have been following you. Your colleagues shot one of Kyle's men in New York. Kyle's son is being moved as we speak. Kyle stayed behind to clear out his things. And he, too, will be gone soon. The last clue led you to the Archer Mansion. You have the complete formula and the one remaining dose of the Materia Prima. Give it to me now. I like you, Alex. I don't want to kill you."

CHAPTER 37

"Where is Alex?"

Grumps leaned in over the bed rail to answer his daughter. "I don't know, honey. He's on his way."

"Where's Lily?" Lily was Grumps's first daughter and Rose's older sister. She lived in Sacramento.

"She's on a flight right now. She should be here first thing in the morning."

Rose's weary eyes gazed past her father and fell upon Benedict's mother. Rose smiled.

"Hi, sweetie," Katherine Benedict said, walking to the bedside and extending her hand to grasp Rose's. "Where is that son of mine?"

"He's taking care of some very important business," Grumps replied. "He promised he'd be here soon."

$$\Omega\Omega\Omega$$

"How did you escape the explosion at the university?"

Benedict shrugged off his confusion. "You know about that?"

"I know everything. You fucked everything up, Alex. Kyle had seen the first clue. Like you, he'd memorized it. It would only be a matter of time before we could find the rest of the recipe. You were expendable. Unfortunately, you figured out the clues before we did. Kyle in a desperate attempt to get some of the formula had the plane followed to West Point."

"You're a part of this?" Benedict said.

"I'm more than a part of this, Alex. I'm the reason behind it."

"Kyle was giving all the orders, making all the decisions?"

"Dr. Kyle works—I should say—worked for me. I'm the silent partner."

"Where is Kyle now?"

"I'm not exactly sure, at the moment. Probably cleaning out his office. You almost ruined our plan, Alex. But we have the answer, we have—you have—the formula. Our work paid its dividends. I want it. Now." Harrison raised the gun slightly.

"I don't have it with me. If you kill me, you'll never find it."

Benedict turned to move towards the door. He took a step away from his Director of Pharmacy.

The burp of the silenced weapon echoed in the enclosed space of the stairwell. Benedict ducked as the round embedded itself in the door just beyond his head. He turned back to Harrison who had the gun in both hands.

"Give me the vial and the formula, Alex. Or the next one ..."

ΩΩΩ

"Is he safe?"

J. Edward Kyle sat in his office inside Tidewater talking on the speaker phone. The room was dark except for the light emanating from the lamp on the large oak desk.

"Yes," Ashan replied. "They will be at the facility in about forty-five minutes. Nurse Gretchen is at his side and will stay with him until we can find more help. I will be out back in about ten minutes. Did Harrison retrieve the formula?"

Kyle had just dumped the entire contents of one drawer into a cardboard box. He replaced the drawer but did not reply. Ashan and Kyle had returned to the hospital after Benedict escaped them in the museum.

Kyle had phoned Melissa Harrison explaining that Benedict had escaped. Harrison had cursed him violently and said she would take care of getting the formula herself. The Director of Pharmacy had also explained to Kyle that the police had shown up at the hospital asking questions about the disappearance of a nurse named Penny Lewis. It was then that he made plans to flee.

"She is attempting to get it now."

"Are you going to get it from her after she obtains it?"

"No. It is vital that we leave soon. I will make arrangements to get it from her later. I will meet you at the rear entrance."

Kyle pressed the talk button and ended the call.

He withdrew another drawer from the desk and was about to empty it when a knock sounded at the office door. Kyle paused then placed the drawer on the desktop.

He rounded the desk, stopping at the door. Another round of knocking started. Kyle swung open the door and faced Ben Roberts, Tidewater's President.

Kyle's eyes shifted to the layers of people behind him. The two uniforms were Newport News police officers. The other two uniforms were Tidewater security personnel. A suited man had a gold shield hung from his suit jacket pocket.

"John," Roberts said. "This detective needs to speak with you."

"This is not really a good time."

"I'm sorry, but it's not a request. He will speak to you now."

The suited man beside Roberts said, "I'm Detective John Palmer with the Newport News Police Department."

"Stop," Kyle demanded. "This is my private office."

"I have a warrant to search your office," the detective replied.

"For what?"

"For evidence in the disappearance of Penny Lewis."

"You have no right!"

Detective Palmer waved the legal document. "This piece of paper says otherwise. Now step into the hallway or I'll have these officers remove you."

Kyle turned to Ben Roberts. "Ben?!"

Roberts smirked. "It's out of my hands, John."

The uniformed officers stepped to either side of the physician and escorted him out of the office.

"Start with the desk," Palmer demanded.

ΩΩΩ

"Come and take it from me, Mel. I told you I don't have it. But if you think I have it, come and get it!"

"Why so you can take the gun? I don't think so."

"You're responsible for all this?" Benedict asked.

"You think a pharmacist can't coordinate such an undertaking?"

"I don't ... know ... what to think."

"Dr. Kyle is the foremost expert in his field. I chose him to lead this project. He's being paid very well. I decide what, when and how things happen. Not Ben Roberts! Not J. Edward Kyle!"

"And the financing for all of it?"

"I provided every penny."

"But...."

"Again, you doubt a pharmacist would have access to such ... resources? My father was a captain of industry for over forty years back in Kansas. I was his only heir. When he died, he left me more than forty million dollars. He died a terrible, agonizing death from liver cancer. I did this for him. So others would not suffer. After he died, I moved to Virginia to start over. I vowed to use his money to find a cure."

"That explains the expensive clothes and car. It was all a charade? You acted like the dutiful director of pharmacy, taking orders from Kyle, acting like he was in charge, letting him have his say with the Pharmacy and Therapeutics Committee. And yet, you were telling him what to do?"

Harrison nodded.

"We had to keep the natural appearances in order. Dr. Kyle is a researcher without equal. A good leader surrounds herself with people who are smarter and more capable. J. Edward Kyle and Michael Watson were the best in their fields. I just gave them the resources to complete the work."

"Where did the Materia Prima come from? How did you know about its ... power?" Benedict wanted to keep her talking. He inched his foot closer to her.

"That's a long story. One for another day. Suffice it to say the formula has been sought after for centuries. My father traveled the world before he became ill. He was given a book by a shaman on one of the Mariana Islands who found it in a cave. The man claimed to be over a hundred and fifty years old. The shaman's tribe was being decimated by disease. They had run out of resources, ingredients to make the Materia Prima. Of course, they didn't call it Materia. They had some other tribal name for it. My father befriended the man, saved his wife from death by administering simple antibiotics. The shaman repaid him by giving him the Book. But unfortunately the recipe in it didn't work. That's why we hired Michael."

Benedict shook his head. It was all too incredible to believe.

"And the deaths?" he pressed. "How can you justify the patient deaths?"

"We certainly didn't intend for the deaths to occur."

"But the incorrect formulas were killing the animals. How could you use them on humans knowing it wasn't perfected in the monkeys?"

"Kyle argued that the formula only worked on humans. In hindsight, I believe his judgment was clouded by his desire to see results for his son. It was a mistake."

"A mistake? That's how you justify it?"

Harrison ignored the question. "After we obtained the formula, Kyle would be given credit for the discovery. I would finance production of the Materia Prima on a wider scale and the creation of a new pharmaceutical company producing it. Once the patients started dying, we were committed. We were all involved, no one was innocent. Kyle's reputation and career as a doctor and a researcher were on the line. He would be ruined by implication. I convinced him he wouldn't survive the fallout so we forged ahead."

"Even Michael?"

"Michael was kept in the dark. He didn't need to know about the human testing until the very end. That's why he took his own life. His job was to perfect the formula. And obviously he did. Margaret Queen proved that. But he managed to find out patients were dying and he couldn't handle the guilt."

"And you, how do you handle it?"

"Setbacks are a nasty side effect of research. People die every day in the name of progress. Look at the space program. Astronauts died in the shuttle accidents, in the Apollo project. No one intends for it to happen. It just does. It's the price of progress."

"But those people, those astronauts knew the risk, Mel. They knew what they were getting into. The patients you're testing this stuff on don't!"

"People die driving cars that have faults that aren't discovered until they are driven. Even in the pharmaceutical industry, drugs reach the market that hurt people all the time and are recalled: Vioxx and its risk of heart attacks; Trovan and liver failure; Cylert. This list goes on and on. Those patients didn't know what they were getting into. They were casualties."

"It's not right!"

"Maybe not, but it's the way of the world, Alex. Now give me the clues and the vial Michael left for you."

"Mel, Rose is down the hall—dying—right now. I can save her. This dose can save her."

"Oh, so now it's okay. You'll give this drug to Rose, knowing it works, to save her life. Even though you abhor the way it was discovered. That makes you as guilty as the rest of us."

"It's different. I was not a part of the Materia's creation. It exists now. All this happened before I was involved. I have it now and I will use it on her."

Harrison wagged the gun back and forth. "No, you won't."

"Mel," he began. "This compound, if released, would turn the world's healthcare systems on its head. Doctors, nurses, pharmacists and countless other healthcare professionals, for the most part, would no longer be needed. Hospitals would empty. Curative drugs would no longer be needed. The pharmaceutical industry would collapse. And how could you produce enough of it to make a difference?"

"Those details will be worked out." Benedict was now a lunge away from the outstretched weapon.

"Only the wealthy would be able to afford it. How would you decide who gets it? You'd be deciding who lives and who dies."

"You're thinking too much, Alex."

"No, we need to be cautious with it. Just like when Nobel invented dynamite, did anyone stop to think about the long-term consequences? When the Manhattan Project produced the A-Bomb, no one considered what would happen when a rogue state could produce one. No Mel, I'm thinking just the right amount."

"Who are you to decide? Give it to me! Now!"

"No!"

She raised the pistol.

"I'll kill you, Alex. I mean it. You see there's one additional problem. After Margaret Queen was cured, we recovered the used IV bag with the remnants of the Materia Prima in it. Kyle had the contents analyzed and he was able to reproduce the exact proportions of ingredients. Before the lab was destroyed, he compounded another formula using those exact ratios. But, you see, it didn't work. Kyle tested it on a monkey in the lab and found that it didn't work. Michael did something else to the formula, something that was not written down as part of his formulation. So you see, Alex, we believe you have the exact formulation and the last real dose of the Materia Prima. So you are going to give them both to me now so we can analyze it. Surely, you understand the significance the last remaining dose. You understand, if you give it to Rose, the rest of the world will lose."

Benedict reached into his pocket with his right hand and removed the final clue. He left the vial in his pocket and dangled the paper between his first and second digits. With his left hand he removed, with difficulty, the gold lighter Rose had given him. He clicked it open and depressed the igniter with his thumb. A tiny sword of flame licked at the air. Benedict moved the flame to the corner of the crumpled paper. The flame began to devour it.

Harrison's eyes dilated, bulging with horror.

"No!" she screamed, lunging at Benedict, clutching at the lighter in his hand.

Benedict swung at the wrist holding the weapon with his left hand. The gun went off. The lighter fell from his hand, clattering to the floor of the landing.

Ignoring the pain, Benedict bent his left arm, cocked his elbow and unleashed a wicked blow to Harrison's head. The weapon fell from her fingers and bounced down the stairs. The Director of Pharmacy fell backward into the wall behind her. Benedict leaned over her.

She looked up at Benedict as blood flowed from her nose. Her gaze fell upon the burning piece of paper.

Harrison dove to Benedict's right, aiming for the paper. Benedict reached out and tackled her. They fell to the floor as Harrison tried to grab the paper. Benedict pulled her down and out of reach of the burning paper.

The vial fell from his pocket and clinked on the floor.

"No!" she cried.

Benedict held her in his arms as they watched the crumpled paper disappear into a curled, black shard. She was face down with her left arm outstretched inches short of the burning paper. Her right was pinned beneath her. Benedict had both arms around her pulling her out of reach, straining with all his might, holding her back.

When she realized it was too late, Harrison let her head fall forward. Then the words came. He didn't understand them. Harrison spoke them into his arm. He grabbed her by the hair and lifted her head.

"What ... have ... you ... done?"

"It's over," he said.

Benedict tried to slide out from under her. Harrison reached out with both hands and clawed at his face, digging her nails into the flesh. Benedict slashed at her hands and arms, whipping them away. But her hands and arms were everywhere. Harrison' strength was beyond that of a frail, demure woman. She was now a crazed defeated animal with nothing to lose. Benedict felt the sting of his already raw facial flesh tearing away beneath her nails.

He reached out, ignoring the tearing at his face. His hands, one wrapped in bandages, found her neck. His fingers wrapped easily around it. His thumbs met under her chin as she flailed wildly, incoherently.

Benedict pressed his thumbs into the flesh. Harrison's clutching and digging weakened as her windpipe closed off and her face reddened. Harrison stopped flailing and tried to pull Benedict's hands away from her throat.

He could feel his own blood rushing to his face as the circle created by his fingers narrowed. Harrison alternated between pulling at his arms and hammering her closed fists into the side of his head. With every passing second, her strength weakened.

Benedict watched her lips turn blue. Harrison tried to hit him one last time. But her hand opened at the last minute and weakly slapped his cheek. Her body went limp and the color drained from her face.

He felt his body begin to shake. He could not catch his breath. Benedict wiped at his face with his hand and his fingers came away, once again, stained in crimson.

He stood up, straightened as best he could. He picked up the vial and his lighter, resting in the corner. One long breath later and he pulled open the door.

CHAPTER 38

"He's administering Last Rites," Grumps said as Benedict approached the room. Benedict's mother and Grumps were standing in the doorway watching.

"Where have you been?" his mother whispered. Then his appearance and facial wounds became visible to her. "Oh, my God, Alex!" She hugged him hard. He winced as she squeezed his shoulder wound.

"It doesn't matter. I'm here now."

"I'm glad you're here. She said you wouldn't let her down," Grumps said, placing a hand on Benedict's shoulder. Grumps looked into Benedict's eyes, looking for a sign that Benedict had achieved the goal. "Did you ... you know?"

"We'll find out," Benedict said.

"What happened to you, son?" his mother persisted.

"Mom, not now. I need to be with Rose."

His mother explained, "Rose just gave her confession. Father Donnelly is now performing the Anointing of the Sick."

Benedict turned to Grumps and his mother. "I want both of you to wait outside for a minute."

Benedict stepped inside the room pulling the door closed. The priest clad in a black cassock with a purple cloth draped around his neck was at the bedside, leaning over the bed. A cross sat on the bedside table.

The slight rise and fall of her chest comforted Benedict. He was not too late. Her cheeks had sunken deeper. Her color was ghastly. She did not seem to notice that he'd arrived. Rose was shriveling before his eyes. She did seem to be coherent at the moment.

The priest placed his hands on Rose's forehead. His words were soft and clear. "Through this holy anointing, may the Lord in His love and mercy help you with the grace of the Holy Spirit."

He then took Rose's hands in his. "May the Lord who frees you from sin save you and raise you up."

The priest then whispered a few words to Rose. She weakly made the sign of the cross. The priest moved to Benedict and blessed him before leaving.

When the door clicked closed behind the priest, Benedict moved to the window looking out on the hallway and the nurse's station. Then he closed the blind. He did the same with the window looking into Angel's room. He was not wearing the protective clothing as the others had been. But that did not matter now. He rushed to action.

He turned and found a wheeled cart along the wall, housing various medical supplies sporting three large drawers. Benedict walked to it and opened the top drawer. He found a ten-millimeter plastic syringe and needle combination wrapped in plastic and paper and some alcohol pads. Benedict removed them and kneed the drawer shut. He retrieved a small bag of saline from a second drawer along with some IV tubing.

Back at the bedside, Benedict laid the syringe and the alcohol pads on the bed near Rose's left arm which had an intravenous line inserted and taped to the back of her hand. A vinyl bag of five percent dextrose and ringer's lactate hung from the IV pole and was dripping into the chamber at the top of the tubing.

Benedict peeled back the wrapping of the syringe and needle. He was about to do the same thing Harrison, Kyle and their whole band had been doing for months to the patients of Tidewater. Benedict didn't care. He would be arrested for Harrison's murder. It wouldn't take long for someone to find her body in the stairwell.

He pulled back the plunger to the ten millimeter mark, filling the chamber with air. Benedict shoved the pain into the recesses of his mind and removed the vial from his pocket and set it on the bed. He tore open an individually wrapped alcohol swab and wiped the top of the vial with it.

Benedict lifted the vial up to eye level and inverted it. After uncapping the needle of the syringe, Benedict aimed the beveled needle at the rubber top of the vial.

His hand began to shake as he moved the needle towards the vial. His head began to swim and the lightheadedness caused him to catch himself on the bedside rail. He tilted his head back, sucked in a lungful of air and tried to relax.

Benedict repositioned the needle under the inverted vial and slowly inserted it through the rubber. With his hands still shaking slightly, he depressed the plunger, pushing the prescribed volume of air into the glass container. Inside the vial, bubbles ejected from the needle. Benedict withdrew the end of the needle back towards the cap in order to withdraw the maximum amount of liquid.

He pulled back on the plunger with his thumb and met stiff resistance due to the thickness of the glowing fluid. He applied continuous pressure and let the liquid seep through the needle until the entire volume had been withdrawn. It seemed to take an eternity.

He tapped the body of syringe with his index finger dislodging the air bubbles stuck along the side of the chamber. He injected the green liquid into the small bag of saline, connected it to the IV tubing and moved to the IV dripping into Rose's arm.

ΩΩΩ

Benedict positioned the Luer-lok end of the tubing an inch from the port in her main IV line. He was about to screw it into place when Rose moved.

Rose's opposite hand grasped his wrist.

Her eyes were rheumy and distant. She managed a half-smile as she looked up at him, lost in the soft, deep pillow.

"What are you doing?"

A single tear tracked along his cheek. "I've got it. I've got the Materia Prima. It will work, Rose." Pleading filled his words as his voice cracked.

Rose's lips formed a tight thin line as her own eyes welled. Her head was shaking before she spoke.

"Do you have any more?" she asked.

Benedict shook his head. "No, this is it."

"You don't need to give it to me."

Benedict felt like a knife had pierced his abdomen. "Of course, I do. Rose, this is the...."

"It's my time. I've had a great life and a great love. You are a wonderful man. But the Lord is calling for me."

Benedict held up the bag and the tubing, shaking it for emphasis. "This will take away your pain. You'll be cured, Rose. I've seen its effect. I've spoken to a patient that...."

"I love you," she whispered.

Rose moved her head in the direction of the other bed beyond the window connecting the two rooms.

"There's someone else who needs it more than I do. Her life has not yet begun. Give it to her. Give it to Angel."

Benedict screwed up his forehead as he tried to absorb the request. The words registered but his brain refused to comprehend. He looked at Rose with a swirling mixture of confusion, anxiety and fear.

Finally, he spoke.

"I don't understand. This is what I've spent the last two days...."

"I know, baby, and I love you all the more for it. But I never thought this would all be real...."

"But it is real. We can have a family and grow old together."

Benedict saw Rose's eyes fill with moisture, overflowing into a stream of tears. She squeezed his hand with both of hers. "Baby, I'm sorry I let you down. I'm so sorry I never gave you a child. I know how much you wanted to be a...."

She choked on the word and looked away. Benedict lowered the bed rail and held the tubing at arm's length away from Rose. He crawled onto the bed and nuzzled his cheek into her forehead, crying along with her.

"Don't ever think that you let me down, honey. I've had the most wonderful life a man could ever imagine because of you. I wouldn't trade it for anything."

Rose caressed the back of Benedict's head. They kissed each other as if it would be the last time. And it would be. She nodded towards the IV bag in his hand, dangling from his arm over the edge of the bed. "Go give that to her and come back to me. I want to feel your arms around me."

Benedict pulled back from her, looking into her eyes, hoping she would change her mind.

CHAPTER 39

The full weight of her choice came crashing down on him as his eyes locked onto hers. Rose was nanometers from a cure that would end her suffering and renew her life. And she still had the strength and selflessness to shun it so another could live. And Benedict didn't think he could love this woman anymore than he already did.

Her choice was now his choice. It was an agonizing one. No matter which way he decided someone was going to die. He contemplated forcing the tubing into her IV line and holding her down until the dose was administered. She was in no condition to fight him.

It was like she was reading his mind. "You'll never forgive yourself if you don't give Angel that dose," she said.

Benedict went to the window, louvered the blind open and looked through it. Angel Blair lay in bed with her mother snuggled up beside her now. Lauren Blair, the hardworking mother who managed a career while caring for her dying child; the widow who had lost her husband in Afghanistan. Could he allow this woman to suffer the loss of her only child, inflicting on her another un-imaginable heartache?

He met Rose's eyes and walked back to the bed, his eyes plead-ing with her. Benedict could see Rose appreciating his torment. He lowered himself and hugged her.

"Go," she said again.

Benedict pushed himself away from the bed. That act was like tearing off his arm. Physical distance from her was not painful, it was excruciating.

Rose nodded her permission. Benedict stepped back and began to turn. He stopped and turned back unable to sever the unseen tether. Rose lifted her thin arm and pointed to the next bed.

Benedict lowered his eyes. He wanted to look at Rose again. But he knew if he did, he would not be able break away. Stepping around the bed, the tears began to flow. As much as he wanted to make his wife's wish a reality, the thought and the action he was now undertaking was tearing him apart. Every step he took away from the bed towards the young girl sent eruptions of anxiety and paralyzing fear coursing through him.

Benedict was about to save a young girl's life, to give her back her future, to ease her suffering and rid her body of the deadly cancer slowly inching it towards death, to relieve the anguish of a tormented mother. Yet, he felt no sense of pride, no sense of self-satisfaction. Someday, perhaps, he could come to grips with the he-roic action he was undertaking or feel some sense of accomplishment.

He moved into the next room and looked on the two forms lying in a loving death grip. Angel was buried deep within the arms of her mother who even in sleep displayed a haggard visage. Benedict stood there momentarily watching them for two reasons. First, he was delaying, postponing what he knew he must do de-spite protestation by every fiber in his body. Second, he was pon-dering what the administration of this material would mean for Angel Blair.

Would Angel earn what she was about to receive? That simple question morphed and multiplied into a myriad of deeper, more complex questions.

Would this young child who would probably never know who had given her this gift reward humankind with a life's work worthy of distinction and merit? Would she cure the cancer that had nearly killed her? Would she grow up to end hunger or child abuse or poverty? Would she be the first person to set foot on Mars?

And if those possibilities lay in her future, what course would humanity be resigned to if Benedict refused her the drug? How would his selfish decision change the unseen outcome of the world?

Or would she squander her opportunity? Would she drop out of high school and become pregnant, give her child up for adoption? Would she take up with the unworthies of the world and become a drug addict or alcoholic or a thief or murderer?

Was this single dose going to be wasted?

Or would Angel Blair just grow up like the majority of humans on the planet, get a job, meet someone, have a family and toil away, letting the years roll by watching her children grow up, perhaps just getting by, or maybe making a good living, saving her dollars for retirement so she could travel to Europe and dote on her grandchildren, only to be finally planted in the earth?

Of course, the answer to these questions lay in the months and years ahead. Benedict would never see how her life turned out. In the days that followed Benedict's—more correctly—Rose's gift, she'd walk out of the hospital and grow up like millions of other children never fully knowing what she had been given.

Benedict knew what kind of woman his wife was. He knew Rose's character and her goodness. Rose would make the most out of another chance. That's exactly why she deserved it.

Lauren Blair would think her daughter's recovery was a miracle, a gift from God?

That's exactly what it was.

Benedict walked to the bedside, cradling the tubing and IV bag. He ran his hand down the IV tubing, tracing it from the bag all the way to Angel's hand. In the darkness, he found the port just above the young girl's wrist.

As with moments before, a hand reached out and grabbed his arm.

"What are you doing?" Lauren asked with a voice leaden with sleep.

Benedict could feel the tears streaming down his face.

"Alex, is that you?"

He nodded.

"What are you doing? Why are you crying?"

Lauren's grip on his arm, the one holding the tubing, grew tighter.

"I'm helping her," he whispered.

"What is it? Why isn't the nurse giving it?"

"Lauren?" Benedict asked. Several moments passed.

"Yes, Alex. I'm listening."

"Lauren, have I earned your trust?"

"Yes."

"Let me do this. It's what's best for Angel. Rose wants it."

"What are you talking about?"

"Someday, you'll understand."

Benedict twisted the Luer-lok into the port and hung the bag beside the larger one. The child stirred in her sleep and rolled tighter into her mother's arms, but did not wake.

"Let this all go in, Lauren. Don't touch it." He turned and walked away.

Lauren called after him with an urgent whisper. "Alex?"

Benedict ignored her and returned to his wife's side. He walked over to the bed, lowered the rail and carefully crawled into bed with Rose. She had her back to him. He nestled in, spooning her. He wrapped his arm around her emaciated body.

A relief washed over him, releasing the stress and exhaustion he felt. His body was racked with pain and wounds. But none of it mattered. He was connected with Rose again. Their oneness communicated through the touch of his hand on her skin. The relief brought with it a renewed flood of tears.

"It's done," he whispered.

Rose reached behind her and squeezed his thigh, whispering back. "Thank you, baby. I know that wasn't easy. You did the right thing." Her voice was filled with fear.

Benedict sighed, his breath caressing his wife's neck. "I'm going to miss you. I don't know how I'm going to live without you."

"You'll find a way baby. I'll always be in your heart."

Rose rolled over with effort and faced Benedict. He kissed her. She kissed him back.

"Yes, you will, baby. You will always be with me."

"It hurts less when I'm on this side." Rose rolled back over into the spoon. He kissed her lightly on the back of the neck.

Benedict and Rose lay there, not speaking and not sleeping, playing a tug of war with death, trying to slow its march, squeezing every nanosecond out of the time that was left.

CHAPTER 40

H er body was cold, curled on her side in the same way she was when Benedict came to her. Rose was gone. For the first time in days, brilliant sunlight spilled into the window. But Benedict did not notice its brilliance nor did he feel its warmth.

He got out of bed, knowing it would be the last time he would ever feel Rose beside him. As his feet hit the floor, he heard Angel's voice chattering from the next room.

Grumps and Benedict's mother appeared in the doorway. They looked upon Rose's body, knowing from its stillness that it was over. His mother was crying as she hugged him.

"She was an angel. I'm so sorry, dear. I'll get the nurse."

Grumps wept openly and moved to Rose, placing a hand on her floral head scarf. He leaned over and gave her one final kiss on the forehead.

He went to Benedict. "It didn't work?"

Benedict shook his head. "No, Grumps, it worked." Benedict looked through the window at Angel Blair in the next room, sitting up, smiling and talking to her mother.

Grumps followed Benedict's gaze to the young girl. His features filled with confusion. "Why did you give it to...."

"It's what your daughter wanted," Benedict said.

ΩΩΩ

"Good morning, Mr. Alex," Angel said.

Her blue eyes held a sparkle Benedict had never seen. Her cheeks were infused with color. Angel Blair had an insatiable energy about her now.

"Good morning, Angel. How are you feeling?" Benedict said without much conviction.

Lauren Blair stood beside her daughter's bed and could not repress a smile. Her face was stained with dried tears. But her countenance was lighter, unburdened. She knew something had changed with her daughter's condition.

"I feel happy," she said. "I'm hungry. Mommy said I can have whatever I want for breakfast." The tray table was loaded with food. Blueberry pancakes dripping with maple syrup, eggs and hash browns slathered in ketchup.

Benedict remained silent. No words would come to him.

"I went downstairs to the hospital restaurant and brought it back," Lauren said. Then she pulled him into the hallway.

"What did you do? What did you give Angel last night?"

Benedict forced a tight smile. "I gave her a second chance."

Lauren hugged him. "I don't know what that was. But thank you." She hesitated then said, "I have questions."

"I'm not sure I have answers."

Lauren asked how Rose was doing. Benedict lowered his eyes and Lauren Blair knew.

"I'm so sorry," she said.

At that moment, a nurse approached and spoke to her. "Ms. Blair, your boss, Senator Paige is on the phone at the nurse's station."

"I'll be right there."

"I know at a time like this, it's an imposition. Would you mind...."

"I'll sit with her for a few minutes. Right now, it would be good for me," Benedict replied.

Benedict sat in the chair and watched Angel cutting her pancakes with a plastic knife in that awkward way children do. She chomped away, savoring each bite.

Angel began to slice her next piece. The needle inserted into Angel's arm came loose and blood began to ooze out. Benedict watched the girl grab at the needle.

"Ouch," Angel exclaimed. She held up her finger and a plump drop of blood emerged from the small wound where the plastic needle had punctured it.

"Are you okay?" Benedict asked, grabbing two tissues from the box near the bed and wiped the blood away.

He pressed another tissue against her finger and did the same with the now-exposed IV site. He thought about the possibility of infection considering she was a cancer patient. But he knew she no longer was. And that the risk of infection for Angel was also gone.

"Press that tight against your finger," he instructed her. "I'll get you a Band-Aid."

Benedict pressed the nurse call button. A nurse appeared at the doorway two minutes later.

"Angel's IV came out and she cut her finger. Can we get some bandages?"

"Sure," the nurse replied. "I need you to put on a gown, mask and gloves. This child is under neutropenic precautions." The nurse pulled them from a cart in the hallway and handed them to him. "You work here, right?"

Benedict nodded.

"Then you should know better."

"You're right. I should," Alex replied with a wry smile.

The nurse also pulled two small bandages from the cart and approached Angel. "Now, where is that cut?"

Angel removed the bloodied tissue from her finger and held it up. The nurse inspected it and looked at both of them in turn.

"I don't see anything."

The nurse inspected all the fingers on both hands. "Did you cut yourself, Angel?"

Angel looked at Benedict with raised eyebrows. "I guess I didn't."

She pulled away the bloody tape from the IV site. "Where was the needle in your arm?"

Angel pointed to the spot. "Right here."

"I don't see where it was," the nurse replied. She left shaking her head. "I'll be right back to start another line."

Benedict said, "Let me see."

Angel showed him her hand and her arm. The small laceration was completely healed without any trace of an injury. The IV site was also completely healed.

Angel said, "It didn't even hurt that much."

Benedict sat back in the chair, stunned. "Oh my God!"

EPILOGUE

Two Months Later

The answer eluded him.

Benedict sat at his desk in the spare bedroom he and Rose had used as an office. It was late, well past one in the morning. He had been reading, researching and taking notes for five solid hours. Open books lay spread across the desk, surrounding his laptop. Benedict had borrowed every book he could find at the Main Street Library about the Materia Prima and had asked for some copies to be loaned from other libraries across the country.

He sharpened the pencil and jotted more notes. They were questions that needed answers, more than notes.

What piece was missing from the formula?

Michael Watson had left him the complete formula. Or did he? Harrison said that Kyle had compounded the formula using the ratios he'd discovered from the used IV bag Benedict had found after Margaret Queen was cured. Benedict knew that the two doses, Margaret Queen's and Angel Blair's, were the correct ones. But

Harrison said when Kyle compounded the formula in the exact ratios as it was in Margaret Queen's dose, it did not work.

Benedict could only conclude that Watson had done something else to the compound, something he'd not reduced to writing. He had hinted as much in his recording. It was in the writings of H.P. Lovecraft, he'd said. There must be another clue, another step, one embedded in the information he'd left for Benedict. Michael Watson had done a superb job of hiding his creation.

An anthology of Lovecraft's work sat opened on the desk among the other tomes. Benedict had read it from cover to cover. Somewhere in this book lay the answer. But, Benedict had yet to realize what it was.

What other properties did the Materia Prima possess?

Margaret Queen had been discharged three days after being given the Materia Prima with an unblemished bill of health. Though Alex had been busy attending to Rose's funeral in the days after Angel was given the dose, he'd later learned that she, too, had been cured of her disease. Her blood work returned to normal and was wheeled out with no sign of blood cancer in her body. Only time would tell if their situations would remain permanent. But somehow Benedict knew they would.

Kyle had spoken about the compound's ability to cure. Of that, there was little doubt. Benedict had witnessed its power twice. Once, after the fact, on Margaret Queen and a second time, he'd witnessed it first hand on Angel Blair. But the other phenomenon he'd witnessed the morning after Rose's death still perplexed him. Even though he'd seen it with his own eyes, Benedict still was having a hard time believing it.

Angel had cut her finger. It was a minor incident. In a matter of minutes, Angel's laceration was gone, healed as if it never happened. And that healing transpired in no more than a few minutes. This was an entirely different kind of power. Benedict understood now why Michael Watson had been so paranoid.

If it became public, such a revelation would send shock waves through the world. And the hysteria it would create would be catastrophic.

Queen and Angel had been sick and they had been healed. But the healing of Angel's laceration had occurred after she'd been given just the one dose.

Did that mean that Angel and Margaret Queen possessed the power to heal themselves now and forever?

Were they immune from disease?

Could they be injured in a car accident and heal their injuries in minutes?

Had the Materia Prima imparted some kind of immortality?

Benedict placed the pencil on the paper and stretched. He was exhausted but trudged to the kitchen. The pot of coffee was six hours old. But he poured himself another cup anyway.

Benedict had been arrested in Melissa Harrison's death in the afternoon the day Rose passed. He'd been released into the custody of his lawyer, Devin McGuire, to tend to his wife's burial. A week later, videotapes were produced showing Harrison pointing a gun at him in the hallway. She had forced him into the stairwell, where there were no cameras. Benedict's lawyer argued with the Commonwealth's Attorney that Benedict had acted in self-defense. The physical evidence confirmed it. Eventually, the charges were dropped.

Though he'd not been fired from his job, Benedict had been placed on administrative leave with pay. News of Harrison's death quickly hit the papers. After the charges were dropped, Tidewater Regional Medical Center offered him a generous severance package which he accepted.

Word had leaked about the patient deaths, though no one could prove any wrong doing. The press tried to connect Harrison's death with the patient deaths. Benedict, of course, knew they were intimately connected. But the hospital managed to sidestep the issue in the court of public opinion. They were unfortunate, but unrelated incidents, their spokesman had said.

It had been assumed but could not be confirmed that Michael Watson had left information about the illegal and unethical experiments with the Joint Commission. The hospitals records had been examined. And no proof of any tampering with intravenous medications could ever be established since no other IV bag had ever been found. The IV bag Benedict had removed from the trash can had not come to the attention of the Joint Commission. Benedict had never seen it again since turning it over to Melissa Harrison. He assumed it had been destroyed. And no connection between the administration of Nonarc and the deaths could be established. They found many examples of the drug being given to patients who had not died. Watson's accusations were found to be groundless. The Joint Commission had returned two weeks after Rose's death to interview Benedict. Benedict told them he had no knowledge of any specific wrongdoing. The interviewers left with more questions than when they'd arrived.

The Joint Commission had found several violations in the hospital's processes during their routine survey but nothing major. They promised to return to re-survey within a year. Tidewater Regional Medical Center would survive. However, rumors of its imminent purchase by several health systems still loomed.

J. Edward Kyle had been questioned in the disappearance of the nurse, Penny Lewis. A recording had been left for the authorities, probably by Watson. Benedict learned from Ulysses Lee, the former cop, that Kyle had been heard on the recording discussing the death of the woman. The nurse was still currently listed as missing. Without any concrete physical evidence or corpus dilecti, no charges would be filed unless additional evidence turned up. Katherine Diehl had not shown up for work and had also never been heard from again. Benedict suspected she also had become a victim of the Materia Prima plot.

Jablonski and Lee had been injured when their vehicle had been struck by a downed utility pole. Among the cuts and lacerations, Jablonski suffered a neck injury which had required surgery. Lee had broken his arm.

Devin McGuire, Joseph Bellini, and Tyrone Manville had survived the plane crash. McGuire had maneuvered the craft as close to one of the highways as he possibly could. But they ended up two hundred yards short, clipping the treetops before plunging into the canopy of the forest. The left wing buckled, cart wheeling the cabin. The Cessna dropped twenty feet, stopping upside down nestled above the ground in the strong branches of three large oaks.

The three men were largely unhurt except for minor scrapes and lacerations. McGuire needed thirteen stitches in his head and Bellini complained of whiplash while Manville barely missed being impaled by a branch. They'd hung upside down in the forest and strapped in for nearly two hours somewhere west of I-495 just north of Reston and Dulles airport in northern Virginia. Rescuers from a Coast Guard helicopter rappelled into the trees to bring them to safety.

All five men, battered and bruised, made it to the funeral.

McGuire's first comment to Benedict had been a half-serious: "You owe me an airplane."

Benedict smiled to himself as he remembered the pained grin on his friends face as he spoke the words.

Though he was relieved his friends would recover from their battle scars and grateful for their selfless assistance, Benedict was still a tortured man. When Rose was alive, he was tortured by her impending death. Now, that she was gone, he agonized over a compound that might promise eternal life.

In the weeks following her death, he'd grieved, struggling to get out of bed each day to an empty house sprinkled with reminders of her everywhere, tugging at him. There were days in which he numbly wandered the house. A gaping hole existed that would never close. He left any reminder of her in the house undisturbed, afraid to move even a hairbrush, for fear it would widen the gap and aggravate the hurt.

Ten days after Rose's funeral, Ari Spanos had invited Benedict to play golf. At first, he'd declined. But Spanos insisted and they hit the links the next day. Benedict played miserably. By the time they reached the back nine, Benedict had had a few beers and relaxed. Spanos had him laughing at some corny jokes. They managed to play eighteen holes once a week. Golf with Spanos was the only human contact Benedict had these days. During Rose's illness, the nights were hell. Now, a different hoard of demons haunted him when the sun went down.

Nighttime was a darkness-infested jungle filled with psychological predators. Benedict's mind and body refused to rest. A full night's sleep was a memory. So he began to occupy his time with research, especially in the wee hours. He returned to the mystery that had been thrown in his lap. Now, it obsessed him.

Benedict sipped his acrid coffee and sat back down, spinning the lighter in his hand. He rubbed the nick on its base. A nick caused by dropping it during his struggle with Melissa Harrison. He wondered what Margaret Queen's and Angel Blair's lives were like. He scribbled Angel's name on the yellow pad, underlined it and drew a box around it.

He lifted the folded, wrinkled page holding his wife's final message to him. She must have penned it before she'd been admitted to the hospital. Benedict had read it at least once every day since he'd found it in her nightstand drawer the week after they put her in the ground.

Alex,

You're so very much a part of me
I close my eyes and feel you in the heart of me, honestly
No night will hide me from your sight
In dreams, you see, I'll always be, with you!

Rose

Rose's words and his torment pushed him. Alex Benedict promised himself he would find the answer to Michael Watson's riddle. He would find the answer to the mystery of the Materia Prima.

And when he did, it *would* change the world forever.

THE END

Jason Rodgers returns and is thrust back into a world of shadows, suspense and intrigue as the dark international forces from Rodger's past seek retribution and to wreak havoc in this riveting sequel to Perry's national bestseller, The Cyclops Conspiracy. . .

The Cyclops Revenge

...will put you back on the edge of your seat and take you on an incredible, breath-holding adventure.

Turn the page for an excerpt of bestselling author David Perry's latest thriller. . .

PROLOGUE

Friday, October 13th

One Week after the Christening of the *Jacob R Hope*

"You are still distressed, Miss Lily?"

The words were delivered as a question. But they hit her with the force of a statement speaking the bold truth.

Delilah Hussein lay on the beach lounge chair with a tall exotic libation sitting on the glass table beside her, untouched. The warm tropical breeze was strong this late afternoon whipping her silk sari. The wind on the secluded, well-secured, mountaintop villa was a constant.

Hussein looked up at Oliver with a distant gaze. Despite her distraction, she could see true concern etched on her man-servant's face. They had been through a lot together. And he had stood by her without a hint of trepidation.

"Would you like a cool, wet towel?" he asked.

Hussein did not speak. She simply looked up at him with unfocused eyes. The trauma of the events of a week ago was still too painful to bear.

Oliver extended the white towel towards her. Her eyes moved lower to see it clutched in his dark-skinned hand. The fingers were long, all except the pinky which was nothing more than a stump.

Hussein had been responsible for its loss. She had snipped off both pinky fingers on separate occasions. Each time he'd let her down, failed her in a mission. And on both occasions, Oliver had paid for his incompetence with the loss of the smallest digit. The most recent failure had been not more than a few weeks ago; though his mistake had not had an effect on the outcome of their calamitous failure.

"Thank you," she replied in a whisper barely audible over the wind. "You are a good man, Oliver. A true and valuable companion."

Oliver was a tall, muscular specimen. His silk shirt was unbuttoned at the neck revealing the sculptured muscles of his chest. Adept in many forms of hand-to-hand combat, he was also deadly at medium distances with many small arms. He had killed countless times for her. And, Hussein knew, he could kill her quickly if he so desired.

Hussein sighed. "I can't believe we failed. The last three years had been planned to the smallest detail."

"It was a bold mission, Miss Lily. Very risky."

"And they're both gone now."

"Unfortunately, it does seem that is the case."

"Are you sure, Oliver?"

"Yes," Oliver replied. "Hammon sent the message twenty-four hours after the christening. Jasmine was killed. Your son was taken into custody. He does not know where he is being held or if he is even alive."

Hussein closed her eyes and tilted her head back, shaking it slowly. She pushed out a long breath. "*Mon Dieu*, I still can't believe it."

"It is not good for you to lie around like this. You must move about. It will make you feel better, get the blood flowing."

Hussein smiled. "Are you worried about me?"

The tall man-servant smiled and nodded. "We must get you back into circulation, *n'est ce pas*?"

"I suppose so."

Oliver kneeled beside her chair, looking deeply into her eyes.

"You have been despondent for a week now," he said. "We must move on. I will help you forget."

Beginning at her bare foot, he gently ran his hand along the inside of her leg. When he reached her knee and his hand had begun to disappear under the cloth of her garment, Hussein held up her hand.

Oliver's hand froze in place. She could see the confusion in his eyes. They were asking a question: *Have I gone too far?*

Hussein knew Oliver was only trying to help. He would not kill her. He would never raise a hand against her.

He owed her too much. She held a marker Oliver could never repay. One she would always hold over him.

She had saved his life from her lover and dictator, Saddam.

His four fingers remained against her soft skin, the pads of each digit connecting with the inside of her thigh, just above the knee. They were four electrodes, pulsing current into her, bringing her flesh back to life. Hussein tilted her head back again and slowly sucked the Caribbean air into her lungs. She held that position for a long time, weighing the events and trying to kill the pain.

Was it too soon?

Hussein felt her nipples become erect and a warm flush swam over her body, back and forth like a violent, storm-laden tide.

"Oliver, help me forget."

Hussein reached for him, clutching the fabric of his shirt in her clenched fist, pulling him to her. His hand resumed its trek inside her sari, inching higher.

When it reached the confluence of her thighs, Oliver spread his fore- and middle fingers gently as a cue. Hussein responded and separated her legs, elevating her knees. The length of silk along her legs drifted towards her abdomen as the warm breeze caressed her exposed womanhood.

Slowly with the deftness of a master craftsman, his fingers crept towards their goal. His fingers dipped slightly, touching the skin just beneath the moist haven.

Hussein arched her back and sucked in a loud, sharp breath. The electricity of his touch arced with mounting voltage. She reached up with her other hand, desperately clutching another fistful of cloth and pulling his lips to within an inch of hers.

Oliver moved his fingers higher touching her moist mound with the gentleness of a moth landing on a leaf. Hussein's body spasmed. His lips made contact with hers as he pushed two fingers inside her.

ΩΩΩ

"Are you feeling better?"

"Yes, *mon ami*," Hussein replied. Her head rested on his bare chest as they lay naked in bed. "Much better."

Hussein ran her hand down his belly under the sheet. His skin, coated with a patina of perspiration, was taut and firm.

"Thank you, Oliver. I needed that."

"Pleasing you is my only mission."

With the blood coursing potently through her veins again, Hussein's mind began to race with more coherent thoughts for the first time in seven days.

As if sensing her impatience, Oliver asked, "You are thinking of something, Miss Lily?"

"*Oui*, I am."

"What do you need me to do?"

"Nothing yet," she answered. "I am still upset. I've lost a daughter and my son is gone. And even more, the failure was my fault."

"The pharmacist?"

"You realized my mistake was allowing the pharmacist to get involved?"

"Yes."

"And you said nothing?"

"It was not my place."

Hussein rose up and looked into his eyes. "You are right. It is not your place. And the pharmacist was the problem. It was my fault that I allowed him to come so close to our operation. I misjudged him."

"Again, what should I do?"

"Nothing. I will need your help in the coming months. Our compatriots in Washington are, no doubt, in a state of crisis. Have you been able to contact Hammon?"

"No, Miss Lily. The secure phone number is dead. I have tried each of the last three days."

"I feared as much. They are going deep underground. Word of the assassination attempts has spread quietly through the American government. . ."

"I have been monitoring the newspapers and news shows. There has been no mention of anything."

"Nonetheless, the FBI, Secret Service and the CIA are tracing all clues. And, I fear, they are torturing my beloved Sharif, trying to extract any shred of information from him."

"I fear you are correct," Oliver replied, running his fingers across her naked back.

"They will come after us."

"Yes, they will."

"I want you to contact Damascus. I will need to meet with them in the coming days. Arrange a meeting for a month from now. They are probably most concerned. I must smooth the waters and make them understand that this was only a temporary set back. We must continue with the mission. We must strike at the Americans again.

"Just as Bin Laden did after the first attacks on the World Trade Center, we will strike them once more. They will beef up their security of all government officials. But we will hit them in a different way. . .in a way they will never expect."

Hussein pulled herself up to Oliver's lips and kissed him deeply as she reached for his groin. She massaged him and felt him growing firmer in her hand as her tongue probed his lips. Hussein ripped the bed sheets from his body and straddled him.

Without warning, she slapped him hard across the cheek, whipping his head to the side. She leaned in and hovered over him, her breasts caressing his chest. "Make love to me again. Then we have much to do."

"What?"

"I will fill you in when the time is right. The details must be worked out. But, trust me, the Great Satan will feel our wrath and we will not fail. I want you to track the movements and communications of Jason Rodgers, the pharmacist. I want to know everything he does and everywhere he goes. Every aspect of his life is to be scrutinized. When we strike again, I will avenge my daughter and my son. And Jason Rodgers will know the pain I have felt and will feel for the rest of my days. He will suffer as I am suffering. Do you understand?"

"Yes, Miss Lily."

"He doesn't know it yet. He is, no doubt, recovering right now. When the time is right, I want him to know that I am the one who has rained down vengeance upon him."

"Yes, *Madame*."

Delilah Hussein slapped Oliver, once more, on the opposite check. With her hand still stinging from the blow, she reached down and grasped his swollen manhood.

"Make love to me, Oliver. I need to ease the pain but not forget the mission."

She lowered herself onto him as she whispered a verse from the Quran to herself. "Help me ease the pain."

PART ONE

CHAPTER 1

Friday, April 10th

Two and a half years later

Jason Rodgers was about to implement the plan to finally bury his ghosts.

The carefully laid plans had been in place for weeks. Tonight marked their new beginning. The first step to making his life whole again. In the days to follow, he would put his past behind him and keep it there.

He leaned back, satisfied, pleased with himself. Everything was going perfectly. *Almost perfectly*, anyway.

The meal had been fantastic, the service exemplary. Everything had gone off without a hitch. Except, that is, for Chrissie's demeanor.

"Are you okay?" he asked Christine Pettigrew. "You seem tired."

Chrissie sat across from him on the balcony level of the restaurant, looking uninspired and melancholy for most of the evening. Jason had noticed a change in her in the last few weeks. She had been working very hard lately. But tonight, she seemed particularly bothered.

She has no idea, he thought, sipping his coffee. *She will be pleased and surprised. That will change her mood! It will change everything.*

They had just completed an exquisite dinner. Jason had had a thick, moist steak with a baked potato and asparagus while Chrissie had barely touched her shrimp scampi. Jason had insisted that they cap it all off by with mountainous dessert of chocolate cake dripping in thick fudge.

The Freemason Abbey in downtown Norfolk, Virginia had been one of the premier dining establishments for decades. Nearly a century and half old, it, as the name suggested, began as church, changed hands numerous times throughout history, and had finally been converted into a beacon of fine dining, sating the appetites of Hampton Roads residents ever since.

Jason had chosen it because they had never eaten there together.

This was a special occasion. It was going to be a night neither one of them would ever forget. It demanded the perfect ambiance of the old cathedral.

Chrissie looked over the half-eaten dessert they had shared, pressing her lips into a thin line. Jason had scarfed down most of it. Chrissie had only tried a small forkful, maybe two.

"Yeah, I am," she replied in a lifeless tone.

"Chrissie, something's been bothering you all night. I can tell. You should be excited. You finally got the partnership you been shooting for. The firm is exploding with business. The Colonial ownership has transferred back to you. That process is finally over with. And we are filling more prescriptions than we did last year. This year is going to be a very lucrative one. And I'm talking about in more than just dollars."

"What is that supposed to mean?"

Jason turned to look for their waitress. She was standing of to the side, waiting for his signal. He made eye contact with her and winked so Chrissie couldn't see it.

"I said," Chrissie asked again, "what's that supposed to mean?"

"You'll see."

The waitress appeared pushing a narrow cart on which sat a large bottle of champagne and two flutes. She showed the bottle to Jason and began uncorking it.

"Jason, I've already had three glasses of wine. I don't need any more."

"Just a small taste," he replied. "Just take a sip."

The waitress poured a small sample into Jason's glass. He placed his nose over the glass and inhaled, pretending he knew something about champagne. He sipped it and nodded his approval. Then the server poured two glasses and placed before both of them.

"A toast," Jason said, lifting his glass. "I love you, Chrissie. To you and me, we are a great team."

The waitress had her back to them. Just as Jason finished making his toast, she turned around to face them. She placed a round, white bread plate on the table between them.

On it rested a small velvet box.

ΩΩΩ

"You've been acting like an ass all day, Michael?" Jenny asked her son. "Do you want to talk about it?"

She was sitting on the edge of Michael's bed. Michael was lying on his back staring at the ceiling. His face was a palate of frustration and worry.

"My life sucks," he hissed.

"I know it seems that way," Jenny counseled. "But your father getting remarried isn't the end of the world."

Michael rolled on his side and propped himself on an elbow. "You knew and you didn't tell me?"

"I'm your mother, Michael. Your father told me what he was going to tell you yesterday. It was the proper thing to do."

"Why didn't you tell me?"

"Because it wasn't my place."

"I don't like her."

"Chrissie? I've met her several times. She seems like a nice person. Why do you say you don't like her?"

"Because she's making him move. When they get married they're going they're going to live at her house."

"I know your father. She's not making him do anything. If he's moving, it's because he thinks that's what's best for them."

"I didn't like it when you moved us out here to the Salt Ponds. What was wrong with the house in York County?"

"There was nothing wrong with it."

"Then why did we move?"

"It was just time," Jenny replied, looking away.

"Bullshit!"

"Watch your mouth!" Jenny slapped his leg as he lay there. "I don't want to hear language like that again."

"You put the house up for sale a week after whatever happened to dad. What happened that night?"

Jenny sighed.

"I know it was something bad. And don't tell me it was a car accident. Because I know you're lying."

Jenny looked out the window into the darkness shrouding their oceanfront home.

"Aren't you going to tell me?"

"I'm not having this conversation now," Jenny declared. "Your father loves you very much. You're still going to see him, Michael. He has a right to live his life. These are the types of issues we all deal with as adults."

Michael got up from the bed and walked to the window. It looked out on the waves of the Chesapeake Bay crashing in the dim wash of light. He studied the line of rotting pilings disappearing into the water.

"I still don't like it!"

"Your father's told me that you really haven't given Christine a chance. You've been distant since the first day you've met her. Has she treated you badly?"

Michael stared into the darkness as his mind wafted back to the night. He'd heard her voice before he'd ever met her. And the words he'd heard spoken that night between his father and *that* woman had stung him to his core.